GET YOUR
S#*T ACT
TOGETHER

GET YOUR
SH*T
ACT
TOGETHER

DEBRA DRUMMOND

booktopia editions

This guide has been created as a resource to assist young Australian adults to become independent, away from the support of home and school. It provides a range of practical skills and lessons to help deal with the demands of life in the real world.

First published in Australia 2018 by Real Life Youth Support
PO Box 302, Mona Vale, NSW, 2103 Australia
ISBN 978-0-646-98523-7

ISBN 9781925995787 (print)
Published in Australia and New Zealand by
Booktopia Editions, an imprint of Booktopia Group Ltd
Unit E1, 3-29 Birnie Avenue, Lidcombe, NSW 2141, Australia

Printed and bound in Australia

booktopia.com.au

CONTENTS

INTRO: **ARE WE THERE YET? WHEN DO WE START TO 'ADULT'?**

When you turn 18, you're officially an adult in the eyes of the law. What now?

This is where you're supposed to know how to conform to all the rules and protocols, like the other good law-abiding citizens.

Only no-one's told you what the deal is. What IS expected of you as an adult?

My son, Jack, gave me the perfect example of how easy it is to get tripped up.

He was 19 at the time when he bought his first car with the help of a mate. They had it all under control, only he didn't know he had to transfer the registration at the motor registration department. (Q: Doesn't the seller do that?) Plus, he didn't check when the registration was due. (Q: Don't you get a notice to remind you?)

So, he's driving home from his girlfriend's place late on a Saturday night, and he gets pulled over by the police. He's not drunk, drugged or driving recklessly.

The thing is, his car isn't registered. This doesn't seem like a big deal, right? But because it's not registered, it's not insured either, which would've been *a very big deal* if he'd had an accident and had to pay for damage to his car, the other car/s *and* any personal damage. Yes, everything! And if the 'other' car were a Maserati and a write-off, it could be a hefty $100,000 mistake.

Jack copped a $700 fine and was understandably not happy!

As a mum, I thought that was a bit tough. When I mentioned it to a local police officer, she said, "Well, he is an adult. He should've known better." Yes, technically that's true, but he's a newbie at this stuff. They could have cut him some slack, except the law's the law.

The fact is: this s*** happens a lot in life. It doesn't end with one or two things.

What I did notice when my kids finished high school was that neither of them received the heads-up on surviving life out in the wild – the real world (one attended a public school and the other a Catholic school). It struck me that there was a big gap on the market around 'life skills', even to the point of giving graduating students a list of contacts and hotlines explaining where to go for support.

I've compiled this resource primarily around practical skills, however, there's no substitute for real life experience.

And while I can't help you with matters of the heart, I can give you some tips and tricks on the practical things. Everyday stuff-ups and disasters *can* be avoided, provided you've done some homework. You definitely don't need to learn *everything* the hard way!

So, in this guide, I've put together everything I wish I'd known at 18. Although, admittedly, I thought I knew it all at 15 when I left home but abruptly realised I was wrong. I couldn't even put a load of washing on.

The problem is, we don't know what we don't know! I'm not saying I got it all right. The reason I know what to include in here is because I DID screw up a lot. I've had my share of drama, mistakes and loss...and popped out the other side, alive and kicking. No doubt you'll have hiccups to overcome too.

Unfortunately, sometimes we have to fall really hard on our butts to get the biggest lessons.

That's where you just pick yourself up, dust yourself off, get on with it, and say "thanks for that crappy lesson."

It's my hope that this guide will help you, in some small part, to get your s*** together.

Warmest wishes, Deb x

ABOUT THE AUTHOR
DEBRA DRUMMOND

Lives: Sydney (Northern Beaches and Central Coast). Previously lived in Wellington, Johannesburg and Los Angeles. Born and bred in the Adelaide hills.

Work: A business owner for the past 14 years, she began her career as a model through her teens and 20s and progressed to journalism, PR, communications and marketing management.

Kids: Grace 23 (primary school teacher), Jack 21 (golf professional).

Milestones: Sole mum to two incredible humans, property investor, business graduate, Miss Australia finalist, federal political candidate in 2013, and a community and youth advocate. Her life-lessons have helped her dig deep and learn plenty of coping strategies, after experiencing abuse at an early age and the loss of her first child.

Main inspiration: She's a long-held fascination with human behaviour, personal development and what makes our minds tick.

Social concerns: One of the reasons she wrote this guide was in response to a spate of suicides on Sydney's Northern Beaches a few summers ago. Having attempted suicide as a teenager, she felt that many of these deaths were avoidable and was drawn to help in some way to relieve some of the stresses for young people.

The goal of Get Your Act Together is to fill in the gaps not taught at school or home and help students transition to adulthood confidently and empowered.

Debra's reality check: Her biggest wake-up call is in knowing that many of the issues addressed in this guide are around First World problems. The millions of people starving in developing countries are thinking only of how to get clean water and food.

ACKNOWLEDGEMENTS

First and foremost, I'd like to thank my kids, Grace and Jack, for their love and support and unwittingly motivating me to keep writing this guide and not give up on it.

I'd also like to thank the many experts, contributors and sources collated in this guide. I've selected each one based on their area of expertise, or because they were the most relevant resource for the topic and have acknowledged each person in the individual sections.

A special thanks to Steve Panozzo (Cartoon Factory), who has been a much-valued sounding board and supporter from the start. Also, thanks to Paul Lewis (Total Legal), Julie Lewis (Jaffle Creative), Sarah Taylor (Spicy Broccoli), Deanne Bennett, Mary-Jane Partridge and Dayna Lingard (for adding her ideas from a 21-year-old's perspective).

Throughout this guide I've aimed to remain neutral and unbiased, therefore there's no reference to religion, political party policies or polarised debates, such as vaccinations or fad diets.

I don't claim to have all the answers to (real) life and with each update the content grows and evolves with the input of others, and as new realisations arise for me.

If you have any feedback, please make it constructive and within the positive intent of this guide.

If you've had a real-life 'aha' moment that you think others would learn from, please share your story or video on the website.

Real Life Youth Support
PO Box 302
Mona Vale NSW 2103
Australia
www.real-life.com.au

SPECIAL NOTES

This guide is for general informational purposes only, with the goal of making it easier for you to transition from life at school or home, to real-life (and living independently).

I recommend you seek professional advice for any specific issues or circumstances, such as (but not limited to) medical, legal and financial matters.

All specialist information has been reviewed by experts; however, you should rely on your own inquiry and research relating to all products, services and life subjects.

Any reliance you place on the information in this guide is at your own risk. I take no responsibility for the integrity or relevance of the sources or recommendations, which are for your information only.

While I have checked the facts and details of this guide many times, I make no guarantees as to the accuracy, currency or completeness of the information presented and therefore disclaim all liability for any loss suffered as a result of any errors, use or misuse of the information.

All links to websites and sources were current at the time this guide was published.

Every effort has been made to contact all sources, however, if I have missed anyone please accept my apologies and advise me of my error so that I can correct it.

Any of the trademarks in the guide are the property of the relevant owners. I have no commercial connections or endorsements with any of the companies or individuals referenced. I have referenced them as recommended resources should you need further information.

Illustrations thanks to Steve Panozzo of The Cartoon Factory.

Government images are used with the permission of the Australian Government Department of Human Services and the Australian Taxation Office, for which I thank them.

LIST OF CONTACTS AND HOTLINES

ALL EMERGENCIES (24-HOUR): Call triple zero **000**

POLICE ASSISTANCE in non-urgent matters: 131 444

LIFELINE for immediate crisis support (24-HOUR): 131 114
lifeline.org.au

ALCOHOL AND DRUG ADDICTION

ADIS: 1800 250 015, yourroom.health.nsw.gov.au/getting-help – 24-hour support line (Alcohol and Drug Information Service NSW.)

Alcohol and Drug Foundation: 1300 858 584
adf.org.au/alcohol-drug-use

Directline: 1800 888 236, directline.org.au – 24-hour free confidential phone and online counselling, information and referral service.

Family Drug Support: 1300 368 186, fds.org.au – 24-hour family drug support service.

Gambling Help Online: 1800 858 858 gamblinghelponline.org.au – Support for anyone affected by gambling.

Lifeline: 131 114, lifeline.org.au – Substance abuse/addiction helpline (drugs and alcohol).

Quit Helpline: 137 848 quitnow.gov.au – Quit smoking support service.

Youth Support and Advocacy Service (YSAS): ysas.org.au – Supporting young people and families to overcome problems associated with substance use and mental health issues.

CONSUMER RIGHTS

ACCC Consumer Rights and Guarantees: accc.gov.au For information on consumer rights and guarantees.

FAIR TRADING NSW: 133 220, fairtrading.nsw.gov.au – Know your rights (see chapter on Your Rights).

Ombudsman: 1300 362 072 ombudsman.gov.au – Complaints against Australian Government organisations.

DOMESTIC VIOLENCE AND TRAUMA

1800 RESPECT: 1800 737 732, 1800respect.org.au – A free confidential 24-hour national domestic family violence counselling service.

Blue Knot Foundation: 1300 657 380, blueknot.org.au – Phone counselling for adult survivors of childhood trauma, and for family, friends and support people. Additional service with Blue Knot Foundation: 1800 421 468 – Support for people with disabilities, experiencing abuse, neglect or violence.

Domestic Violence Hotline – White Ribbon: 1800 RESPECT – 1800 737 732 whiteribbon.org.au – A global movement working to end violence against women and girls.

Domestic Violence Line: 1800 656 463 domesticviolence.nsw.gov.au – 24-hour help service in NSW. (Google: domestic violence services near me.)

GENERAL MEDICAL AND SEXUAL HEALTH

24-Hour Health Advice: 1800 022 222, healthdirect.gov.au – Free Australian health advice and Symptom Checker.

24-Hour MEDCARE: 139 247 – 24-hour phone service to discuss general and mental health and psychology.

National Home Doctor service: After Hours My Doctor Service, 137 425 homedoctor.com.au

Pregnancy, Birth and Baby Helpline: 1800 882 436 pregnancybirthbaby.org.au

Sexual Health: healthdirect.gov.au – Symptom checker.

+ **Google:** GP/doctor or medical centre near me.

LEGAL SERVICES

Community Legal Centres Australia: clcs.org.au – info@clcs.org.au. Free legal assistance, not-for-profit organisation.

Legal Hotline: 1300 636 846, gotocourt.com.au/legal-advice 7am-midnight 7 days – Legal advice (Note: this is not a free service.)

Legal Aid numbers (National): info.australia.gov.au (legal aid)

+ **Google:** Legal Aid near me. e.g. NSW: 1300 888 529 legalaid.nsw.gov.au

LIFE-SKILLS TRAINING AND SEMINARS

Australian Apprenticeship Support: 1800 363 831 apprenticeshipsupport.com.au – Australian Government run service, providing support and advice to apprentices, employers, career advisors and parents.

Awake Academy: awakeacademy.com.au – A transformational online course by 7-times world champion surfer, Layne Beachley.

Landmark Forums Life programs to empower teens: landmarkworldwide.com (services for young people) – A program to empower young people.

Leading Edge Life Skills: leadingedgelifeskills.com.au/youth-programs – Interactive youth program working with horses.

Mentoring programs: raise.org.au
Early intervention mentoring programs.

Red Cross: redcross.org.au/get-help/community-services
Youth services and programs for young people.

Salvation Army: salvationarmy.org.au (youth support networks and programs) – Youth support networks and programs for disadvantaged young people.

Tomorrow's Youth (EmpowerU) Life-skills program: 1300 039 662 empower-u.com.au – Australia's leading personal development and life skills program.

Tony Robbins courses. tonyrobbins.com/events
Transformational courses, e.g., Unleash the Power Within.

Uniting Church: uniting.org (youth services)
Youth support programs and services.

Year13: 02 8084 6422 year13.com.au
The home of post-school options.

+ Google: Life skill camps, youth programs and self-development courses.

LIVING AND ACCOMMODATION

Burdekin: 02 8976 1777 – Support to prevent homelessness for 12 to 24-year olds (Northern Sydney). Google search in your state.

Link2Home: 1800 152 152 – Homeless and accommodation support. Google your state. facs.nsw.gov.au/families (support to find a home)

Rental Assistance (Centrelink): servicesaustralia.gov.au/individuals (Centrelink rent assistance)

Salvation Army: 13 SALVOS (137258) salvationarmy.org.au – Provides a large range of social services without discrimination, even positive lifestyle programs, legal help and learn to drive services for those who are eligible.

Student and Trainee Assistance: servicesaustralia.gov.au/individuals (student and trainee payments) – Government help for students, trainees and apprentices.

Youth off the Streets: youthoffthestreets.com.au – A safe place for disadvantaged and homeless youth, and support with drug addiction, family breakdowns and debt.

MENTAL HEALTH

Barnardos: barnardos.org.au – Works with young people and families to break the cycle of disadvantage and homelessness.

Batyr: batyr.com.au – Preventative mental health organisation run *by* young people *for* young people. Online, or face-to-face, or share stories.

Beyond Blue: 1300 224 636 beyondblue.org.au – Support to help all Australians achieve their best possible mental health. Provides online and email chat and online forums.

Black Dog Institute: blackdoginstitute.org.au – Support for mentally healthier lives. Offers a free mental health assessment tool.

Connected Space: connectedspace.com.au – A safe space for young people to share experiences and 'tricky times' and ask any questions.

GriefLine: 1300 845 745 – griefline.org.au/phone-counselling – A free and confidential counselling service 7-days a week nationwide, for people experiencing loss or grief.

Headspace: headspace.org.au – Free mental health support for youth. Headspace centres are one-stop shops for young people, at 100+ locations throughout Australia.

eheadspace: 1800 650 890 – 24-hour free confidential phone and online service for 12 to 25-year-olds. (Fees may apply if you call from a mobile. Let them know and they will call back.)

Kids Helpline: 1800 551 800 kidshelpline.com.au– 'Anytime. Any reason.' Confidential webchat or email for all ages. Email: Counsellor@kidshelpline.com.au (Email inbox is checked 8am – 10pm daily.)

Lifeline: 131 114 (24-hour) lifeline.org.au – Confidential crisis support and suicide prevention service, which includes referrals to other services. Or text a crisis supporter on 0477 131 114 (6pm to midnight Eastern Standard Time, 7 days/week).

Lifeskills Australia: 1800 870 080 lifeskillsaustralia.com.au – Psychologists and counselling advice 24-hour.

Mensline: 1300 789 978 mensline.org.au – Free counselling for Australian men, anytime, anywhere (call, online or video chat).

Mindspot: 1800 614 434 mindspot.org.au – Programs to build emotional resilience. Includes confidential MindSpot Online Assessment.

ReachOut Australia: au.reachout.com – ReachOut is here for whatever life throws at you, with practical support, tools and tips for young people to get through anything from everyday issues to tough times.

Suicide Call Back Service: 1300 659 467 suicidecallbackservice.org.au/phone-and-online-counselling – 24-hour free service for anyone affected by suicide.

The Butterfly Foundation. 1800 334 673 thebutterflyfoundation.org.au – National support service for eating disorders and body image issues.

Way2Wellness: 1300 120 446 way2wellness.org.au – Support service for anxiety, stress and general mental wellbeing concerns, run by Lifeline.

Wesley Mission: wesleymission.org.au – Programs and life-skills for youth 12 to 25. You can also find a mentor, accommodation, financial counselling and legal support services.

+ **Google:** Youth and mental health centres and services near me. E.g. Youth Point and PCYC (Police Citizens Youth Club Centres NSW).

MONEY AND FINANCE

Australian Taxation Office: 132 861 ato.gov.au
Taxation information and advice.

Budget planner: ASIC's MoneySmart website. moneysmart.gov.au – Easy-to-use budget planner.

Credit and Debt Financial Rights Hotline: 1800 007 007 financialrights.org.au – Advice for consumers in financial stress. Financial rights legal centre.

National Debt Helpline: 1800 007 007 ndh.org.au – Free financial advice to help with debt problems. Live chat with financial counsellors.

Personal Tax Information Line: 132 861 ato.gov.au/individuals For all taxation information for individuals.

RELATIONSHIPS

1800 MYLINE: 1800 695 463 – National relationship support.

Child Family Community Australia: aifs.gov.au/cfca (publications and phone counselling) – Comprehensive resource sheets for each state, with helplines and counselling services.

Family Relationship Advice Line: 1800 050 321 (8am – 8pm Mon-Fri) – Advice line for relationships.

Kids Helpline: 1800 551 800 kidshelpline.com.au/young-adults – Help with anything, like mental health, life issues, sex and relationships (for young adults 18 to 25).

QLife: 1800 184 527 qlife.org.au – A national service to support and connect LGBTQIA+ communities, including Webchat 3pm-midnight every day.

Relationships Australia: 1300 364 277 relationships.org.au – A national relationship support service, including counselling, mediation and family dispute resolution.

SEXUAL ABUSE AND RAPE CRISIS

1800 RESPECT: 1800 737 732 1800respect.org.au – A free confidential 24-hour national sexual assault, family violence counselling service.

Bravehearts: 1800 272 831 bravehearts.org.au – Telephone counselling for survivors of institutional child sexual assault, and a child protection advocacy.

Living Well: livingwell.org.au – Online support for male survivors of sexual assault.

HOTLINES: Rape and Domestic Violence Hotline: 1800 424 017 rape-dvservices.org.au and in NSW nswrapecrisis.com.au – Telephone and online crisis counselling for rape and domestic violence.

LGBTIQ+ Violence Service: 1800 497 212 – Specialised line for LGBTIQ+ support.

Sexual Assault Counselling Australia: 1800 211 028 – Specialised line for sexual assault support.

STUDY, CAREER AND BUSINESS

ASIC: asic.gov.au – Australian Securities and Investment Commission. Registers and regulates companies.

Centrelink (e.g. ABSTUDY and Newstart): 136 240 or 1800 132 317 – For a current list of numbers go to: servicesaustralia.gov.au (Centrelink phone self-service)

Myskills: myskills.gov.au –
National vocational education and training.

Study Assist: studyassist.gov.au –
Government assistance for financing tertiary study.

TAFE: tafecourses.com.au/resources/guide-to-tafe-courses-in-australia; **e.g. TAFE NSW:** tafensw.edu.au – TAFE is Australia's largest vocational training provider.

TRAVEL

Australian Passport Office: 131 232 passports.gov.au – For all passport services.

Emergency Helpline: Outside Australia +61 2 6261 3305 or SMS +61 421 269 080 dfat.gov.au (contact us) – 24-hour consular emergency centre in Canberra.

Smart Traveller: smartraveller.gov.au/consular-services – Travel and insurance advice.

Smart Traveller Guide: smartraveller.gov.au (guide), and australia.gov.au (passports and travel) – 'Before you travel' information, and consular services.

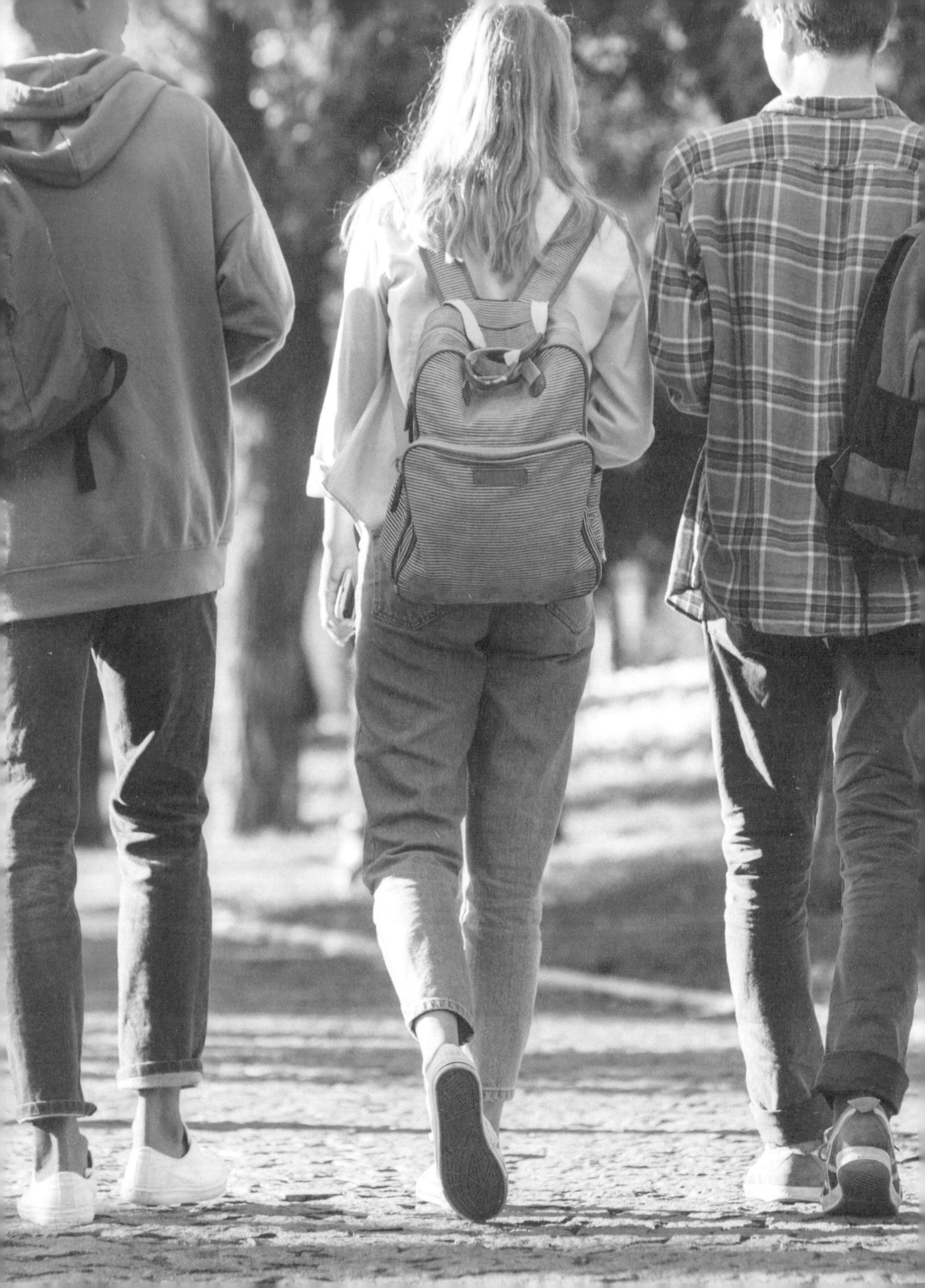

1. YOU'RE AN ADULT. **NOW WHAT?**

Things to know by the time you turn 18:

- Understand your legal responsibilities as an adult
- Open a MyGov account
- Sign up for Centrelink (government support options)
- Get a Medicare card
- Consider private health insurance
- Enrol to vote
- Set up a tax file number and superannuation fund
- Open a personal bank account
- Start a personal budget and financial plan
- Get control of your spending
- Create a vision for how you want your future to look
- Plan your income (career and study pathway)
- Check your car registration and insurances
- Brush up on your domestic and life skills
- Organise living arrangements and budgets
- Read this guide ☺

"The key to a good life is this: If you're not going to talk about something during the last hour of your life, then don't make it a top priority during your lifetime."

Richard Carlson

When you turn 18, there are some requirements of you as an Australian citizen, now that you're no longer under the umbrella of your parents or guardian.

They include signing up for (and understanding the roles of) government services, such as:

REGISTER FOR MYGOV MY.GOV.AU

MyGov is a secure one-stop shop for government services, including:

- Centrelink
- Medicare
- Australian Taxation Office (ATO)
- My Health Record
- Australian JobSearch
- Child Support
- Department of Health Applications Portal
- National Disability Insurance Scheme

WHAT IS ASIC? AUSTRALIAN SECURITIES AND INVESTMENTS COMMISSION

ASIC is an independent Australian government body that regulates laws around company and financial services to protect Australian consumers, investors and creditors.

It helps you deal with disputes around **financial services and products**, such as loans, bank accounts, credit cards, insurance and investing.

It also manages **business and company registrations and fees**.

ASIC also manages a comprehensive money management website, called ASIC's MoneySmart.

ASIC: asic.gov.au, Asic's MoneySmart

CENTRELINK

The Department of Human Services manages Centrelink, Medicare and Child Support agencies.

Centrelink is a government agency that delivers a range of payments and services for the unemployed, families, carers, parents, people with disabilities, indigenous Australians, students (aged 16 to 24) and apprentices.

The service provides support for Australians who are disadvantaged, out of employment, or going through major changes.

Department of Human Services, humanservices.gov.au

MEDICARE AND MEDICAL TREATMENTS

Medicare is the basis of Australia's health care system, which provides free or subsidised services on many healthcare costs, including treatment in public hospitals.

Most permanent Australian residents are eligible for Medicare. You can choose whether to have Medicare cover only or a combination of Medicare and private health insurance.

EXAMPLES OF MEDICARE SERVICES

- **HOSPITAL COVER:** Under Medicare, you can receive free care as a public patient in a public hospital and be treated by a doctor appointed by the hospital.
- **MEDICAL COVER:** Medicare gives access to a range of medical services for free or a lower cost, including doctors, specialists, optometrists and lower-cost prescriptions. When you visit a doctor, Medicare will reimburse 100% of the Medicare Benefits Schedule (MBS) fee for a general practitioner, which is called 'bulk-billing'. Note: Your doctor may charge more than the MBS, so you may have to pay more.

WHAT AGE CAN YOU GET TREATMENT ON YOUR OWN?

- If you're over 16 years old, you can get medical treatment without your parents' or guardians' consent.
- If you're over 14 years old, you may consent to your own medical treatment provided you adequately understand and appreciate the nature and consequences of the medical procedure or treatment. However, if you are 14 or 15 years old, a doctor may still wish to obtain the consent of your parent or guardian.
- If you're 14 years or younger, you will normally need the consent of your parents or guardians to get medical treatment.

WHAT DO YOU NEED TO CHECK BEFORE GETTING MEDICAL TREATMENT ON YOUR OWN?

- Do you have a Medicare Card? See previous page for information on Medicare.
- Find a doctor who 'bulk bills', so it's free of charge.
- Book an appointment and advise them that you will attend without a parent and would like confidentiality.
- Talk openly with your doctor and listen to their advice.

TIP

If you need x-rays or scans, shop around to see who bulk bills. It can be the difference between getting a free scan or paying hundreds of dollars.

Medicare services, humanservices.com.au, Lawstuff (source)

AUSTRALIAN TAXATION OFFICE

The Australian Taxation Office (ATO) is the government's revenue (money) collection agency.

It collects individual company income tax, goods and services (GST) tax, excise and the Medicare levy.

TIPS

- Tax returns are due October 31 following the end of financial year (June 30).
- Tax returns submitted via a tax agent are due April 30 of the following year.

WHAT ARE THE TAX RATES?

Tax Rates for financial year ending June 2021		
Taxable income	Tax on this income	Rates
$0 - $18,200	Nil	0%
$18,201 - $45,000	19c for each $1 over $18,200	19%
$45,001 - $120,000	$5,092 plus 32.5 cents for each $1 over $45,000	32.5%
$120,001 - $180,000	$29,467 plus 37 cents for each $1 over $120,000	37%
$180,001 and over	$51,667 plus 45 cents for each $1 over $180,000	45%
Compulsory superannuation rate: 9.5%.		
The above rates do NOT include the Medicare levy of 2%		

ATO (Australian Taxation Office tax table, individual, rates, Medicare levy) ato.gov.au

What's GST? Goods and services tax (10% on goods and services) was introduced in Australia by the Howard government in July 2000.

GST is levied on most transactions in the production process but is refunded to all business parties in the chain of production.

What's BAS? The business activity statement (BAS) is a form submitted to the ATO by all businesses reporting their taxation obligations, usually on a quarterly basis.

What's a TFN? When you go into the workforce, you will need a TFN (tax file number) so employers can legally employ you. The easiest place to apply for a TFN is via an Australia post office.

Complete the form online, print out the summary and take it to the interview at the Australia post office with proof of your identity.

You will pay tax if you earn more than $18,200 per annum. (2020-2021)

What's an ABN? The Australian Business Number (ABN) is a unique identifier issued to businesses by the Australian Business Register (ABR) which is operated by the Australian Taxation Office (ATO).

What's the Medicare levy? Medicare gives Australian residents access to health care. It's partly funded by the Medicare levy, which is 2% of your taxable income. You pay the Medicare levy in addition to the tax you pay on your taxable income.

GOVERNMENT SUPPORT - WHAT FINANCIAL SUPPORT CAN I GET WHEN LEAVING HOME OR STUDYING?

If you're between 15 and 24 years of age, you may be eligible for payments and services to support you if you're looking for work, studying, training or if you're becoming independent from your parents or carer. Contact Centrelink to see if you're eligible for support.

EXAMPLES OF GOVERNMENT SUPPORT SERVICES:

- **Newstart allowance** is the main income support while you're unemployed and looking for work.
- **Austudy** is the main income support payment if you're 25 or older and a full-time student or Australian Apprentice.
- **ABSTUDY** is financial help for Aboriginal and Torres Strait Islander students and Australian Apprentices.
- **Education entry payment** is a yearly payment you can get when you start to study and get certain income support from the Department of Human Services.
- **Student start-up loan** is a voluntary loan you can get up to twice a year if you're an eligible higher education student.
- **Fares allowance** helps with travel costs between your permanent home and place of tertiary study if you get certain payments from the department.
- **Relocation scholarship** is a once-a-year payment if you get Youth Allowance or ABSTUDY. You must also move to or from a regional or remote area for higher education study.
- **Rent assistance** is an automatic payment if you pay rent and get certain payments from the government.
- **Low-income health care card** is a card to get cheaper health care and medicines if you're on a low income.

- **Australian apprenticeships** provide information and resources about Australian apprenticeships and the support available.
- **My skills** is the national directory of Vocational Education and Training (VET) organisations and courses. It lets you search for and compare courses and providers.
- **Study assist** provides information for students about Australian government help for tertiary study, including information about subsidised fees and government loans.
- **JobSearch** is a free online jobs website. It runs JobActive.

Department of Human Services humanservices.gov.au, (individuals, leaving school, Centrelink, JobSearch), online estimator online estimators, Centrelink payment and service finder

WHAT ARE THE LAWS IN AUSTRALIA?

The rules governing criminal law in Australia are generally set by the individual states and territories, although the Commonwealth Government also has a criminal code covering such things as border control, terrorism and postal offences.

The laws vary from state to state and so legal advice should always be obtained if a criminal law issue emerges. Each state has a legal aid service or community legal services, which are usually free, that you can approach for initial assistance.

WHEN CAN I BE CHARGED WITH A CRIMINAL OFFENCE?

You cannot be charged with a criminal offence until you are **10 years old**, except in Tasmania and the ACT where the ages are 7 and 8 respectively. This is known as the 'Age of Criminal Responsibility'.

If you're between **10 and 14 years,** you may be responsible for the offences you commit if it can be proven that, at the time of the offending behaviour, you knew the behaviour was wrong. It's recommended to get legal advice.

Once you're **14 years old,** you will be responsible for any offence you commit.

WHEN DO I NO LONGER GO TO THE CHILDREN'S COURT?

If you're under 18 years old when the crime was committed and are charged for that crime before you are 21, you'll usually go before the Children's Court. (Except in the Northern Territory, Tasmania and Queensland, where you will be dealt with as an adult once you turn 17.)

Once you turn **18 years old,** you will go to the District Court or Supreme Court depending on the offence.

Note: All matters start in the Local Court and, if serious enough, get referred to the District or Supreme Court. In states, other than NSW, Local Court = Magistrates Court, District Court = County Court.

WHEN WILL I GET A CRIMINAL CONVICTION?

You will not usually get a criminal record for offences committed when you are under 16.

However, although you might not get a 'criminal record' when underage, the system records everything, so if you appear before a court years later the magistrate or judge might still see every entry on the record. Magistrates and judges do not get to see your criminal record until after you have pleaded or been found guilty of the offence for which you're before the court.

LawStuff website, Total Legal. Paul Lewis (source)

LEGAL STUFF - WILL, POWER OF ATTORNEY AND GUARDIANSHIP

WHAT'S A WILL?

A Will is a legal document that clearly sets out your wishes for the distribution of your assets after your death. You'll need a Will if you have any personal assets in order for your assets to go to the people of your choice.

Studies show that **an estimated 45% of Australians die without a Will.**

If you die without a Will, it means you have died 'intestate'. When this happens, the intestacy laws of the state where you reside will determine how your property is distributed upon your death. This includes any bank accounts, securities, real estate, and other assets you own at the time of death.

A Will does not need to be a formal document. It can be on a piece of toilet paper, as long as it's a clear statement of your intentions, it's signed, it's dated, and it's witnessed by two people who are not beneficiaries of the Will. (i.e., won't benefit or get a gift). The witnesses don't need to be lawyers.

TIP

Make sure a copy of your Will is stored safely and your loved ones know where it is.

WHAT'S POWER OF ATTORNEY AND ENDURING POWER OF ATTORNEY?

A power of attorney (POA) is a document you can sign appointing another person to act for you regarding your financial matters. An enduring power of attorney has effect if you lose mental capacity.

WHAT'S ENDURING GUARDIANSHIP?

When you're arranging a Will and POA it's worthwhile to also appoint an enduring guardian, which appoints someone you trust to make medical and living decisions due to incapacity or disability. (Note: a parent would have this role for a minor, but not after you turn 18.) Guardianship is often something considered later in life, but in all fairness, any of us can become incapacitated at any time through an accident or illness.

WHAT ABOUT ORGAN DONATION?

You need to be 16 years or over to register to donate organs or tissues.

You can register online through MyGov or Medicare or the Donate Life website or the Department of Human Services.

Find Law, What is a Will, Human Services - Organ donor register, Donate Life

> "In life, as in business, it's about give-and-take. Don't expect from anyone more than you're willing to give yourself."
>
> *Entrepreneurship.com*

DO YOU KNOW YOU HAVE LEGAL RIGHTS AS AN AUSTRALIAN CITIZEN?

NOTE: This section is an introduction only, to make you aware that you have rights.

Whether you're an employee, buying products and services, renting a home, or simply going about everyday life, you have rights under government laws. Each state's laws vary, so Google search your state and your particular area of concern (e.g. NSW trading laws, Fair Trading).

You also have legal rights under Human Rights legislation to ensure you and others are treated fairly in all areas of life (including at school, at work, at doctors, and in law enforcement).

If you feel you've been unfairly treated or received a fine or been unfairly charged with a crime, then do your online research and seek legal advice.

Free legal advice, Lawyer near me, Community legal centres (CLCS)

WHAT ARE YOUR RIGHTS AS AN EMPLOYEE?

Young people often do not know their rights and are taken advantage of in the workplace, especially in retail and trades.

It's important to read up on your rights, read the employment contract closely and do not do tasks that require formal certifications that you do not have, such as serving drinks without a Responsible Service of Alcohol (RSA) qualification.

Is there a minimum wage I should be paid? Yes. The current NATIONAL MINIMUM WAGE is... $19.84 per hour for employees who are 21 years or older (per 38-hour week before tax, as of 22 April 2021. Fairwork.gov.au), which applies to employees not covered by an award or registered agreement.

Juniors (employees under 21 years of age) get paid a percentage of the relevant adult pay rates. The rate will vary depending on your age, employment type, allowances and your industry. Calculate your specific pay rates here:

fairwork.gov.au/pay/minimum-wages/junior-pay-rates
calculate.fairwork.gov.au/CheckPay

What about sick leave? An employee can take as much paid sick leave as they have accumulated to get better from an injury or illness. Provided you provide proof of your sickness, you can't be fired because you're sick, even for an extended period.

Employers can ask you to give evidence to confirm why you have been away from work at any time, even if you have only been off sick for one (1) day. If you cannot provide evidence of your sickness, you may not be entitled to the sick leave. (You also have rights around personal leave, such as carer's leave, which helps you deal with caring responsibilities or family emergencies.)

What if I am sacked unfairly? If you think you were sacked unfairly, contact the Fair Work Commission first. You have 21 days from the day you were sacked to lodge an application with the Commission.

TIPS FOR EMPLOYEES:

1. Getting cash for work means you're 'off-the-books' and not protected by law. You probably won't get your entitlements (like annual leave, sick leave and penalty rates, superannuation and Workcover insurance, etc).
2. Ensure your employer gives you a PAYSLIP. Check your bank account for the payment.
3. Casual and part-time workers are not entitled to sick leave. They can request leave without pay.

Fair Work Commission, Fair Work Commission minimum wages (source), ACTU (Australian Council of Trade Unions) website – Young workers often ripped off and checkyourpay.com.au

WHAT ARE YOUR RIGHTS AS A CONSUMER (CUSTOMER)?

Read the retail store's terms of trade to see if they allow returns for a refund (money back) or exchange of products. For example, in NSW retailers by law must allow the return of faulty products for a refund. However, return for change of mind is different.

Businesses must guarantee products and services they sell, hire or lease for under $40,000.

Consumer rights, e.g. NSW Fair Trading, ACCC website

HOW DO I AVOID GETTING RIPPED OFF BY TRADESPEOPLE?

It's advisable to get three (3) quotes before deciding on a tradesperson. This allows you to check if the quote is 'around the mark' and reasonable (but remember that cheaper might mean 'cutting corners'). Preferably get a referral from a friend and mention the referring person's name to the tradesperson on requesting a quote.

Ask for references and check if the tradesperson is licensed.

If you're unhappy with the workmanship or with the final price you can contact your state's equivalent to NSW's Department of Fair Trading.

Department of Fair Trading NSW Is my builder or tradesperson licensed? (search for your state)

HOW DO I TO PROTECT MYSELF AGAINST CREDIT CARD SKIMMING?

Credit card skimming is a form of card theft where criminals use a small device (or 'skimmer') to steal your card information.

HERE ARE SOME TIPS TO PROTECT YOU:

- Keep your card in sight in a store or restaurant at all times.
- Never share your PIN and cover the keypad when you enter your PIN.
- Look for signs of tampering at the ATM, like loose or moving parts. Avoid outdoor ATMs.
- Check your credit card statement regularly for fraudulent transactions.
- Report suspicious activity to your bank, or the police or Crime Stoppers on 1800 333 000.

Crime Stoppers, AFP Identity crime

TIPS WHEN CHOOSING A PHONE PLAN

1. SHOP AROUND to get the best deal. Contact your current provider each year to check you're on the best plan, as new deals come out regularly. Note: Telecommunications companies generally don't contact you with cheaper plans. You need to ask.
2. Know your rights if you have a problem.
3. Make sure you know exactly what you need. If you use lots of data and go over your plan, this is where the costs rise fast!
4. Check there is NO LOCK-IN CONTRACT and that the phone is NOT LOCKED to a provider.
5. Don't sign anything without reading the fine print! Be sure you understand the terms before agreeing to anything. Check if there is down-time when changing over from one provider to another (i.e. you may not want to go without a phone for 24 to 48 hours).

Consumer rights ACCC; ACCC - internet and phone

WHAT DOES AN OMBUDSMAN DO?

An ombudsman is an independent person who investigates complaints about the decisions and actions of Australian Government agencies when you feel you've been unfairly treated.

More than 500,000 complaints are made to the public sector and industry ombudsmen in Australia each year.

The ombudsman's services are free and are usually the last port of call after you've exhausted all other avenues to deal with the dispute.

Ombudsman, ACCC Dispute Resolution

CYBER SAFETY - DO YOU EVER WORRY ABOUT STAYING SAFE ON THE INTERNET?

NOTE: The lock next to the URL must be closed. An open lock is NOT SECURE.

THINGS TO CHECK WHEN SHOPPING ONLINE:

- Ensure the site has a secure SSL.
- Read reviews and ratings to feel satisfied the website is not a scam.
- What fees apply? Is the currency in Australian dollars? Is there an international transaction fee?
- Use a secure payment option, such as PayPal.
- Are there other potential delivery costs?
- Check you're not agreeing to contracts or on-going membership.
- Is there a warranty or guarantee (if things go wrong)?
- Have you read the fine print before committing to a purchase?

THE TOP 5 CYBER-SMART TIPS FOR UNDER 25s ARE:

- Create long, strong, unique passwords. Set two-factor authentication where possible to protect accounts.
- To avoid scams, check authenticity first and be careful of clicking on links in emails.
- Backup your device or laptop to the cloud or a hard drive, in case of loss, a virus, or damage.
- Don't post anything online you wouldn't want on the evening news!
- Use social media for positive connections, fun and friendships. Don't live your life online.

Leonie Smith The Cyber Safety Lady (source), ASIC's MoneySmart shopping online, StaySmartonline Current cyber threats, eSafety Commissioner, ACCC Scamwatch

HOW DO I DEAL WITH CYBERBULLYING?

Cyberbullying can occur on any online social media platform. Harassing comments can be shared and spread rapidly 24/7, while the bully's identity can often remain hidden.

Under current Australian law it's an offence for a person to use the internet or technology in a way that's threatening, harassing or offensive.

Such behaviour can result in very heavy fines or even prison sentences. The maximum sentence varies depending on which state or territory you are in. In NSW, as of October 2020, offenders could face up to five years in jail and a potential fine of more than $30,000. (Source: ACORN)

Police have the power to arrest serious offenders and take out apprehended violence orders (AVOs).

Check the laws in your state or territory.

There are also stalking offences in each state and territory, which carry heavy maximum penalties.

Consult your local police website for further information or contact the **Police assistance line on 131 444.**

4 WAYS TO DEAL WITH TROLLS:

- Don't be tempted to respond or react. When they fail to get a response, they'll usually lose interest.
- Report the troll to the social media provider. Delete or block the user.
- Tighten your security settings on social media accounts.
- Have 'time out' from social media and talk to real people.

(Also, refer to the 'how to deal with bullies' section of this guide.)

Report cyber-bullying via Australian Cybercrime Online Reporting Network (ACORN) Youth Central Web social safety, eSafety Stay safe online young people

TOP TRAVEL TIPS FOR UNDER 25s

PASSPORTS

When you're applying for a new passport, organise it well in advance of your travel date as it can take **up to four weeks** to process.

Passport Applications (passports.gov.au) can be done through Australia post offices (including passport photos).

Documents you'll need (Unless you qualify for streamlined renewal of a previous passport):

- Birth certificate – original copy of your full birth certificate
- Australian citizenship proof – evidence that you're an Australian citizen
- Identification – identity documents with your photo, signature and current address
- Any documents that prove change of name or change of gender.

TIP

If you still have a child's passport, it's only valid for five years, not 10 years.

VISAS

Check if you need a visa for the country you're visiting (Visa Quick Check) and any other entry requirements. *E.g. some countries won't let you enter unless your passport is valid for six months after you plan to leave the country, and some require you to have proof of a flight out before they will let you in.*

TRAVEL INSURANCE

Depending on the level of cover, insurance can compensate you for cancelled or delayed flights, medical treatment, theft, lost valuables, accidents and loss of luggage, etc. SmartTraveller Travel insurance guide

Remember: Travel insurance companies will often require a police report for crimes.

> **TIP**
>
> There is NO insurance payout if you engage in illegal behaviour, such as having no license, no helmet, or using drugs or being over the legal limit of alcohol.

IN CASE OF AN ACCIDENT OR EMERGENCY ask for help from the local police, and contact family and friends. If you need Australian Government assistance, you can contact the consular section of the Australian Embassy, High Commission or Consulate-General at your destination. Visit: Australian Government embassies and consulates.

> **TIP**
>
> The Australian Government provides 24-hour consular assistance: +61 2 6261 3305 or SMS service: +61 421 269 080.

TRAVEL VACCINATIONS

Some countries may have a condition of entry that you're vaccinated against certain diseases.

> **TIP**
>
> You might require several doses spread over weeks. Visit your doctor at least 6 weeks prior to travel (preferably 12 weeks). **Health Direct website** Travel vaccinations

TRAVEL DOS AND DON'TS

DO:

- Keep your passport and credit cards safe, preferably in a bum-bag or clothing close to your body and not in a handbag. Alternatively, keep your passport and credit cards in the hotel safe.

- Take copies of your passport, travel documents and insurance papers and leave them in your hotel, as they're your most important documents, and having copies can speed up the replacement process.

TIP

If you lose your passport overseas it can take two weeks to get a replacement via the Australian consulate in the country that you are in.

- It's recommended you have at least six (6) months' validity on your passport before you leave for overseas.
- Know your budget and the costs in the country to ensure you have enough money to cover the whole trip.
- Have a buddy system and connect with other travellers (watch out for each other).
- Travel insurance is recommended (see page 38).
- Understand the laws and customs of the country you're visiting and be aware of any unsafe areas.
- Beware of unwelcome interest from strangers. Don't be too trusting.
- Blend into the crowd and don't look like a tourist. Do walk with purpose.
- Ask the hotel concierge what to be careful of. In some countries only use Uber, as taxis might be fake.
- Register your destination for free with SmartTraveller 1300 555 135 (option 3).
- Check your luggage and have clear ID labels on all pieces.
- Pre-book travel to your hotel on arrival in a new country and have the first night's accommodation (at least) booked.
- See your destination 'as it truly is', not just how it's advertised.

DON'T:

- Don't drink too much or accept drinks from strangers. Don't leave drinks unattended (to avoid spiking). Don't leave venues alone with strangers or give information to new people about where you're staying.
- Don't wear bling jewellery or display other valuables, such as expensive

cameras or phones, which can attract potential thieves.
- Don't walk alone or in poorly lit areas. Instead, walk where there are other people and not in quiet lanes or alone late at night.
- Don't carry a lot of cash and don't flash cash around if you have it.
- Don't break the law. Don't carry or take drugs, as laws in some countries are severe, including jail terms and even the death penalty.
- Remember: Keep your passport and other important documents in a safe place!

Youth Central Advice for travellers, Countries with harshest drug laws

DO YOU REALLY NEED HEALTH AND INCOME INSURANCE?

Note:for car insurance refer to Car section in this guide

1. HEALTH INSURANCE:

If you decide to take out private health insurance, choose the most suitable insurance for your needs to keep monthly premiums down.

TIPS

1. Review your health cover annually to see you're getting the best deal that suits you.
2. You can avoid the 2% Medicare Levy surcharge if you have private health insurance (hospital cover).
3. Consider extras cover for non-hospital services, like physiotherapy and optical.
4. Having private health insurance can avoid waiting lists in the public health care system.

Compare health insurance

2. INCOME PROTECTION AND SAFE-WORK:

Income protection insures against injury or accidents and is advisable if you have a high-risk job or high cost of living, such as a mortgage to cover in the event of being unable to work.

Higher risk jobs include construction, building, truck driver, refuse collection, roofer, tree feller, miner and labourer.

WHAT'S A WHITE CARD IN THE BUILDING INDUSTRY?

A white card (or general construction induction card) is required for workers who want to carry out construction work.

MoneySmart income protection, Safe Work licences and registrations, high-risk occupations

VOTING AND POLITICS (IN BRIEF)

As the future leaders of this country, it's important to care about politics and make your vote count instead of casting an informal vote that does not indicate a clear voting preference or is left blank, and therefore is invalid (a.k.a. a donkey vote).

VOTING IS COMPULSORY FOR AUSTRALIAN CITIZENS AGED 18 YEARS AND OVER.

Once you turn 18, you need to ENROL to vote and advise the Australian Electoral Commission of any changes of address. If you don't vote you may receive a fine.

WHY SHOULD I VOTE?

Voting enables you to choose your representatives in parliament, as part of the democratic process in this country.

You should choose the candidate whose policies you agree with the most. Usually, each candidate belongs to a political party, such as the two main parties in Australia (Labor and Liberal) or the Greens. Some candidates stand as independents.

WHAT IS POLITICS? (IN CASE YOU WEREN'T LISTENING IN CLASS)

Politics controls everything in society, including the economy, taxes, education, development decisions, environmental issues, the social security system, laws, the health system and international affairs.

WHAT IS THE AUSTRALIAN CONSTITUTION?

The Australian Constitution is the supreme law of the country. It sets out the way that Australia is governed by three tiers of government: federal, state and local.

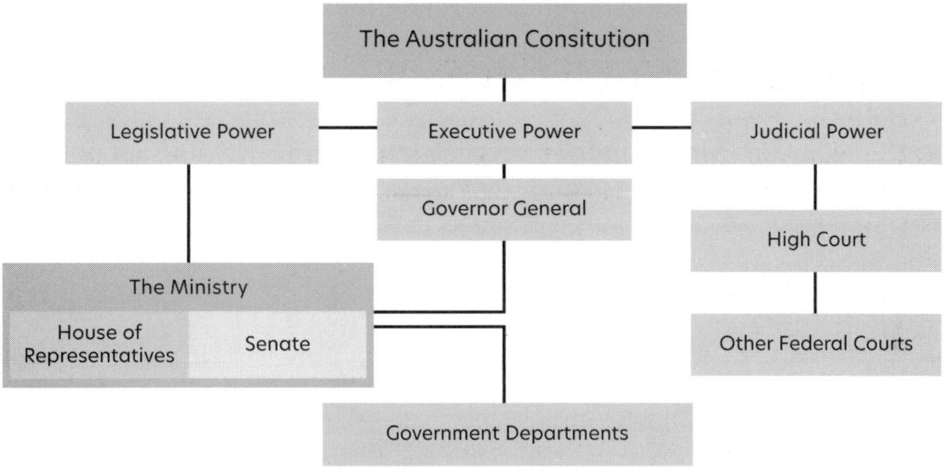

The legal system administers justice, including judges and magistrates, according to legislation/law.

Parliamentary Education Office, Parliament Explained, AEC - how to enrol to vote

WHAT DOES IT MEAN TO BE SOCIALLY RESPONSIBLE?

Social responsibility is about us 'doing our bit' for society and the environment, to safeguard the planet for future generations and sustainability.

By increasing awareness of our collective environmental footprint, both businesses and individuals can maintain a balance between the economy and the ecosystems.

Doing good stuff also has a feel-good spin-off.

10 EVERYDAY EXAMPLES TO CONSERVE OUR LIMITED RESOURCES:

- Using eco-friendly shopping, produce and (compostable) garbage bags.
- Using reusable coffee mugs and water bottles.
- Being aware of your carbon emissions (Carbon footprint calculator).
- Choosing products that have been produced ethically.
- Being careful to recycle goods properly.
- Reducing the use of plastics, such as drinking straws.
- Setting up a compost bin.
- Conserving water and 'going green' with washing and cleaning products.
- Using fans (and only using the air conditioner when really essential).
- Picking up rubbish and/or getting involved in clean-up Australia day.

HOW TO ADDRESS AN ENVELOPE (THE OLD-FASHIONED WAY)

If you've never had to post a letter, you may be unaware how to do it.

The mail service in Australia is Australia Post. It has many other services, such as payment of bills for some Australian services and the processing of Australian passports and passport photographs.

The cost of a stamp for sending a small letter or postcard is currently $1.10 (as of 12 January 2021).

You then take the letter to the post office or post it in an Australia Post red street posting box.

FRONT OF ENVELOPE – RECIPIENT'S DETAILS:

1 – Name
2 – Street address. If it is a business, the business name must be written first. If there is a Unit or Level number then this must also be written.
3 – Suburb and state/territory in CAPITAL letters
4 – Postcode
5 – Place a stamp on the top right corner

BACK OF ENVELOPE – SENDER'S DETAILS:

Remember to include your details on the back, as per the front (but without the stamp ☺)

Australia Post, address an envelope

2. HOW TO GET SAVVY WITH MONEY

Please note: All information in this section is provided as a general, practical guide to finance. If you require financial advice, contact a registered financial planner or chartered accountant.

THE SECRETS TO GETTING SMART WITH MONEY

Having control of your money gives you more freedom to do the stuff you enjoy.

However, most students leave school understanding mathematics, but have very little idea how to manage their own money so they have security for the future.

> "Money isn't everything. Not having it is!"
>
> *Kanye West*

There are a lot of things that you can do to get smart with your money. The top tips include:

- Spend less than you earn. i.e., live within your means.
- Get savvy and save. i.e., get in the habit of saving.
- Know where you're at with your finances. i.e., budget = Track your spending against income.
- Have a goal to invest (in things that go up in value) and grow your money.
- Avoid debt. i.e., don't over-spend on things that go down in value, like cars.
- Prioritise your money. i.e., have a financial plan.
- Don't get in the credit card trap. i.e., if you don't have it, don't spend it.
- Always manage your own money, even in a relationship. i.e., have separate personal accounts.
- Show self-control and don't buy for quick gratification. i.e., only buy necessities.

BEST MONEY-MANAGEMENT SITE IN AUSTRALIA:

ASIC's MoneySmart (website moneysmart.gov.au) offers FREE advice on managing money, budgeting (interactive budget planner), financial calculators, superannuation calculator, income tax calculator, investor tool kit, mortgage calculator, personal loan calculator, help with debt, avoiding scams, building wealth, financial counselling and what to do if you lose your job.

ASIC's MoneySmart budget planner, ReachOut Australia How to manage your funds, tips for young investors, *Rich Dad Poor Dad* book by Robert Kiyosaki

"Do not let making a living prevent you from making a life."

John Wooden

A SIMPLE BUDGET GIVES A SNAPSHOT OF YOUR FINANCES

CATEGORY	WEEKLY	MONTHLY	ANNUALLY
INCOME			
Job # 1			
Job # 2			
Support from parents			
Support from Centrelink			
Study loans / financial aid			
Miscellaneous income (e.g. tips)			
INCOME SUBTOTAL =			
EXPENSES			
Rent / board			
Home utilities (gas, power)			
Food / groceries			
Mobile phone			
Car petrol / running costs			
Car insurance			
Car repayments			
Transport (bus or train)			
Parking			
Uni fees / books			
Tuition			
Computer costs / internet			
Going out / entertainment			
Personal care / hair / pharmacy			
Clothes / personal Items			
Health care / insurance			
Loan repayments			
Miscellaneous expenses			
EXPENSES SUBTOTAL =			
INCOME - EXPENSES = SAVINGS			

"If you fail to plan, you are planning to fail."

Benjamin Franklin

HERE'S AN ESTIMATED COST OF LIVING BREAKDOWN:

Illustration by Steve Panozzo, The Cartoon Factory

NEEDS - LIVING / FIXED EXPENSES (50-60%):

- Mortgage or rent
- Food / groceries (note, some financial experts put food as a discretionary spend)
- Home utilities (water, power, gas, phones, internet, broadband)
- Personal phone
- Transport and/or motor vehicle
- Other bills, like insurances and uni or tuition fees

WANTS - PERSONAL COSTS / DISCRETIONARY EXPENSES (20-30%):

- Fun stuff (e.g., hobbies and gifts)
- Clothing and personal care
- Entertainment and going out
- Membership and subscriptions

SAVINGS - PLANNING AND EMERGENCY (15-25%):

- Holiday savings
- Future plans
- Emergency reserves

Experts and financial advisors variously put fixed, or necessary, living costs at between 50% to 60% of total net (after tax) income. This will depend on factors such as city-living and high accommodation costs, which can increase your fixed expenses and, therefore, reduce your discretionary spend and savings plan.

(Note: this is a guide only. Its intention is to raise awareness around the importance of budgeting.)

ASIC's Money Smart budgeting, budgeting on a low income, 50-30-20 budget, Services Australia's help to budget

10 THINGS ABOUT MONEY YOU'LL WISH YOU'D KNOWN EARLIER!

Author of The Money Factory**, Lillie Cawthorn says:**

> "I was lucky enough to be in a home where money beliefs were solid. Unfortunately, not all people get this," according to Lillie.

It's really powerful to forgive the money stories that played out around you when you were a child, which frees you to create a new money story for yourself. Believing that money is 'available' and abundant is the key to bringing more into your life.

"Money can be attracted to you by putting your focus on getting a job, being disciplined with your savings and spending, and by understanding the principles of wealth, i.e., don't spend it unwisely and save to invest, so your money works for you," says Lillie.

TOP 10 TIPS:

1. **Start saving:** Get into the habit of always saving something every pay day. It will accrue quickly.
2. **Be transparent:** If you get in strife don't put your head in the sand. Be honest with your creditors. Call them up and explain, as they're usually able to help if they can see you're being proactive.
3. **Have a budget:** Track your spending. If you don't have a budgeting app on your smart phone, use a notebook to jot down your spending, so you know your expenses and income.
4. **Is it a 'want' or a 'need'?** Know that there's a difference between a WANT and a NEED (e.g., we need a new pair of shoes, or we want a pair of Converse).
5. **Avoid credit cards:** Use a debit card which uses your money from your own account. Credit cards are deceptive. Once you get one it's like a rabbit getting caught in a trap. "It's like a drug, having access to easy money, but it's an evil spiral." (Plus, only the banks benefit from the big interest rates charged.)
6. **Be clever and be frugal:** Limit household services like Foxtel. You don't need the highest services. But you don't need to feel deprived.

You can get Netflix or a SmartTV. Also, don't eat out all the time... Eating in is cheaper and healthier.

7. **Is your account fee-free?** Check your bank account is FEE-FREE. Many banks now have fee-free online accounts with unlimited free transactions.
8. **Check bank accounts regularly:** Download your bank statement and check if those debits are really yours and are accurate. Look for places you're overspending and find savings opportunities.
9. **Keep receipts to return goods:** You'd be surprised how many businesses process mistakes. Look at the bill. Also, it's good practice to keep your receipts as a warranty, if you need to replace or repair any goods.
10. **Recycle stuff:** You can sell what you don't use on Gumtree, Facebook or Buy Sell Swap.

Lillie's words of wisdom:

- "90% of humans are scared of maths, because they don't understand it."
- "Make a friend of money, not an enemy."
- "Give and be generous as it will return to you."
- "Support a charity each month or give a dollar to the homeless. Money is energy and recycles."

5 SAVVY FINANCIAL PLANNING HACKS FOR UNDER 25s

Julia Blenkhorn is co-owner of Blenkhorn Financial Planning, where they have a strong passion for financial education. **Blenkhorn Financial Planning**

1. SET FINANCIAL GOALS

Set yourself a savings goal for each week. Set financial goals around your income and savings as well as lifestyle goals. Create a budget for spending. There are some great apps as well that help you manage your money and save. They help you set a budget for a set period of time to ensure you don't overspend.

2. START SAVING – DON'T SPEND MORE THAN YOU EARN

Your earnings should **exceed** your spending.

Saving money is simple with easy-to-implement strategies. For example, one simple one is to put away every $5 note you have in your purse or wallet. You will be surprised what you can save if you employ this strategy.

Two nice ways to ensure you save some money each week are by structuring your bank accounts correctly and finding a good savings account, which, of course, allows you to buy things in the future.

3. TRICKS TO SAVE ON YOUR MOBILE PHONES

There are many different types of mobile phone contracts. Consider these points before you buy:

- How much does the phone cost? How much does it cost to use your phone?
- How much data do you realistically need?
- Buying a phone outright will save you a lot of money in the long term.

4. CREDIT CARDS ARE THE FASTEST WAYS TO BURY YOURSELF IN DEBT. HERE ARE SOME TIPS TO AVOID CREDIT DEBT:

- Save or layby for the things you really want instead of using credit.
- Use your savings account as your own personal (debit) 'credit' card and be sure to pay yourself back.
- Understand that credit is 'borrowed' money which has to be paid back with interest and bank fees.
- A maxed-out card with a limit of $5,000 could take you 45 years to pay off with an interest rate of 20% (if you only make minimum payments).

5. CARS ARE EXPENSIVE AND DEPRECIATE QUICKLY

Cars are expensive to purchase, run, insure and maintain. By making an informed decision, you could save yourself a lot of money.

Also, cars depreciate very quickly, especially new cars. Do your research on cars that have affordable parts and good feedback from mechanics and independent expert reviews. Consider buying a well-maintained second-hand car, but not too old, as you may end up spending more money on repairs and parts than the initial cost of the car. A smaller car means less petrol and more money to save.

CREDIT CARDS ARE A POTENTIAL 'MONEY TRAP' FOR YOUNG PEOPLE

Once you get on the credit card merry-go-round it's hard to get off. Saying to yourself "I'll just put it on the credit card" makes it too easy to over-spend, and before you know it your debt has exploded.

It might look like easy money, but credit cards have high-interest rate charges compared to car or home loans.

TIP

If you don't have the money now, don't buy it (save up for it!). In other words - don't get a credit card at all. Use a debit card instead, so you pay from your savings and know you can afford whatever it is you're buying.

If you've done your research and decide you still want a credit card, **shop around for a card that has a low-interest rate.** **Interest is calculated daily and is charged once per month.*

What's a credit account? (-): When you use a credit card, you're borrowing money from the account's credit limit, up to a maximum amount approved by the bank/lender. Just like any other loan it has a % interest charged on the balance.

What's a debit account? (+): A debit account is when you already have money in a bank account and draw money out from your savings. There's no interest charged, as you're drawing off your own money.

3 RESOURCEFUL TIPS:

1. Afterpay is a form of credit. i.e., buy now, pay later. Like a layby, you 'save' to buy, by paying in instalments. However, be careful, as afterpay fees are very high if you miss the repayments.
2. If you're married or in a partnership, always manage your own daily finances, as money can be a manipulative tool. Even if you have a joint home account, keep your independence, check your account regularly, know your PINs and have money for emergencies.
3. It's easy to get tricked into getting a credit card. Some banks and retailers (such as electrical goods or furniture stores) entice you to get a credit card because it's an incentive for you to spend with them. They might offer two years interest-free terms, however, at the end of that two-year term, the interest rates can be sky high... and you might have accrued even more debt on the card in the meantime. Be careful and aware when you sign up for anything.

ASIC's MoneySmart credit card calculator, Canstar minimum payments, Debt Help Australia lower debt repayments

WHAT'S A CREDIT RATING?

Your credit score estimates how trustworthy you are as a borrower to a prospective lender, based on your previous financial dealings.

A bad credit rating can affect your chance of getting a mortgage or personal loan.

Your credit rating (or credit score) is a rating, usually between zero and 1,000. A low score means you're a higher lending risk.

THE CREDIT SCORE IS CALCULATED BASED ON:

- How much money you've borrowed.
- Whether you pay your debts on time or fall behind on payments.
- The number of credit applications you have made.

WAYS TO DAMAGE YOUR CREDIT RATING:

- Applying for several credit cards or loans at once.
- Lots of credit inquiries.
- Missing repayments.
- Maxing out your credit limits.
- Court writs and summons.
- Applying for balance transfers too often.
- Bankruptcy and insolvency.

ASIC's MoneySmart understanding credit scores, Finder credit rating, get credit score

WHEN DO YOU HAVE TO START PAYING YOUR HECS-HELP LOAN?

Once you earn over $46,620 (2020-21), you'll need to start repaying your HELP loan through the tax system (through the Australian Taxation Office), even if you're still studying.

Check the sites listed below for information about when you need to start paying off your HELP loan and how you can repay the debt faster.

You can visit ATO voluntary repayments or contact the ATO on 132 861 for further information on how to make your voluntary repayment.

Please note: the compulsory repayment threshold is adjusted each year.

2020-21 HELP repayment rates	
2020-21 Repayment Income (RI)	**Repayment % rate**
Below $46,620	Nil
$46,620 - $53,826	1.0%
$53,827- $57,055	2.0%
$57,056 - $60,479	2.5%
$60,480 - $64,108	3.0%
$64,109 - $67,954	3.5%
$67,955 - $72,031	4.0%
$72,032 - $76,354	4.5%
$76,355 - $80,935	5.0%
$80,936 - $85,792	5.5%
$85,793 - $90,939	6.0%
$90,940 - $96,396	6.5%
$96,397 - $102,179	7.0%
$102,180 - $108,309	7.5%
$108,310 - $114,707	8.0%
$114,708 - $121,698	8.5%
$121,699 - $128,999	9.0%
$129,000 - $136,739	9.5%
$136,740 and above	10%

Study assist paying back my loan, ACCC help when you're in debt, ATO repayment thresholds and rates

TAX DO'S AND DON'TS FOR UNDER 25s

By Stuart Boyers - Owner/director of Sydney-based accounting practice, SME Business Accountants, which has been providing professional services to small businesses and their owners for the past 17 years. SME Business Accountants

So, you're becoming financially independent – starting to earn your own way in life. There are a few matters to consider regarding your tax obligations.

In 2020/21 your first $18,200 is tax free; however, you can earn as much as $21,884 before paying any tax when taking into account the Low-Income offsets, as long as you have a Tax File Number (TFN).

First of all, you need to apply for a TFN to take advantage of the tax benefits above. Without it, you will be taxed at 47% on all your income.

TAX RETURN TIPS:

At the end of each financial year, which runs from 1 July – 30 June, you will receive a summary from your employer (via MyGov) of what you have earned and how much tax they have deducted.

You should then complete a tax return by 31 October, which can be done yourself online using your MyGov account if it is a simple return, or a tax agent if you are self-employed and have completed many jobs during the year and may find it hard to complete.

You will need to include ALL your earnings on your tax return, not just those paid to you by your employer, which includes interest earned, dividends received, etc. and even some Centrelink payments.

You are also entitled to claim for some expenses, most of which are directly related to your income.

To claim work-related expenses:

1. You must have spent the money yourself and not been reimbursed.
2. It must directly relate to earning your income.
3. You must have a record to prove it. (Keep all your receipts – find a handy place to keep them all together, this will make it simple at tax time, or use the ATO app's myDeductions tool.)

(You can only claim the work-related portion, if the expense has been used for both private and work purposes.)

COMMON DEDUCTIONS INCLUDE BUT ARE NOT LIMITED TO:

- Motor vehicle – be careful with this – you can claim up to 5,000km at 72c per km but NOT for travel between home and work. You must be able to substantiate this claim. Alternatively your basis for a deduction could be a % of all your motor vehicle-related expenses; however, you will be required to complete a 12-week valid logbook to determine the business use %. Be sure to get some advice on how to complete a valid logbook.
- Travel expenses – once again, this is not between home and work.
- Tax agent fees.
- Compulsory uniform – this identifies you as an employee of an organisation and is strictly enforced or a non-compulsory uniform that your employer has registered with AusIndustry (check with your employer).
- Protective clothing and footwear to protect you from the risk of illness or injury, or to prevent damage to ordinary clothing.
- Tools.
- Donations (not if you have received a personal benefit, e.g., raffle ticket, items, fundraiser dinners, etc).
- Mobile phone usage – you will need to substantiate your business use percentage (%).
- Investment expenses.

WHAT ABOUT SUPERANNUATION? WHAT IS IT?

Once you start work and are 18 years of age, or work more than 30 hours per week, you will be entitled to superannuation guarantee contributions by your employers if you earn $450 or more in a month.

Most Australians have the right to choose their own super-fund, however certain industrial awards determine the fund on behalf of their employees.

These can usually be changed by contacting the fund.

If you do have the choice, take the time to choose the right fund for you. Talk to people and do a bit of research. Once you choose your fund, check what they will be deducting from your super contributions, e.g., life insurance.

Starting young with a good superannuation plan can make a big difference to your financial situation in the future.

Superannuation is a tax-effective way to save for your retirement. Your money is pooled with other members' money and invested on your behalf by professional investment managers.

In most cases you can access your 'super' once you reach 60, when you retire from your current job; or at 65 you can get total access to your super without any questions asked.

Your employer pays the super on your behalf. The super guarantee contribution rate is currently 9.5% of your gross salary and wages if you earn $450 per month or more before tax.

ASIC's MoneySmart how superannuation works, Super Guide withdrawing your super, ATO calculate your superannuation

DOCUMENTS YOU'LL NEED FOR YOUR TAX RETURN

- **Payment summaries or income statements** – Income from employers, super or government agencies. (Note: If the employer is reporting through Single Touch Payroll (STP) the payment summary information will be available online in MyGov which will be called an 'income statement'.)
- **Bank statements** – Details any interest you have earned and fees you have paid.
- **Shares, unit trusts or managed funds statements.**
- **Buy and sell investment statements** – Needed to calculate capital gains and losses.
- **Records from your rental property** – Annual tax statement.
- **Foreign income** – Details of foreign pensions or other foreign income.
- **Private health insurance policy statement.**

ATO tax deductions you can claim, ASIC's MoneySmart tax return tips

> "If you don't find a way to make money while you sleep, you will work until you die."
>
> *Warren Buffett*

INVESTING – IT'S NEVER TOO EARLY, OR TOO LATE, TO START INVESTING

"You can start investing for as little as $50 a month. You've got to take that step and start doing something," according to Jeff Rose in the video below.

If you're looking to start investing in share portfolios or real estate, consider getting advice from financial and investment advisors who have the latest data and research.

As a rookie investor, start by doing your research into investments that suit you and that have the best return on investment. You might look at the property market, depending on your borrowing capacity, or the stock market, where shares are bought and sold (much like at an auction, where there are sellers, bidders and an auctioneer).

WHAT'S ASX?

In Australia it's called the Australian Securities Exchange (ASX), where around 2,000 companies (like BHP, Westpac, Woolworths, and Telstra) are listed on the exchange. When starting out, it's best to invest in quality shares from the top 20-50 on the ASX that are highly liquid, according to Wealth Within's Dale Gillham's blog (below).

The author of *The Barefoot Investor*, Scott Pape, says "start small, but just start! The sooner you can get into the property or investment markets the better."

Investing for beginners, ASX start investing, Wealth Within investing, Jeff Rose first time investor tips, Listcorp companies listed

3. A GUIDE TO BUYING YOUR FIRST CAR

WHAT DO YOU NEED TO CONSIDER WHEN BUYING YOUR FIRST CAR?

Buying your first car might be the first major purchasing decision that you make, so you want to make sure you get it right.

Start by researching the type of car that fits your specific needs and budget. E.g., do you like compact and sporty, or an off-road SUV (sport utility vehicle)?

If you're buying a second-hand car, be especially vigilant and do your homework. An older car can come with a heap of mechanical problems if you don't do your due diligence, which is costly, leaves you without a car while it's in the garage and may be less safe if it doesn't have all the safety features of a newer car. However, a new car also loses value the minute it's driven out of the dealership, so consider a demo model with 1,000 or 2,000 kilometres (plus newer cars have long warranties).

We highly recommend ASIC's MoneySmart guide to buying a car start-up pack to help you to:

- Avoid common car buying traps and identify hidden costs.
- Find out the real cost of your car purchase.
- Find alternate ways to finance a car... and many more tips.

CHECKLIST BEFORE YOU PURCHASE A CAR

- What can you afford? Know your budget. Can you get finance if you need it?
- What type of car do you need or want? Is it for work or private use?
- Are you licensed to drive a manual or automatic only?
- Will the car have good re-sale value? Does the model/year of car have good independent reviews?
- Have you got the money to pay for insurance and stamp duty?
- Check P-plate driver restrictions in your state. (Some states restrict the cars allowed to be driven by P-platers, based on a power-to-weight calculation. e.g., in NSW, there are restrictions on vehicles with a ratio of 130kw-per-tonne.)

TIP

Know all the up-front and on-going costs.

CHECKLIST WHEN SHOPPING FOR A SECOND-HAND CAR:

- **Age and mileage** of the vehicle.
- When does the **registration expire**? Registration can be costly, so this is a cost consideration.
- Check **proof of ownership** via the personal properties securities register (PPSR). If money is still owing on the car, it could get repossessed.
- Go online for the car's **accident history check** (via the VIN or registration number).
- Arrange a **pre-purchase mechanical report**, e.g., NSW Fair Trading, vehicle inspections.
- Has the car been **serviced regularly**? Check the service manual.

- Some state authorities require **proof that the car being sold is roadworthy.**
- If you buy through a **dealer there are usually guarantees**, but not with a private sale.

TIP

With a dealer, check there are no dealer delivery costs.

- After the purchase, remember to **transfer the registration** into your name at the motor registry office (or online). The seller also does the transfer, but don't rely on this because your address details need to be accurate so that you receive registration expiry reminders.

ASIC's MoneySmart guide to buying a car, Carsales.com.au P-plate prohibited vehicles, car accident history, vehicle inspections, Check if money is owing on the vehicle - PPSR

CAR COSTS - REGISTRATION, STAMP DUTY AND INSURANCE

Before you buy a car, ensure you've budgeted enough money to cover the transfer costs (stamp duty) and on-going costs (registration, insurance and maintenance).

CAR REGISTRATION FEES

You will need to pay an annual fee to register your car. This fee varies between different states and territories.

IS A MECHANICAL OR OTHER INSPECTION REQUIRED?

Safety certificate requirements vary in each state. Google your state's requirements. (E.g., In NSW, an e-safety check, called a pink slip, is required for a car more than five years old as a condition of registration renewal.)

WHAT IS STAMP DUTY?

Stamp duty is the one-off tax payable to the government on the purchase of a motor vehicle.

Ensure you pay the stamp duty promptly, as it may cost more two weeks after purchase.

Check this site: savings.com.au/car-loans/stamp-duty for the various stamp duties payable on cars in each state in Australia.

WHAT HAPPENS IF YOUR CAR REGISTRATION EXPIRES?

If your registration expires, you're not insured in the event of an accident.

Police can trace your registration plates from their cars to check if your car's registered.

If it's not registered, you'll receive a fine.

Put your date of renewal for registration in your phone as an auto-reminder, so you don't forget.

Cars Guide cost to register a car in Australia, vehicle inspections

CAR INSURANCE – COMPULSORY THIRD PARTY VERSUS COMPREHENSIVE INSURANCE

As a general rule, you should not be paying more than 10% of the car's value each year in (non-compulsory) insurance premiums. Of course, compulsory third party is required by law, however, you'll notice in the table below, that the other insurance options cover you, in varying degrees, for other people's cars and full cover on your own car.

"Whether you drive a bomb or a sports car, insurance is essential," according to *Choice.com.au*

1. **Compulsory third party (CTP)** insurance is included in your car registration cost (except in NSW where it's called a 'green slip', and you buy it separately). It covers the costs of *compensation claims if you injure or kill other people* in an accident.
2. You have the option to take **third party property** insurance, which covers the *damage to other people's cars* and property when an accident is your fault; or **third-party property, fire and theft** insurance, which covers your car if it's stolen or damaged by fire.
3. **The other option is comprehensive insurance, which** covers *repairs to your car and other people's cars* in an accident. It also covers your car if it is stolen, vandalised or damaged by fire or flood.

Types of car insurance	Covers damage to your car	Covers damage to other people's cars	Covers theft of your car (loss or damage)	Covers injury or death to others in an accident
Compulsory Third Party (NSW = Green slip)	✗	✗	✗	✓
Third Party Property	✗	✓	✗	✗
Third Party Property, Fire & Theft	✗	✓	✓	✗
Comprehensive Insurance	✓	✓	✓	✗

What's the 'excess'? When you make an insurance claim you will pay an out-of-pocket amount called the excess. The excess is decided when you take out the insurance policy and is usually lower if you pay a higher premium. e.g. if your excess is $500 and your damages are $10,000, you pay the $500 and the insurer pays $9,500.

TIP

Check when taking out the insurance policy, as excess for under 25s can be as much as $1,500-$2,000.

What's a no claim bonus? Some policies have a 'no claim bonus' where you pay a lower premium for not making a claim for a period of time.

TIPS

1. Shop around to get a good deal on insurance - Search online for the best insurance for your needs. Check for any exclusions that are not covered under the policy, such as storm damage.
2. Look for insurance that covers anyone who drives your car. Read the fine print before agreeing to anything. If someone else is driving your car, double-check your insurance, and list him/her as a nominated driver to ensure you're covered.
3. If you're driving under the influence of alcohol or drugs (DUI), or driving an unregistered vehicle, you're not insured. You'll need to pay for damage to all vehicles involved.

ASIC's MoneySmart choosing car insurance, Choice car insurance guide, QBE What does CTP cover?

CAR FINANCE - HOW DO YOU GET THE BEST CAR LOAN?

A car loan is like personal finance, where the financier lends you funds for the purchase of a vehicle and secures the loan against that vehicle.

ASK THESE QUESTIONS BEFORE YOU GET A CAR LOAN:

- What are the interest rates? Fixed or variable? Will the car repayments fit your budget?
- Can you make extra payments on your loan without penalty?
- Can you pay out your loan early without penalty? (i.e., no early-exit fee)
- Can you choose your repayment period?
- Are there any additional hidden fees?

- How long does it take to be approved?
- Is there a *balloon payment (lump sum) at the end of the term?
- Is it a secured or unsecured loan?

WHAT'S A BALLOON PAYMENT?

A balloon payment is a lump sum owed to the financier at the end of a loan term after all regular monthly repayments have been made. E.g. A new car buyer borrows $40,000 over 5 years and elects to have a $10,000 (25%) residual value/balloon payment on their loan, which is paid at the end of the contract.

ASIC's MoneySmart car loan, is money owing on the car? PPSR, Repossession financial rights, car finance loan calculator

10 BASIC TIPS ON MAINTAINING YOUR CAR

Regular maintenance of your car is much cheaper than costly repairs caused by neglect. As the saying goes 'prevention is better than cure'.

1. Get familiar with your car. Know where to check and refill water and oil levels.
2. Monitor gauges. Keep petrol out of the empty zone. If a sign comes up, refill as soon as you can.
3. Check, check, check (temperature, air pressure, oil level, lights, battery). If a warning light flashes, take immediate action to fix it. Contact your mechanic. (Don't leave it, as an engine blowing up can be very costly.)
4. It's also a good habit to get into, to check your tyres once a week, as a small puncture can take a week to deflate a tyre.
5. To change a tyre... read the manual (see tips below).
6. Use petrol in 'petrol' cars only (diesel is different and will damage petrol engines, and vice versa). Premium fuel is specified for some makes of cars, especially European cars.

7. Know and trust your mechanic. Ensure you get what you pay for. Get a quote before work starts.
8. If the oil is low, top up to the level, no more. Check the specialised oil requirements for your car by looking at the car's manual.
9. Pay attention to noises or different behaviour of the car. If it's pulling in one direction, check the wheel alignment, wheel balance, and/or the brakes and suspension.
10. Before a long trip, it's a good idea to check tyres, oil and water.

HOW TO CHANGE A FLAT TYRE:

1. Pull over safely. Ensure there's plenty of room for you to change the tyre on a flat (flat as possible) surface, well away from traffic.
2. Turn the engine off and put the handbrake on. Ensure your passengers are out of the car.
3. Find the manual in the compartment and the spare tyre in the boot (sometimes it's a space-saver temporary tyre).
4. Loosen the wheel nuts by one turn (it's easier to loosen the nuts while the tyre is firm on the ground).
5. Place the car jack under the jack-point, usually located under the car's frame (check the manual). Ensure the ground surface under the jack is stable and flat.
6. Raise the car by turning the metal winder.
7. Remove the wheel nuts fully and put them safely to one side; then remove the tyre.
8. Replace with the spare tyre, lining it up with the wheel holes, and lightly put the wheel nuts back on.
9. Lower the car on the jack and tighten the wheel nuts (tighten to the right).
10. As soon as you can, go to a tyre repairer or mechanic to repair and replace the flat tyre.
11. If you've changed to the space-saver tyre, ensure you drive at the limited speed, as indicated, and change the tyre at a tyre dealer as soon as practicable.

TIPS

- It's easier than you think to change a tyre. The hardest part is to get the jack in the right spot (check the manual) and, obviously, don't put your head fully under the car frame at any time.
- If you get really stuck, call the roadside assistance companies and join on the spot. The cost is as little as $80-86/year, and even $9.90/month is not too bad if you have a problematic car.
- When undoing and doing up nuts, it's 'righty tighty' and 'lefty loosey' (That's a real saying!) ☺
- Do you know? There's a little arrow next to the dashboard's fuel gauge to show which side of the car your tank is on (to refill the fuel).

Changing a tyre, Budget Direct car maintenance, Motoring car maintenance tips, RACQ owning and maintaining a car

DRIVING LAWS - SPEEDING AND DUI LAWS

Drivers under 25 are at most risk of having a fatal accident because they're more likely to drink alcohol and drive, take risks, ignore speed limits and drive older vehicles, according to a report by Transport for NSW.

It takes some time for young drivers to get savvy on the roads and gain some experience around the dangers of 'it'll be ok' attitudes while driving a 1,500kg vehicle (average weight of a car).

Become familiar with the road rules in your state (for licences and motor registration for cars and motorbikes).

Demerit points can quickly accumulate if you break the laws during holiday double-demerit periods.

Know that you get a different number of points with your learner (L), provisional (P) and full licences.

It varies in each state, but you will lose varying numbers of points depending on the type and severity of the infringements.

6 TOP DRIVING TIPS

1. **Double demerits.** Holiday periods mean double demerits and big fines for driving offences.
2. **Speeding** is the leading cause of death and injuries on our roads, contributing to 40% of road fatalities (source: NSW Centre for Road Safety).
3. **Feeling unsafe?** If you're feeling unsafe as a passenger in a car, it's important to speak up. Ask to be let out in a safe place. If necessary, pretend to be sick, or that you want to vomit, or make another excuse.
4. **Don't travel with a driver who is under the influence of alcohol or drugs.** If you believe they are drunk or drugged, try to convince them not to drive in the first instance.
5. **Stay up to date on the rules in your state** (e.g., In some states, drivers who use a mobile phone are penalised 5 points. During double demerit periods, that's 10 demerit points.)
6. **Using a mobile phone is illegal at all times**, even when stopped at traffic lights. (It's one of the most common infringements for young drivers, as well as DUI and speeding.)

DO YOU KNOW? You're 'travelling blind' when looking down at your phone

(*based on average conditions and average car and braking system)

In the example above, the FIRST CAR travelling at 60km/hour will take 32 metres to stop at the position of the LAST CAR (or 8–9 car lengths). It takes 3-4 seconds to stop.

Taking your eyes off the road to look at your phone for 3 to 4 seconds means you're **effectively travelling blind for 32 metres** if you're travelling at 60km/hour.

In an emergency, the average driver takes about 1.5 seconds to react. Stopping distances increase exponentially the faster you go.

Road rules in each state, Allianz stopping distances, young driver trauma trends report

DO YOU KNOW HOW TO DRIVE DEFENSIVELY? HERE'S SOME ROAD-TESTED TIPS:

- **Don't assume or trust other drivers:** Be aware that other drivers don't always turn the way they indicate. Make sure you can see their intention before assuming they'll turn or change lanes.
- **Keep your phone out of sight:** If it's out of sight, you're less likely to be tempted to peek. A quick look at a text could result in 3 seconds of reading and a very high risk of rear-ending the vehicle in front... or worse.
- **Take extra care in the rain:** When the roads are suddenly water-soaked, they can become extra slippery. Drive more slowly to adapt to the conditions. Don't brake when turning, especially going down steep wet roads, as this can cause the tyres to lose grip on the road and cause the vehicle to hydroplane.
- **Don't tailgate:** Allow 3-4 seconds when following another vehicle (or more in rainy conditions).
- **Beware of blind spots:** A blind spot is where drivers cannot see another nearby vehicle from the rear-view mirror without turning their head and before taking their eyes off the road. Get to know the blind spots in your car, and also be aware of travelling in other drivers' blind spots.
- **Veering off road onto the verge:** If your vehicle veers off the road (onto the shoulder or verge), don't harshly pull the car back to the right, as you'll risk rolling or fishtailing the car. Instead, slowly recorrect or allow yourself to straighten up and either pull up on the shoulder, parallel to the road, or regain control with the four wheels on the bitumen.
- **Steering out of a skid (to avoid 'over-correcting'):** If you find yourself driving in icy or wet conditions and the back end slipping out, don't brake or 'over-correct'. Instead, 'turn INTO the slide' in the direction the back end is sliding (i.e. if the car's backend is sliding left, steer gently to the left to straighten the vehicle). The reason you don't brake is because the tyres need to be turning freely, to get traction, for the correction to work. Once the car straightens out, straighten the steering wheel. (Note: If you lose control on a dirt road, release your foot off the brake and the accelerator and gently steer out of the situation.)

- **Stay to the left on multiple-lane motorways:** If you are travelling at a lesser speed to other vehicles, move into the left lanes to allow others to pass on the right.
- **Be courteous:** Allow others to merge. Being stubborn on the roads achieves little. You might advance a few cars, but end up stuck at the same intersection, having achieved nothing but aggravation.
- **Practice quick lookdowns:** We all have to look around the vehicle at times when driving (whether to look at our speed, the radio, or put a window down). Practice mini-1-second lookdowns, e.g., if you're changing music, do it in quick bursts.
- **Driving while tired is a no-no:** If you're tired, pull over safely and take a nap, or leave your departure for another day. Driver fatigue is a big killer on the roads (playing a role in an estimated 13-17% of accidents).
- **Seatbelts save lives:** Even if you have an accident travelling at 60km/hour, a seat belt will prevent you from being thrown around inside the vehicle or propelled through the windscreen. If you're giving friends a lift, don't be tempted to squeeze an extra person in the vehicle where they wouldn't have a seatbelt. If you have an accident, that person can be hurled out the side or rear window, and you know the rest of the story...
- **Am I safe to drive?** Before getting behind the wheel ask yourself 'am I safe to drive?' i.e., tired, ill, medicated, or possibly still over the DUI limit, etc.

DRINK DRIVING – WHEN IS IT SAFE TO DRIVE AFTER A NIGHT OUT?

Young drivers are most likely to drink and drive, often because they underestimate how alcohol metabolises in their bodies and don't fully understand the high risk of an accident.

In Australia, **a standard drink refers to 10 grams of alcohol** which, on average, is how much the body can process in one hour (i.e., blood alcohol concentration drops by about 0.015, or roughly one drink, every hour, however, factors like your weight, gender, metabolism and how much you've eaten all contribute to how your body processes alcohol, so everyone has different limits.

Random breath testing (RBT) can be conducted anywhere, anytime. Drink driving is a serious offence. It is also an offence if you refuse to take a test.

Refer to this guide to find out the average amount of standard drinks in different beverages and to the DrinkWise calculator Standard Drink Calculator (*Note: this is intended as a guide only*).

> **TIP**
>
> If you're planning to drink, don't drive. Have an alternative plan to get home.

Blood Alcohol Concentration (BAC)	Number of drinks	Effects on driving
0.02% BAC		• Decline in visual functions • Inability to perform two tasks at the same time • Loss of judgement • Altered mood
0.05% BAC		• Reduced coordination • Reduced ability to track moving objects • Difficulty steering • Slower response to emergency situations
0.08% BAC		• Reduced ability to concentrate • Short-term memory loss • Lack of speed control • Impaired perception and self-control
0.10% BAC		• Clear deterioration of reaction time • Reduced ability to maintain lane position • Reduced ability to brake appropriately • Slurred speech
0.15% BAC		• Substantial impairment in vehicle control • Loss of auditory information processing • Major loss of balance • Vomiting may occur

DRUG DRIVING AND MOBILE DRUG TESTING (MDT)

Taking illegal drugs before driving puts you at risk of injuring or killing yourself, your friends or other innocent people. You're also not insured if there's an accident.

Mobile drug testing (MDT) detects drivers who have recently used four common illegal drugs: MDMA, cannabis, cocaine and methamphetamine.

MDT can be conducted at police roadside operations or by police in vehicles patrolling our roads, at any time.

If you fail the test, you'll immediately have a 24-hour driving ban placed on you and your car will be left at the side of the road. The test will be sent to a laboratory for further analysis.

Saliva tests guide: According to the Alcohol Drug Foundation, saliva tests can detect THC (the active ingredient in cannabis) for around 12 hours after use for infrequent users, however THC may be detected in urine samples of frequent users for around a month after it was last used (because the body stores THC in fat cells for a period of time).

Methamphetamines (i.e., speed or ice) and MDMA (i.e., ecstasy) can be detected in saliva for about two days after use.

If you are taking any medications, "it's best to talk to your doctor about the combined impact on your ability to drive," according to the ADF.

Different types of drug tests can trace whether you've consumed drugs for different amounts of time. When you use a drug, it doesn't just leave metabolic by-products in your urine and blood, it also can leave traces in your hair and fingernails.

ADF -roadside drug testing - cannabis in saliva (main source)

A GENERAL GUIDELINE OF HOW LONG DIFFERENT DRUGS STAY IN THE BODY

Drug	Blood (hours)	Urine (days)	Hair (days)
LSD	3 hours	3 days	3 days
Alcohol	12	5	90
Amphetamines	12	3	90
Barbiturates	48	4	90
Cocaine	48	4	90
Cannabis	336	30	90
Heroin	12	4	90
MDMA	48	4	90
Methamphetamine	36	6	90
Morphine	8	6	90

(*Data is an estimate only. Detection times may vary depending on a person's height, weight, age, health and conditions and usage, strength of drug)

Science alert How long drugs stay in the body

Note: This is a guide only. Each drug can take varying lengths of time to leave the body, depending on its strength, your metabolism and if you have used a combination of drugs. The same drug can affect you differently on separate occasions.

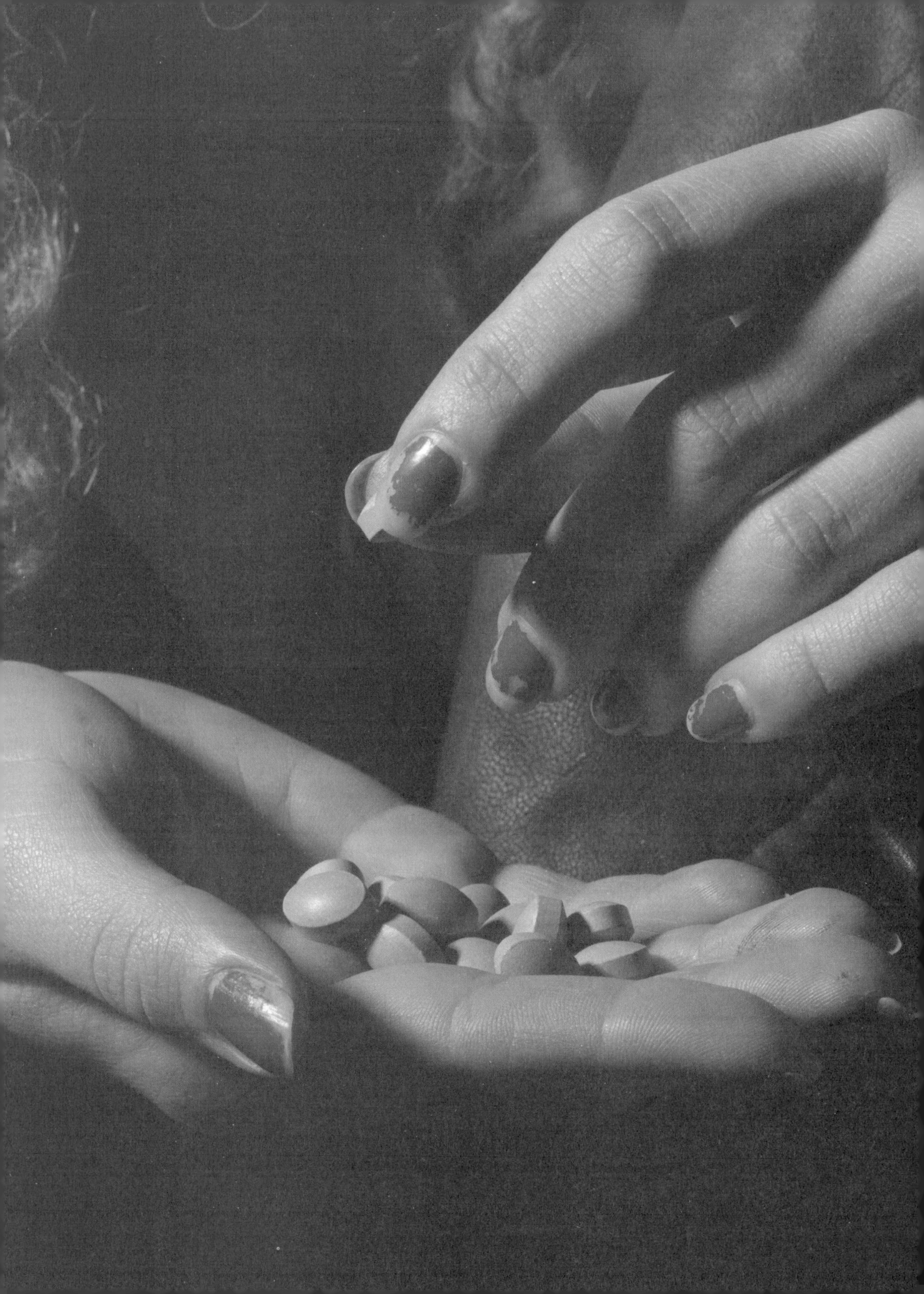

4. THE FACTS OF LIFE: **SEX, DRUGS AND GOING OUT**

Please note: This chapter gives you some background on these topics and how to stay safe when going out. It is for information purposes only. If you have any specific issues, we recommend contacting a medical professional with expertise relating to your needs.

Most of us learn about sex, drugs and alcohol the hard way. But there are potential risks involved in learning by experimentation.

HOW TO STAY SAFE WHEN GOING OUT

One of the main risks when going out is that drinking alcohol and taking drugs affect your judgement. Plus, getting home safely can be a challenge, especially if you're separated from friends.

SOME SAFETY TIPS WHEN OUT CLUBBING:

- Never accept an open drink or leave a drink unattended, as it may get spiked.
- Drinks lots of water and stay hydrated.
- Eat carbohydrates before going out, or while you're out.
- Pace yourself. Set yourself a limit on how many drinks you'll have.
- It's ok to say 'no' and not to drink. Say no to rounds and shots (pretend they make you feel sick). Don't drink multiple drinks too quickly, as they catch up on you.

- Have a plan to get home or where to sleep (or get an Uber if you're stuck).
- Stick together with your friends.
- If you must walk alone anywhere, be aware of the surroundings and walk with purpose. Hold your keys between your fingers if you need to use them for protection. This is called situational awareness (see 'self-defence' section).
- Charge your mobile before you go out to ensure you have enough battery later in the night to get home safely.

HOW TO LOOK AFTER A FRIEND WHO HAS DRUNK TOO MUCH:

If a friend needs your help while you're out, try to contact a family member or friend to see if they can help and collect your friend. When you get your friend home, put him or her in the RECOVERY POSITION (See next page). Ideally, once home, advise a family member so that they can observe your friend.

FIRST AID BASICS TO HELP FRIENDS WITH ALCOHOL POISONING:

- Stay with them.
- If they're conscious, try to keep them sitting up and awake. Give sips of water.
- If they're unconscious, put them in the recovery position (so if they vomit, they don't choke) and keep checking their breathing.
- Keep them warm.

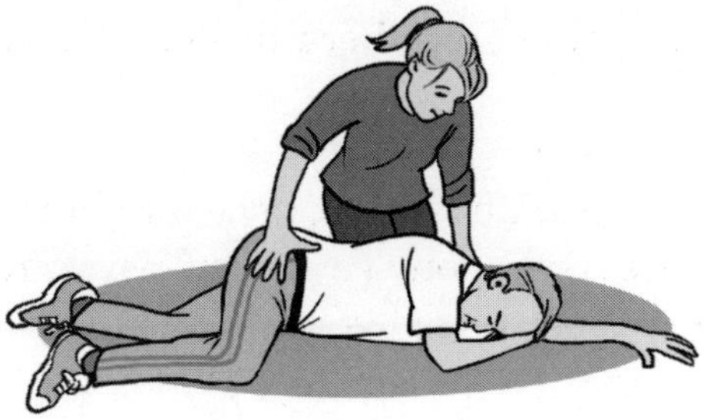

Recovery position

WHAT TO DO IF YOUR FRIEND HAS PASSED OUT:

1. If your friend is not responding or you're concerned, **call an ambulance on triple zero 000.**
2. Put them in the **recovery position if they're breathing ok** (see diagram, above).
3. Continue to check their breathing.
4. **If they stop breathing, start CPR (for adults, it's 30 chest compressions, followed by 2 breaths) until the ambulance arrives. (Note: rescue breaths are optional if you're performing CPR on someone you don't know.) For the latest information on how to perform CPR, visit** Healthdirect.gov.au

HOW MUCH DOES AN AMBULANCE COST?

In NSW, the call out fee in an emergency (as of 20 April 2021) is **$401 to the person who receives the treatment** (plus $3.62/kilometre to the hospital).

AN AMBULANCE IS FREE ONLY IN THE FOLLOWING CASES:

- If the patient has private health cover (or their parent's insurance covers them).
- If you have a health care card or pensioner card.
- If the accident is a work injury and covered by WorkCover.
- In some States, if you were in an accident on a public road in a car registered in that State. (Check the rules in your State.)
- If you were a victim of sexual assault or domestic violence.

TIPS

1. If your friend is drunk, it's important NOT to let them fall asleep on their back. If they vomit, they can choke, and potentially die. Put them in the recovery position (see previous page).
2. Ambulance officers are not required to call the police for incidents, unless there's a death or a threat of danger.
3. Know the law when out drinking, as the police can detain you for being drunk in a public place, or fine you if you're disorderly. Know that you can be refused entry into clubs if you're considered drunk under responsible service of alcohol laws.

Health Engine how to help a drunk person, Life Hacker is my friend asleep or unconscious? Drink Wise when drinking turns toxic, Ambulance service e.g. ambulance fees, St John Ambulance recovery position, (Search ambulance service near me)

ADDICTIVE SUBSTANCES - WHAT ARE THE MOST ADDICTIVE DRUGS?

Alcohol is such an intrinsic part of the Australian culture that the warning signs of excess drinking, and potential addiction, are often masked.

Young people see drinking advertisements endorsing alcohol, or friends and parents drinking at weddings and dinners, and really don't think of alcohol as a 'drug', which it is... just a legal one for those over 18.

In Australia it seems to have become almost a 'rite of passage' for teenagers turning 18 to go to the pub or bar and have a drink.

Thankfully, young people are trending away from alcohol, but younger teenagers often experiment with alcohol to rebel, relieve 'boredom' or reduce inhibitions.

However, it's one thing to have a drink 'here and there', and another to drink daily or binge drink on weekends. This is when health and social issues can insidiously creep up.

WHAT IS ALCOHOL?

Alcohol is a depressant and slows the central nervous system and alters perceptions, emotions, movement, vision and hearing.

Alcohol risks include: The social risks of excessively drinking alcohol include losing your job, or losing your driver's licence, or losing your relationships.

The long-term health risks include:

- Chronic diseases, such as cancer and diabetes
- Brain damage (impaired memory and concentration)
- Mental health issues
- Liver and kidney damage
- Infertility and sexual problems
- Alcohol dependency

WHAT'S BINGE DRINKING?

Binge drinking is when you drink excessively in a short space of time. For men that is considered more than six drinks, and for women four drinks.

GETTING DRUNK CAN MAKE YOU DO STUPID STUFF, LIKE:

- Taking risks, such as driving drunk, having an accident, or walking or falling asleep in an unsafe place.
- Taking sexual risks and having unprotected sex (risking an STI or pregnancy).
- Getting emotional or aggressive with friends and damaging relationships.
- Getting taken advantage of by predators who look for people who are not on top of their game.
- Being argumentative with the police and getting a criminal record.

WHERE TO GO TO HELP QUIT ALCOHOL

If you feel like you're becoming dependent on alcohol, it's a good idea to visit your doctor to help manage withdrawals, and to develop an action plan. They can also link you up to support services and make you accountable by tracking your progress.

It is helpful to have a clear goal why you want to give up, such as improved health, more energy, better sleep, save money or improve relationships. Become aware of your triggers and how you can avoid them.

(Refer to the 'quit' section in the chapter)

Health.gov.au how to quit alcohol, the alcohol experiment, Drink Wise, ADF website (source), ReachOut what is binge drinking

SMOKING – A HIGH PRICE TO PAY

Cigarettes contain nicotine – a highly addictive poisonous volatile chemical – which is both a sedative and a stimulant drug (resulting from an increase in adrenaline).

While smoking might seem like a cool or rebellious thing to do at first, it's notoriously hard to give up once an addiction sets in. People who suddenly stop smoking can experience withdrawal symptoms, which may include cravings, a sense of emptiness, anxiety, depression, moodiness, irritability and inattentiveness.

REASONS NOT TO SMOKE:

- It costs around $37/ packet. One packet / day = $13,505/ year.
- Smoking is the leading cause of lung cancer in Australia, according to the Cancer Australia website.
- In 2018, there were 8,586 deaths caused by lung cancer (23 people/day).
- Plus, you won't smell or taste like an ashtray.

TIPS TO QUIT SMOKING

It is hard to give up an addictive drug like nicotine. Some people can do it first time, others take multiple attempts.

Start with a quit plan. Be clear on why you want to quit. Learn about the health benefits and what quitting feels like. Consider the cost savings (the immediate savings from not buying cigarettes and long-term savings on sickness expenses down the track). Know your triggers and avoid those situations.

Contact Quitline: 137 848 (13 QUIT)
Refer to the 'quit' section in the chapter.

THE HEADS UP ON VAPING (E-CIGARETTES)

Electronic cigarettes are battery operated devices that heat liquids to create a vapour that looks like smoke, often called 'vaping'. You can legally buy e-cigarettes that do **not** contain nicotine, but the impact of vape fluid on health is still uncertain and research into short-term and long-term effects is on-going.

According to the government's HealthDirect website, "In all states and territories in Australia, it is illegal to sell, possess or use e-cigarettes that contain nicotine. But this does not guarantee all e-cigarettes sold legally are nicotine-free."

The Australian Government made it **illegal from 1 January 2021 to import or purchase liquid nicotine** e-cigarettes or refills from overseas. You will only be able to legally use e-cigarettes containing nicotine if they have been prescribed by a doctor. Learn more at the Therapeutic Goods Administration website.

Cancer Australia (source), Quitline how to quit smoking, Quit Now, ReachOut how to quit smoking, cancer facts, vaping information

TIPS

- Don't start smoking in the first place. If you think it's cool, you won't in 10, 20, 30 years when your health is paying the price.
- Read up on the dangers of inhaling toxic chemicals and the laws around vaping.

DRUGS – THE FACTS AND EFFECTS (SUMMARY)

Please note: This guide supports a healthy, drug-free lifestyle and warns against the use of any illegal drug.

The information included in this section is for reference only and is obtained from a collation of expert sources, as listed. It is not intended as medical or professional advice.

We recommend seeking a professional opinion for specific issues or concerns.

A drug is any chemical substance that can change the way your body works and the way you feel.

Every drug, whether legal or illegal, can have a negative effect on your health.

Almost all drugs are potentially addictive because people can develop a level of dependence on them. Some are far more addictive than others, and just one-time-use can cause dependence.

People addicted to drugs often lose the ability to maintain self-control, maintain relationships, keep their jobs and function in normal, day-to-day activities.

A drug's effect depends on things like your size, weight, height or what other drugs you've taken. It also depends on how much you take, the strength of the drug and if it's laced with other substances (see below).

Drugs can affect your judgement, making you do things – including dangerous and life-threatening things – that you wouldn't otherwise do.

THERE ARE MANY KINDS OF DRUGS, SOME LEGAL (MEDICAL) AND SOME ILLEGAL (STREET DRUGS).

While the manufacture of legal drugs is closely regulated, **there are no controls over what goes into illegal drugs**. The quality and strength of any illegal drug can be completely different each time you take it.

They're made by backyard chemists, so you never really know what you're taking. Plus, there's a higher risk when mixing drugs and combining them with alcohol, which can lead to over-dosing, a strain on the heart, hospitalisation or death.

Note: There's no safe level of illegal drug use.

THE HIDDEN DANGERS OF LACED DRUGS:

Nearly all street drugs can be 'laced', which is the act of adding one or more substances to another to bulk up the original product with a cheaper drug or substance, making it more profitable for the dealer.

Illegal drugs can be bulked-up with dog de-wormers, bath salts, cleaning powder or rat poison, or any drug that's cheaper.

TIP

Many users don't know the strength of the drug they've purchased or if it's laced until they're in trouble and it's too late to call for help, which can lead to accidental overdose and death.

WHAT ARE THE MAIN DRUGS (IN BRIEF) AND SOME EXAMPLES?

Main source and quick reference guide: ADF - Drug facts

A. DEPRESSANT DRUGS, INCLUDING CANNABIS AND GHB

Cannabis - When smoked, cannabis levels in the blood are estimated to peak within 8 minutes, and when consumed orally, they peak within 1 to 2 hours. Users can build up a tolerance to the drug, which can lead to dependence or addiction. Other names are pot, weed, dope, joint, ganja, reefer, hash, etc.

GHB – GHB (gamma hydroxybutyrate) usually comes as a colourless, odourless, bitter or salty liquid, which is mostly sold in small bottles or vials. It can also come as a bright blue liquid known as 'blue nitro', and less commonly as a crystal powder. Other names are G, fantasy, grievous bodily harm (GBH), juice, liquid ecstasy, liquid E, liquid X, Georgia Home Boy, soap, scoop, cherry meth, blue nitro, fishies.

B. STIMULANTS, INCLUDING COCAINE, AMPHETAMINES/ SPEED, ICE/CRYSTAL METH

Cocaine - Cocaine is a short-acting powerful stimulant drug that is highly addictive. After using cocaine, the user might experience a crash that can last from 9 hours to 4 days.

ICE (crystal methamphetamine) and speed (amphetamines) Crystal methamphetamine ('ICE') is a stimulant crystal-appearance drug and is highly addictive.

One-time users can quickly become dependent. It is never safe to try ICE. It is stronger and has more addictive effects than the powder form of methamphetamine, known as speed.

C. HALLUCINOGENS, INCLUDING MDMA/ECSTASY/MOLLY; LSD/ACID

MDMA/ecstasy/molly/caps - Usually taken in pill or tablet form, ecstasy or MDMA is a hallucinogenic drug that can have numerous side effects.The effects of ecstasy can begin in as little as 30 minutes and last for up to 6 hours.

Overdose can occur when the user takes more than one dose at a time. Other risks are heatstroke, water intoxication and serotonin syndrome. High body temperatures can lead to organ damage, heat-stroke, dehydration, heart failure, high blood pressure, panic attacks, seizures, loss of consciousness and death.

LSD is a synthetic chemical belonging to a group of drugs called psychedelics. What is often sold as LSD can actually be other chemicals (e.g. NBOMe or the 2C family of drugs), which are highly dangerous and can be fatal.

D. OPIOIDS, INCLUDING HEROIN AND PRESCRIPTION DRUGS, SUCH AS PAINKILLERS

Heroin - Heroin is highly addictive and can bring devastation to both physical and mental health. It has a high risk of social and legal ramifications for the user. The risk of **death from overdose** is a concern for people because dosing is impossible to measure due to the difference in purity. **It's never safe to try heroin**; first-time users can overdose, and veteran users can overdose.

Prescription pharmaceutical drugs/medicines - There are a number of prescribed drugs that can be addictive. e.g. Benzodiazepines are a group of prescription drugs called 'minor tranquillisers', often known as 'benzos'. They are prescribed by doctors, mostly to help people with anxiety or sleep problems, and are an increasing drug-abuse problem.

TIPS

1. Know the risks before using any drug, legal or illegal. If you or your friends are having bad reactions, seek medical help immediately. Call triple zero 000.
2. If you use drugs and have a 'bad trip' try not to panic as this will increase the effects and your heart rate. You can expect that some drugs can cause hallucinations, fear and paranoia. If you are concerned, and especially if your temperature is rising, call triple zero 000 or contact a friend or family member if you're in trouble and they can call an ambulance.
3. Know the after-effects of drugs: Most party drugs impact serotonin levels and can make you feel anxious, confused, moody and really out-of-sorts next day, or for a few days afterwards. Don't spin out. Go with it and know that hormone levels will repair and rebalance.
4. If you're having a bad week and think a drug will lift your mood, think again. Usually a drug will magnify the mood you're in before you take it.

ADF the effects of drugs (source) drug facts, ReachOut How to tell if you have a drug problem and drug and alcohol info, Science Insider and Mayo Clinic (source), Business Insider (Dragan Radovanovic YouTube - How long drugs stay in your system), Science alert How long do drugs stay in the body, Youth Central drugs and alcohol info, types of drugs, Destinationforteens how party drugs mess with your head

WHAT TO DO IF YOUR FRIEND ACCIDENTALLY OVERDOSES

- Phone triple zero **000** to get an ambulance and tell the operator that the person has overdosed. If your mobile is out of range in your network, then dial **112**.
- Stay with your friend.
- Try to keep calm.
- Try to keep your friend awake. Walk them around, talk to them, and use their name.

- If the person is unconscious, put them on their side, in the recovery position.
- Clear their airway. Check their breathing.
- Do mouth-to-mouth resuscitation if they stop breathing (until help arrives).

(Refer to the section in this chapter on first aid basics, CPR, recovery position and calling an ambulance.)*

TIPS

1. Look after your mates. If you can't get a response from your friend, don't assume they're asleep. They might be unconscious. Don't leave them on their backs. Put them into the recovery position and seek help immediately.
2. Remember: the police will not come unless someone dies, or you call them. Paramedics are NOT obliged to involve the police, and the sooner you get help for someone the more likely it is that they'll make it.

Health Direct accidental overdose, Youth Central drug overdose, ADF what is an overdose

QUITTING AN ADDICTION

WHAT'S AN ADDICTION?

When something that was once pleasurable begins to affect your relationships, work, finances, mental and physical health and everyday life, you might have an addition.

You may not be aware (or want to accept) that your behaviour is causing problems until things start going wrong around you, like losing your job or a relationship, getting in debt, fighting with family, or physical and mental health issues.

Sometimes the most difficult part is identifying that point where you need help.

Types of addiction: Substances (like alcohol, nicotine or illicit drugs) or activities (like gambling, shopping, sex or electronic devices).

WHERE TO START WITH YOUR PLAN TO QUIT:

1. **Seek professional support**. They will guide you through the process and help you identify triggers and how to change patterns. Talk to your doctor or a person you trust.
2. **Be clear about your 'why'**. Why do you want to quit? How is it affecting your life? Write the reasons down. List the positive things that will happen when you quit.
3. **Prepare your environment** to eliminate triggers and the source of your addiction. Change lifestyle patterns and avoid situations where you feel vulnerable.
4. **Tell others**. Once you tell other people (e.g. face-to-face or on social media) it makes the commitment more real. You're likely to be more committed and accountable.
5. **Limit access to money or supplies that feed your addiction.**
6. **Stop on the day you decide.** Know that the first few days will be hardest.
7. **Stay distracted and ride through the urge.** Remind yourself of the reason for quitting. Visualise the positives of how your life will look without your addiction.

ReachOut what is addiction, helpline, Salvation Army addiction rehabilitation, Odyssey House, Better Health addiction information, Lifeline problem gambling, Gambling help online tools for quitting.

(Also refer to the list of contacts at the start of this guide.)

SAFE SEX FOR UNDER 25s

The ReachOut Australia website (au.reachout.com) is recommended as an easy-to-use site for under 25s on everyday questions around mindset, relationships and sex. See the ReachOut guide for safe sex (source) for information on the following:

- Pregnancy
- Abortion
- STIs and HIV
- Sexual health checks
- Safe sex and safe oral sex
- Consenting to sex
- Masturbation
- LGBTQIA+ friendly sexual health services

TIPS

- Always use a condom.
- If it's not on, it's not on.
- It's ok to say no!
- If you have an STI inform your partner of that and take precautions to protect the spread of infection.

THE 10 BIGGEST SEX MISTAKES

1. Forgetting condoms or relying on 'the other person' to have condoms.
2. Not using a condom in the moment and getting an STI (chlamydia is the main STI for under 25s) or getting pregnant.
3. Not checking the expiry date of condoms or if they've deteriorated (in the heat).
4. Getting an STI from unsafe oral sex. Not using condoms or dams during oral sex or when there are sores or cuts on genitals or mouth or when they have a sore throat (as infection can be passed on during this time).
5. Not doing regular STI tests and sexual health checks when sexually active or in a new relationship.
6. Not asking a partner if they're exclusive, i.e. if they have other sexual partners.
7. Getting drunk and not keeping safe boundaries.
8. Not being safe with strangers, including people met online.
9. Trying to be popular and not saying 'no'. Being uncomfortable and not saying anything.
10. Failing to seek consent from the other person.

WHAT TO DO IF YOU'VE HAD UNSAFE SEX

If you've had sex without using a condom, or if the condom breaks or comes off, visit your doctor or sexual health clinic to discuss your options. Refer to ReachOut and Better Health guide to safe sex.

A SHORT SUMMARY OF BIRTH CONTROL OPTIONS

If you're sexually active, you need to be thinking of birth control options.

Don't leave this to chance, because 'pulling out' is not a reliable means of avoiding pregnancy and is best used with another form of contraception, such as a condom. About 1 in 5 women get pregnant this way, according to the website Planned Parenthood.

Do you know? There is a risk with condoms too, due to breakage and user-error. "If you use condoms perfectly every single time you have sex, they're 98% effective at preventing pregnancy. But people aren't perfect, so in real life condoms are about 85% effective — that means about 15 out of 100 people who use condoms as their only birth control method will get pregnant each year," according to the website.

TIP

The risks of pregnancy are far greater than the inconvenience of using contraception (birth control).

THE RISKS OF NOT USING BIRTH CONTROL CAN RESULT IN YOU HAVING...

- A child when you're not ready.
- A child with a person you don't love or want a long-term relationship with.
- To consider adoption.
- To consider termination.
- Regrets.

EXAMPLES OF METHODS OF BIRTH CONTROL

- The Pill
- The condom
- The IUD
- The vaginal ring
- The diaphragm and caps
- The implant
- Abstinence (not having sex at all)

Planned Parenthood birth control, Health Direct contraception options, Health NSW safe sex, Teen Vogue birth control pill, Better Health contraception, Stay Teen birth control

HOW TO PROTECT YOURSELF AGAINST STIs

STIs (sexually transmitted infections) are infections that can spread during sexual contact (vaginal, oral and anal) and are caused by bacteria, viruses or parasites.

Types of STIs include chlamydia, herpes, gonorrhoea, syphilis, genital herpes, scabies, pubic lice (crabs), hepatitis and HIV, which is the virus that causes AIDS.

Many STIs have no obvious symptoms, which can make them hard to detect and treat, and can mean you or your partner could have an STI without knowing it.

However, most STIs are curable and easily treated so, if you've had sex without a condom or if you sense something's 'not quite right', it's a good idea to get tested by a doctor (which is usually a simple urine or blood test).

> **TIP**
>
> As many as 1 in 8 (that's 12.5%) Australian adults have genital herpes, which is an incurable STI (source: healthdirect.gov.au). Condoms are the easiest and most effective way to protect yourself from STIs.

Chlamydia is the most common STI for under 25s, and because there are often no symptoms, it can be hard to know if you have it. If left untreated it can lead to pelvic inflammatory disease and infertility (which means you can't get pregnant in the future).

If you're sexually active, it's important to get an STI test at least once a year (or more), especially if you've had unprotected sex, or when you start a new relationship.

WHAT AGE CAN I LEGALLY HAVE SEX?

16 is the legal age of consent in most states, except South Australia and Tasmania, where it is 17

Young people at the age of consent are viewed by law to have general sexual competence to enforce personal boundaries and negotiate the risks involved in sexual activities. When an adult engages in sexual behaviour with someone below the age of consent, they are committing a criminal offence (child sexual abuse).

AIFS Age of consent laws (Source), Health Direct sexual health

SEXUALITY - WHO CAN YOU TALK TO ABOUT YOUR SEXUAL IDENTITY?

It's possible to have intimate feelings for people, regardless of gender. It might be a passing emotion or curiosity... or it might be more. If you're feeling uncertain about your sexuality, talk to someone you trust and feel safe with and don't be hasty in giving yourself a label.

SEXUAL ORIENTATION

Sexual orientation is how a person describes their emotional and sexual attraction to others.

Heterosexuality is being attracted to someone of the opposite sex, while LGBTQIA+ applies to people who experience their sexuality in different ways.

LGBTQIA+

The term LGBTQIA+ has changed over time as people identify in different ways.

- L **Lesbian:** A female who is attracted to a female.
- G **Gay:** Someone who is attracted to people of the same gender.
- B **Bisexual:** Someone who is attracted to people of more than one gender.
- T **Transgender or trans people:** Someone whose personal and gender identity is different from the one they were assigned at birth.
- Q **Queer:** This term has many different meanings, but it has been reclaimed by many as a term to describe sexuality that is anything other than heterosexual.
- I **Intersex:** Someone who is born with reproductive or sexual anatomy that is not wholly male or female.
- A **Asexual:** Someone who is not sexually attracted to any gender but may have a romantic attraction towards another person.
- \+ **Transsexual:** Someone who has medical treatment to transition from one sex to another.
- I **Gender fluid:** Someone who does not identify themselves as having a fixed gender.
- \+ all other diverse sexual orientations and gender identities.

ReachOut gender and identity (source), HealthLine how to come out, headspace

COMING OUT – HOW DO YOU TELL PEOPLE ABOUT YOUR SEXUALITY?

If you've decided to come out, there are some sites that can help you with what to expect and how to manage the steps. You don't have to go it alone. Your partner (if you have one) can support you too. You might like to tell close friends first before your family, so you're clear on how to express yourself. By being prepared, you can better anticipate any questions.

Due to heteronormative social biases, LGBTQIA+ people can be stigmatised or marginalised. If you're experiencing prejudice or discrimination as a result of your sexuality or sexual identity and think you may need mental health support, speak to a counsellor or call a support line, like Headspace (or refer to the list of contacts at the start of this guide).

SEXTING – IF YOU'RE UNDER 18, KNOW THE RISKS OF SENDING RISQUÉ PHOTOS

Do you know you can get a criminal record for sending sexual photos of yourself if you're under 18?

Sexting can be:

1. Seen as child pornography.
2. Used against you (as sexual bullying or cyber-bullying).
3. Giving opportunities to sexual predators.
4. Placing you at risk of blackmail and shaming.
5. A threat to your reputation. Sexts never go away (they can be on search engines forever).

Sexting a boyfriend or girlfriend can lead to serious legal ramifications.

If a sexually suggestive photo or video is of someone who is under the age of 18, it may be child pornography (even if it is of yourself). Creating, sending and possessing child pornography is a criminal offence in Australia.

When sexting, you risk:

- **Receiving criminal charges for child pornography.** Both kids who send the photos and kids who receive the photos can be charged even if they did not request the photo. If they distribute the photos to friends, then they also may face charges for distributing child pornography.
- Being registered as a sex offender **and jail time.**

- **Exposing parents to legal consequences** if parents know that their child is sexting and do nothing to end it.

TIP

- Be careful when texting/sexting with anyone you've 'met' online. There are people who pretend to be your age when in fact they're preying on younger people to get them to send sexy photos, or worse, meet up.
- Never meet with anyone you haven't seen on a video chat app to confirm their identity and age. And if you meet anyone, always meet in a very public place, like at a mall, where you can call security if you need to.

Very Well Family. S. Gordon What are the consequences of texting, Lynn and Brown lawyers Australian law on teenage sexting (sources)

PORNOGRAPHY – IT'S NOT REALITY, IT'S ACTING

It's easier than ever to find pornography online. Sometimes we see graphic images of sexual acts and might think it's an everyday thing. However, **this is acting and needs to be differentiated from reality.** We don't watch actors in movies like *Pulp Fiction* or *American Psycho* and think they're real characters.

The actors in pornographic videos don't know or care for each other, and therefore it's not reality.

The negative outcome is that many of the demeaning sexual acts shown in pornographic videos give false ideas to some people, who *aren't* aware **this is not normal behaviour in intimate, loving relationships.** A lot of scenes show an aggressive edge to sex, and normalise forceful anal sex, which you'll find are not the norm in caring, respectful relationships.

If people think they can re-enact some of the scenes in real life, it can leave one person feeling 'used', under-valued and disrespected because there's a lack of emotional care, consent and connection.

When two people care for each other in a relationship there's an emotional attachment and it's not about one person's enjoyment but about give and take.

In all sexual relations, each person needs to maintain safe and respectful sexual boundaries. Remember that oral sex is still sex, and respect is paramount.

What most people eventually find out is that pornography is a poor substitute for the intimacy which can only be found in a committed, loving relationship – a relationship that begins with valuing and loving ourselves first.

TIPS

1. If you don't feel ok doing something, don't do it. You can say 'no'. Note: 'no' means no!
2. If anyone demands anything, the answer is 'no'.
3. If you wouldn't have it done to you, don't do it to others.

Psychology Today impact of pornography, Kids Helpline how pornography impacts relationships

SEXUAL ABUSE AND HARASSMENT - WHERE TO GET HELP

NOTE: There is never an excuse for sexual harassment or abuse. Remember you have rights, and it's never the victim's fault.

WHAT'S SEXUAL ABUSE?

Sexual abuse is any unwanted or forced sexual behaviour.

If you've been sexually abused or assaulted, you may feel a range of emotions, including fear, anxiety, confusion, loneliness, guilt and a loss of confidence and self-esteem.

It's important to know that there are support services that can help you.

Sexual assault can occur towards all genders; however, police-recorded sexual assaults are seven times higher for females than males.

Almost 2 million people in Australia have experienced at least one sexual assault from the age of 15.

WHAT YOU SHOULD DO IF YOU'VE BEEN SEXUALLY ABUSED:

1. Ensure you're safe. If you feel in danger contact triple zero 000 and get to somewhere safe.
2. Seek medical help at a hospital or medical centre.
3. Talk to a friend, family member or counsellor who can support you to get help.
4. Contact a confidential support group in your area (Also refer to the list of contacts at the start of this guide) or 1800RESPECT which is a 24-hour service.
5. Find out about your rights, e.g., the Lawstuff website.

THE FOLLOWING ARE EXAMPLES OF SEXUAL ABUSE

- Touching you without your permission.
- Demanding sex and forcing you to do anything against your will (i.e., rape).
- Making sexually degrading insults or comments.
- Exposing you to pornography or photographing you against your wishes.
- Refusing to use safe sex practices or causing you pain.

WHAT'S SEXUAL HARASSMENT?

Sexual harassment can occur in many environments and many different ways, from an inappropriate touch and indecent exposure or comments, through to more aggressive harassment cases.

The #metoo movement, and other recent campaigns, have been the catalyst to bring much-needed media attention to the cause and resulted in a string of convictions of serial sexual-harassment offenders.

The courage of the girls and women (and also men) coming forward is giving victims worldwide more freedom to speak up, without fear of retribution, judgement or losing their jobs.

FYI - The last sexual harassment prevalence survey run by the Australian Human Rights Commission (AHRC) in 2012 found a quarter of women and one in six men aged 15 years and older reported having experienced sexual harassment in the workplace in the past five years.

WHAT CAN YOU DO IF YOU'VE BEEN SEXUALLY HARASSED?

If you experience sexual harassment in school or the workplace, say 'stop'.

Research and understand your rights. Contact helplines and support services (see below).

If it continues, report it to someone in authority and/or speak to a friend, family member, counsellor or helplines to decide the best course of action. If you're being harassed by your boss, consider contacting a lawyer or Human Resources specialist to advise your boss of legal responsibilities of businesses.

Know where the line is: This initiative is a national awareness program which aims to prevent and reduce the harm of sexual harassment in the Australian workplace.

Stop relationship abuse types of sexual abuse, AIHW sexual assault in Australia statistics, Wikipedia Grooming, Raising Children Grooming - recognising the signs, ReachOut what is sexual assault, Human Rights sexual harassment information for employees (See list of contacts at the start of this guide, including 1800respect - 1800 737 732)

THERE IS NO EXCUSE FOR SEXUAL HARASSMENT

Anyone can be targeted as the focus of sexual abuse or harassment, especially the vulnerable. It's never acceptable to violate anyone's boundaries, it's never the victim's fault and there's never an excuse, regardless of what anyone wears or how they behave.

Employers have a responsibility to ensure the workplace is safe and they should have a sexual harassment policy in place. An employer can be held legally responsible for acts of sexual harassment committed by an employee if policies and procedures to protect staff are not put in place by the employer.

CONSENT - SAYING "YES" OR "NO" TO INTIMACY OR SEX

The language around sexual consent and giving permission is important. Whatever Australian state you live in 'no means no' and 'stop means stop'. Silence can mean frozen in fear and does not mean consent.

You might at first get intimate with someone and feel safe (which is a yes to intimacy only). However, this might lead to more expectations and it might begin to move too fast towards having sex. You can change your mind at any time - If you've initially decided to have sex and the tone becomes aggressive or pushy, you can say "stop" or "no" at any time.

WHAT'S GROOMING?

Grooming is befriending and establishing an emotional connection with a person under the age of 16 (a child) to lower the child's inhibitions, with the objective of sexual abuse (i.e. paedophilia). Child grooming is also regularly used to lure minors into various illicit businesses such as child trafficking, prostitution, cybersex trafficking or the production of underage pornography. (Source, adapted: Wikipedia)

In order to establish a good relationship with the child, a predator might gain their trust by befriending the family or looking for opportunities to be alone with the child. Commonly, they give the child special favours, compliments, attention, treats or money, and begin to show them pornography to 'normalise' the behaviour. When online, groomers often pose as children (or their own age) and attempt to arrange a meeting. People of all ages can get caught in the trap, given that social media causes so much contact from people they don't know.

The people most at risk are those who are lonely, vulnerable, or feeling a need for attention.

BEWARE OF SEXUAL PREDATORS

Sexual predators do not stop at minors. If you're over 16, be aware that predators can target you with the objective of sexual abuse. They're not always older people or strangers, but people of a similar age group or people known to you (e.g. neighbours, family members, colleagues, or people helping around the house).

Sexual predators are given a sea of opportunities to trawl the internet and target friends-of-friends on social media sites or use online dating sites to access potential victims. Be extra careful when talking to strangers who have contacted you via social media. DO NOT share any explicit or sexual photos, as they can be shared widely on the internet.

TIPS

- Only share photos that you'd be happy to see on a google search the next day.
- If you're talking to a new person, they may send a sexual photo first to coerce you to do the same. Don't fall for this trick. You don't know this person, and they can easily share photos to friends... or on the internet.
  (Also see the section on 'The risks of sexting')
- If something doesn't seem right, listen to your instincts. If you suspect you're being lured or sexually manipulated, contact 1800 737 732 for advice, or if you're immediately concerned contact triple zero 000.

SELF-DEFENCE – 12 EFFECTIVE WAYS TO AVOID OR DEAL WITH AN ATTACK

NOTE: These are recommendations only. Use your judgement and be strategic. Be careful not to aggravate your attacker if you don't feel you can get away quickly. You might want to wait until the attacker looks away and then make your move.

1. **Stay alert and aware.** Walk with purpose. Walk wide around building corners (so you don't get jumped as you come around a corner). Avoid small gatherings of people. Don't jog or walk with earphones.
2. **Use your instincts.** If it doesn't feel right, it usually isn't.

3. **Keep your phone in your hand and keys if you have them.** You can use your keys between your fingers to hit an attacker in the eyes. In an emergency, spray perfume or deodorant at the face to give yourself a chance to escape. (Note: use caution and common sense.)
4. **Maintain a personal comfort zone.** When strangers are walking too closely or at your pace, cross the road or walk on a different street. Be ready for action or get ready to run!
5. **Attack back if they catch you.** React at high speed, surprise them. Yell or scream, which will surprise your attacker and/or raise the alarm to other people.
6. **Before the attacker gets control, and if they do not have a weapon, do everything you can to inflict injury so you can escape.** Go for the most vulnerable spots on the body if you need to attack back (e.g., groin, eyes, nose, throat, knees). Use your elbows, knees and head, as they're the body's strongest parts and built-in 'weapons'.
7. **Never accept help or a lift from strangers. It's better to call a friend or family member or catch transport.**
8. **Never leave your drink unattended.** Someone could spike (put a drug in) your open drink. Never accept an open drink from a stranger or someone you don't fully trust.
9. **Don't open your home door to strangers.** If someone is knocking for help, call triple zero 000.
10. **During a robbery or carjacking, you need to co-operate!** Don't move quickly. If they're armed (i.e., have a weapon) and ask for money or possessions, hand them over (they are only material possessions).
11. **Download the Panic Alarm app,** which turns your iPhone into a loud flashing alarm with the touch of an icon. (Note: if you are walking alone at night, ensure you have this app open on your phone.)
12. **Learn self-defence:** Watch YouTube videos on ways to defend yourself, and/or attend a self-defence course.

Self-defence courses near me, self-defence tips, apps to use in an emergency

5. HOW BELIEFS SHAPE YOUR SELF-IMAGE

HOW DOES THE MIND TICK?

The brain is a remarkable organ, running everything from stabilising bodily functions to regulating hormones (processes that are outside of our control on a conscious level).

The more intriguing part of the brain is the part that filters and files your thoughts non-consciously (to protect it from actual or perceived danger or attract it to actual or perceived pleasures). This is commonly referred to as the 'mind'.

Importantly, the mind is where the words you say to yourself (your self-talk) shape your reality. e.g., if you're about to speak in front of 100 people, your adrenaline levels will be amplified in order to improve performance (this physical reaction is *not* a conscious process). The conscious part is the words you 'say' to yourself around this heightened experience. Instead of using the words "I'm nervous" you can replace it with "I'm excited", which results in an entirely different (less fear-based) perception and, most likely, a far more pleasurable outcome from the speech.

THE STORY YOU TELL YOURSELF SHAPES YOUR REALITY

The mind works on three levels according to one of the most influential (and controversial) thinkers of the 20th century, psychoanalyst Sigmund Freud.

Freud's psychoanalytic theory emphasised the importance of the unconscious mind in controlling our behaviour.

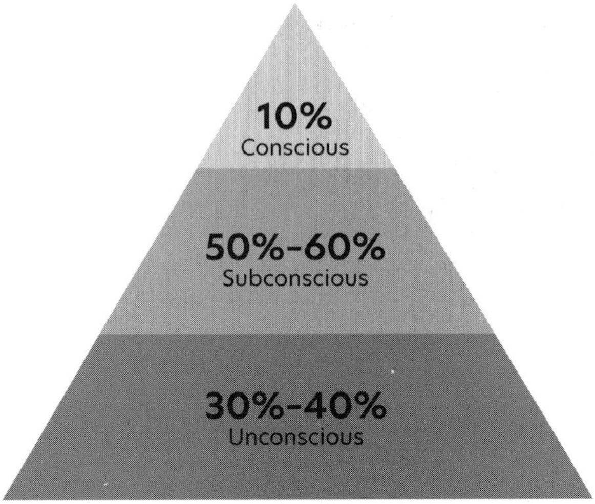

- 10% CONSCIOUS – the thinking part (being aware of thoughts and feelings at any given moment).
- 50-60% SUBCONSCIOUS – where you do things on autopilot (like brushing your teeth or picking up a piece of chocolate 'without thinking').
- 30-40% UNCONSCIOUS – the database of beliefs (about life and yourself) and habits (that can either 'sabotage' or' support' you).

Human motivation has long been the subject of conjecture. Psychologist Abraham Maslow's hierarchy of needs is a well-known theory of motivation, used broadly in marketing to understand buyers' needs and motivations. It's based on the premise that the most basic human need for food and shelter (physiological), must be met before humans can attend to higher needs of belonging, esteem and self-actualisation.

The need for certainty is a core emotional need that is gaining more attention from behavioural experts. Research is showing that you can influence feelings of certainty by your dialogue (or the words) you say to yourself and the pictures (imaginings) in your head. These two factors significantly influence your perception. For example, someone in a city might perceive rain to be miserable, while another person on a drought-stricken farm would be thrilled to get rain.

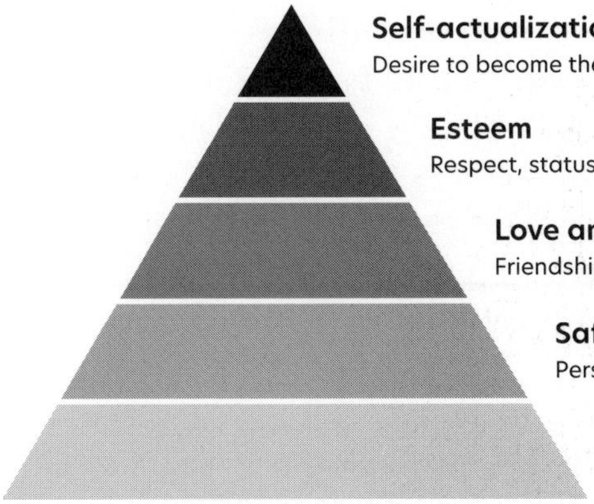

Simply Psychology Maslow's hierarchy of needs, Sigmund Freud theories, Marissa Peer secrets of your mind

> "When you say: 'I can't', your mind immediately begins to find evidence to support that belief."
>
> *Douglas Vermeeren*

BELIEFS - YOUR BELIEFS COME FROM MANY SOURCES

Whether you think you CAN or CAN'T do something is based on your special blend of beliefs.

Since birth, your mind has been taking in information (like putting data into a computer), seeing life through your own lenses, and accepting or rejecting certain concepts.

These concepts become implanted in your mind on an unconscious level.

Let's say someone told you that all dogs are to be feared. That concept will sit around in the back of your mind. Each time you see a dog, your reaction is to pull away because of your belief that 'all dogs are dangerous', regardless of whether the dog is dangerous or a fluffy, harmless old lapdog.

As you go through life, you'll be told or begin to believe many stories just like the dog story, such as: 'I'm a kick-ass basketballer' or 'I'm not good enough'. You will accept whatever you've reinforced in your 'belief-bank' over time.

You can re-write those stories by repeatedly reinforcing a phrase like "I am enough" or "I am amazing".

> "Where the mind goes, energy flows."
>
> Ernest Holmes

Beliefs and perceptions have come from many sources, like your:

- Parents and family (home-life and upbringing)
- Environment (where you live, and your cultural and demographic influences)
- Friends, peers and social/sports groups
- School and work communities
- Interactions with other people in the community
- Impressions from the media (news, social media and advertising)
- Everyday experiences and observations of life events around you

How to eliminate limiting beliefs

From birth, according to the founder of NeuroGym, John Assaraf, your brain is wired for:

1. Survival
2. Bodily functions
3. Safety
4. Energy conservation
5. Pleasure

We're not born with beliefs around *money, emotions, or self-esteem,* says John.

"These core emotions in the subconscious mind are learned from upbringing and habits."

But the good news is, you can change any beliefs that don't serve you well and re-train your brain.

"Just as we exercise our bodies to be stronger, we can exercise our 'neuro-muscle' to be stronger and more resilient," John said.

"If you have limiting beliefs that you're not good enough, your subconscious mind will activate the fear-centre to cause you to procrastinate and resist. When your conscience goals are out of alignment with your subconscious habits and beliefs, this is called 'neural dissonance',

"What's happened is you've moved out of your comfort zone, which causes many people to quit and retreat to safety," he says.

Through mind re-programming and repetition, there are programs, such as NeuroGym's Innercise program, that are designed to develop and encode new beliefs and to get your mind working in harmony for you, not against you.

John Assaraf. MyNeuroGym; Innercise: Fix your Focus, Fix your Fears

"Life is 10% what happens to you, and 90% how you react to it."

Charles S. Swindoll

TWO BELIEFS THAT WILL PUT YOU IN CONTROL OF YOUR LIFE
by Michelle Carlyle

Michelle Carlyle is the founder/owner of Thought Ratio which teaches people how to thrive in life by developing strong psychological foundations. Also see: Thrive Programme

What can you see around you right now? Is it comfortable and happy, or is it uncomfortable and miserable? You're not seeing reality. None of us do. We see reality through our 'belief spectacles'.

Some belief spectacles are **helpful** and **empowering**, while others are **limiting** and **unhelpful**, such as:

1. YOUR SENSE OF POWER AND CONTROL

This is your belief about how powerful and in control of your life you are.

Examples of helpful beliefs:

- I believe I can achieve my goals. It's up to me to put in the effort.
- I believe I can easily calm myself down if I start to get upset.

Examples of limiting beliefs:

- I believe I'm not very good at certain subjects.
- I believe that other people make me angry.

Ways to change these beliefs:

- Every time you have a thought that suggests you are powerless and do not have a choice, take action and change your thoughts.
- Think of how you can take off the 'unhelpful' spectacles you're wearing and replace them with the 'helpful and thriving' spectacles.
- Challenge yourself with a small goal you'd like to achieve. Break it down into even smaller goals. When you achieve the first small goal, congratulate yourself and move on to the next one.

2. YOUR SENSE OF SELF-ESTEEM

This is your belief about how good, kind and likeable you are. In other words, it's your subjective view of **your current thinking about you.**

Ways to change these beliefs around self-esteem:

- Every day for at least 14 days, write down 3-5 positive experiences you've had that day and add these to your growing list of positives.
- As often as possible throughout the day, re-read your positives and enjoy remembering how good they felt. Notice how **positive experiences** in your day have a direct influence on your self-esteem.

SELF-CONFIDENCE – 10 SECRETS TO BUILD UNSTOPPABLE CONFIDENCE

1. **Pay attention to the good things and cast off the negative**. For every negative thought, create three positive thoughts and focus on them several times every day, so they get embedded into your subconscious (like learning your times tables by rote learning).
2. **Observe super-successful people and do what they do.** Do they stand tall and walk strong, or hang their heads and speak meekly? You can see if someone's confident in the way they walk and talk. Do that too! Visualise yourself as them and mimic their confidence.
3. **Embrace the nerves.** Nerviness is an adrenaline rush that's preparing you for change and a challenge, which will take you to the next level. As humans, we're primitively wired to seek security and look for danger (as hunters or the hunted). Everything new is not a threat to our survival. Learn to spend time with your worst fear. What's the worst that can happen? When you're in control, you're not fearful.
4. **Push through self-doubt.** If you're spending your days picking yourself apart, you're focusing too much on yourself. Shift your mind off yourself onto helping others or doing stuff towards your goal.
5. **If you say, 'I can't do that' it's a self-fulfilling prophecy.** You've already told yourself the outcome. Instead, plant the seed in your

mind that you can. Now... water and nourish that seed so that it puts roots into your brain, and you can accomplish anything you put your mind to. Have a 'can-do' attitude.

6. **Talk yourself up.** Your self-talk is going on constantly. Make sure it's talking you up. Are you 'your own best supporter' not 'your own worst enemy'? When any self-limiting belief comes up, push it aside and say: 'I've got this!' and 'I will make this happen'.
7. **What I think, I am.** Your thoughts create your reality and, therefore, your life.
8. **Surround yourself with people who build you up.** If 'friends' put you down, keep them on your outer-circle or eliminate them from your friend-circle altogether.

   Remember, "you're the average of the five people you spend the most time with." (Source: Jim Rohn)
9. **Turn up the volume on self-love.** Be self-assured (with a dose of humility). Be the lead actor in your life story. When you step onto the podium of life, take on the role of your favourite actor. How would he or she walk? Take on their voice and stance and speak with absolute confidence as if you're on the world stage. Win the leading role in your life story! (See the chapter on writing your story, 'This is my life'.)
10. **Be open to new possibilities.** A closed mind cannot create and grow. Be open to opportunities.

How to develop self-confidence, Success.com Mental hacks to be more confident, Tony Robbins build massive self-confidence

"The only impossible journey is the one you never begin."

Tony Robbins

WRITE DOWN MOMENTS WHEN YOU FELT BULLETPROOF

Remember 5 moments when 'You did it!' or a time when you felt super proud of your achievement! It doesn't matter how big or small your 'feel good' moment is. It's a time you felt amazing and on top of the world.

Regularly draw on those examples to feel confident and reinforce that feeling by going over those experiences and imprinting them in your memory bank.

1.
2.
3.
4.
5.

SELF-ESTEEM – THE POWER OF A POSITIVE SELF-IMAGE by Wayne Donnelly

Wayne Donnelly is a hypnotherapist and behavioural expert, who helps clients become the best version of themselves by utilising the power within their unconscious mind. Wayne Donnelly

WHATEVER'S GOING ON IN YOUR LIFE IS A REFLECTION OF WHAT'S HAPPENING INSIDE YOUR MIND.

Your beliefs about yourself, your life's values and especially the image you have of yourself are reflected in your experience of the world around you.

If you have a look at what's happening to the people around you, you may observe that people have varying opinions of themselves. To see the truth of what they *really* believe, you only need to look at the experience of life that they're having. Listen to their self-talk, look at their friendships and get a sense of how they're feeling and notice what they're creating in their world (i.e. happy, joyful and fulfilled, or sad, unhappy and frustrated, etc).

WHERE DOES YOUR SELF-IMAGE COME FROM?

As we begin our journey in the world, we're like sponges, soaking up everything around us as we grow and learn. Some things are good, and some aren't.

As children, our critical conscious factor isn't developed until 10 or 12 years of age. Therefore, we don't say 'yes' or 'no', or 'good' or 'bad'. Instead, all the beliefs and ideas go straight to the unconscious mind.

Here are 3 tips to help you change your self-image and begin to enjoy your life experience more:

1. **Create an image of the ideal version of you:** Imagine you have a magic lamp. You rub it and the genie says: 'You can have the ideal version of yourself right now ... What do you want?'

What type of person would you become? ... What beliefs would you have? ... What would be your highest values? ... What emotions do you want to experience? *Paint the picture, vividly in your mind.*

2. **Practice the ideal you:** Many times each day, practice being the ideal version of you. With your eyes closed, get this picture of the ideal you right in front of you. Make it colourful, bright and strong... in 3D.

   Pretend that you can float out of your chair and into the body of the ideal self. See through ideal eyes, hear through these ideal ears, and feel what it's like to be in this ideal body.

   By practising this, you're programming your unconscious mind that this is where you want to be.

   Over time this will become your reality.

3. **Man in the mirror:** The most important words you hear are those reflected back at you from the mirror. Make these words beautiful. Look yourself in the eye and say, with great meaning and sincerity,

   'I love you. I totally love, accept and appreciate you.' (Do this until you believe it, until there's no doubt in your mind.)

STEREOTYPES – BREAKING DOWN OLD-FASHIONED STEREOTYPES

Gender stereotypes are culturally ingrained views of the roles of men and women in society.

We get impressions about gender roles not only from our parents, peers and upbringing, but also from messages in the print media (magazines, newspapers), visual media (television, social media, games) and audio media (music, lyrics, conversations).

How do outdated gender roles play out in real life? Here's some examples:

- Domestic – men do things around the house; women cook and clean.
- Occupation – women do support jobs or 'look after the kids'; men are the 'bread winners' (e.g., women are nurses and men are builders).

- Appearance – men are 'blokes' and are masculine; women are feminine and are 'pretty'.
- Personality – women are 'lady-like', submissive nurturers; men are tough, dominant and 'don't cry'.
- Psychological – women are inferior and the weaker sex; men assume control at home and work.

Harmful gender stereotypes are beginning to be broken down, but cultural and societal biases and prejudices can take generations to change.

While the education system is working on integrating gender equality into schools, collectively society can contribute to bridging the gender divide by being aware of stereotypical talk and actions, by speaking up and writing to the media...and by 'walking the talk' and allowing people to be who and what they want to be.

Gender stereotypes, Parliamentary initiatives, The Conversation sexualised and stereotyped, ABC gender discrimination driving pay-wedge

"Those who cannot change their minds cannot change anything."

George Bernard Shaw

THE AUSSIE 'BLOKEY' CULTURE IS SHIFTING

Young men are dealing with a range of stereotypes in today's society, with pressures placed on them around male body image, alcohol consumption and expectations around masculinity.

In particular, the 'toxic' culture of 'man up and not cry' has been damaging our men and boys for many centuries (dating back to the Victorian era). Of course, men cry. It's a natural human requirement to express emotion.

Thankfully that culture has shifted and is being viewed as old-fashioned and out of touch.

There's a large movement working to break down this masculine 'blokey' Australian culture and encourage boys and men to speak up and discuss their feelings openly.

The new generation of men is learning that it's important for everyone to express emotions and not bottle them up for those feelings to fester.

Steve Biddulph, author of *The New Manhood,* says there is always a risk that if boys feel unable to express when they're scared or sad, that they may turn that into anger. His ground-breaking books explain how to establish healthy masculinity and how to break these patterns from early childhood.

With support and educational programs, men are becoming more confident in seeing vulnerability as a strength, allowing them to be more open emotionally and form closer connections with friends, family and colleagues...and to cry if they want to.

UnimedLiving real man versus true man, Movember Men's mental health, Gotcha 4 Life program Support for men of all ages, Heart on my Sleeve program Heart on my sleeve, CNN article Benefits of crying wellness, ABC news Steve Biddulph – Toxic masculinity and tips for raising boys

> "I am who I am, your approval isn't needed."
>
> *Jack Nicholson*

BODY-IMAGE – THE REVOLUTION OF THE FEMALE BODY

The weight-debate for Western women has been going on for a long time. Just as fashion changes, so do the often-unrealistic expectations of women's bodies.

HOW WOMEN HAVE CONFORMED AND CONTORTED OVER THE CENTURIES

- The Renaissance era – Soft, pale and curvy.
- The 1890s – Bustles, bodices and boobs.
- The 1920s – Thin and pale.
- The 1930s – Fuller figure again.
- The 1950s – Think Marilyn Monroe.
- The 1970s – Thin, hippie-style.
- The 1980s – Tanned, tall and athletic like Elle McPherson.
- The 1990s – Pamela Anderson 'slim/booby' or the Kate Moss 'waif' look.
- The 2000s – A variety, from slim through to curvy.
- The 2010s – The early part of 2010 saw painfully-thin girls aspiring to be Victoria's Secret models (at that time anorexia cases reached an all-time high).
- The 2020s – Anything goes, as long as girls are healthy. Society and the media are embracing diversity and originality in all aspects of life. The trend is celebrating women of all shapes and sizes.

Today, the average Australian woman is a size 14-16. Here's a comparison over 45 years showing similar height, but a weight increase of 8kg.

- 1966 – 161cm tall and 63kg
- 2011-12 – 161.8cm tall and 71kg

Source: The Australian Bureau of Statistics (ABS) 2011-12 (Published Jun 7, 2013)

ABS average height and weight, what is the average Australian female height, Huffington Post huffingtonpost.com.au/entry/best-plus-size-models

6 SUPER-SIMPLE TIPS FOR A BETTER BODY IMAGE:

1. **Be perfectly imperfect:** You're perfect just the way you are! Create a signature-look. If there's something unique or different about you, then 'own' it!
   a) Use your personality and 'look' to your advantage (it differentiates you!)
   b) Remember – Don't give a **** about others. Do your thing.
2. **You're one of a kind:** Of the 7.8 billion people on the planet, you have a unique fingerprint, like no-one else.
3. **Love yourself unconditionally:** It's a valuable lesson to first offer unconditional love to ourselves. The most gorgeous girls are the ones who walk into a room owning their look and feeling fabulous.
4. **No comparisons, alright!** Comparing ourselves to other people's 'pretend-perfect' or 'high reel' on social media can result in us feeling inadequate, when in fact our social media friends are putting their best foot forward... and who knows what their reality is.
5. **Buy clothes that fit:** If you've gained or lost a size, accept it and buy a size up or down.
6. **Avoid disparaging talk about other people's appearances and your own:** For example: 'I look fat' or 'I look skinny'. That's your self-talk. Those around you aren't thinking that and if they are then ditch them! Friends **who matter** love you exactly as you are, irrespective of your outer layer.

Body Image Movement, Embrace You, ReachOut What is body image??

> "For beautiful eyes, look for the good in others; for beautiful lips, speak only words of kindness; and for poise, walk with the knowledge that you are never alone."
>
> *Audrey Hepburn*

6. MASTERING YOUR FEELINGS AND EMOTIONS

Please note: This chapter highlights a small selection of emotional states, and techniques to manage those emotions. It's a guide only. If you have any emotional concerns, please visit a health professional.

HOW TO TAKE BETTER CONTROL OF YOUR FEELINGS AND EMOTIONS

Do your feelings ever flip-flop around based on things happening to you or things people say about you?

Maybe you've said something like "my friend made me angry," or "I'm down because I lost my job," or "my boss makes me feel like ****".

But in reality, how you feel isn't controlled by others, but by how you perceive (or see) that situation or that person's actions.

Therefore, with practise and self-control, you can learn to rein in your thoughts and control any emotional outcomes, so that you're not a puppet to external influences.

> "It's not what happens to you, but how you react to it that matters."
>
> *Epictetus*

WHAT ARE EMOTIONS?

Emotions are biological states associated with the nervous system brought on by changes in thoughts, feelings, behavioural responses, and a degree of pleasure or displeasure (source: Wikipedia).

While there are very broad descriptors of emotions, such as 'happy', 'anxious' or 'angry', your own experience will be subjective (personal to you) and varied across the spectrum of that emotion.

Biologically, the limbic system is the part of the brain that regulates emotional and behavioural responses (the nervous system), especially in relation to survival, such as fight-or-flight responses, motivation, memory and reward. This 'reptilian', or reactive, part of the brain determines if you over-react or respond to situations. Some research suggests we can control the limbic system by slowing an overactive mind (relaxing) and through diet and exercise (also refer to Hormones section). Khan Academy - Emotion limbic system

HOW TO ACTIVELY CONTROL YOUR THOUGHTS AND STOP SELF-SABOTAGING YOUR EMOTIONS

You may have noticed that when you actively focus on, or even obsess over, a particular thought, it stirs up a deeper reaction in you.

This is because: E-MOTION = ENERGY (thoughts) + MOTION (action). Those thoughts and the resulting emotions are 'energy-charged' (*yes, we're all made of energy).

While negative emotions deplete our energy (-), positive emotions elevate our energy (+).

If they spiral out of control, negative-energy thoughts can sabotage our mind and cause suppressed feelings, such as anxiety, and eventually deeply affect our emotions, causing more serious mental health issues and even disease.

An idle mind *without positive purpose* can quickly go down the rabbit hole of overthinking and negative chaos (not to be confused with sitting quietly and letting the mind wander into creative solutions). You're in the driver's seat of your mind, so either put it in neutral (e.g. meditation) or keep it in gear, moving forward with constructive mental activities (e.g. reading, learning, purposeful thinking, or connecting with positive people).

Only you decide if you'll dwell on the 'negative'... or the 'positive'.

'OPEN UP' BY 'WRITING DOWN'

Writing emotions down gives some distance between you and your emotions. It gives clarity and assists in analysing and accepting your feelings. You are then better able to reflect and understand the origins of the emotions.

POSITIVE INTELLIGENCE (PQ)

Author of *Positive Intelligence* (PQ), Shirzad Chamine, claims mental fitness is a measure of the strength of your positive mental muscle (the SAGE part of the brain) versus your negative mental muscle (the SABOTEUR part of the brain).

"Stress and unhappiness are always a choice. Any negative feelings you experience are because you've chosen to listen to your saboteurs.

"Your highest performance comes from the brain that is calm, centred, focused, able to see possibilities and be creative," he says.

HAVE YOU HEARD OF IMPOSTER SYNDROME?

Imposter syndrome is an internal experience where you feel like a fraud. It can happen to anyone, with any level of expertise or knowledge. You might ask yourself "what gives me the right to be here?" or "who do I think I am to be called an expert?" This is a type of self-sabotage, and can create anxiety, self-doubt, perfectionism and procrastination.

The good news is that if you're feeling this way you've had some level of success in your life. It's helpful to remember that no-one is the definitive expert on anything and that you have something unique to offer. Focus on what you DO know, rather than on what you still have to learn. Avoid the need to be perfect (as there's no such thing), and instead be grateful for what you've accomplished so far. You can't be an imposter if you're being real and being 'you'.

CHANGE HOW YOU FEEL BY MOVING YOUR BODY

If you want to change the way you feel, begin with changing your physicality. When you're stuck your energy is low. Moving your body and using 'power posture' wakes up the nervous system and changes your state of mind, according to life and business strategist, Tony Robbins.

"Make a radical change. Speak with energy. Use your energy," says Tony.

By standing taller and sitting straighter, you'll exude more confidence (plus you open the chest and breathe better). Try using the 'Superwoman' or 'Superman' power-posture.

Tony emphasises that 'emotion is created by motion'. Your body language sends signals to your brain about how you're feeling. When you change the way you move your body, you change the way you feel.

This includes smiling and laughing, which elevates your mood by releasing positive hormones (e.g., dopamine), in turn releasing stress and sending positive signals to your brain.

> "Life is a long lesson in humility."
>
> *James M. Barrie*

NEGATIVE ENERGY VERSUS POSITIVE ENERGY

Here are some examples of negative emotions that pull your energy down, versus positive emotions that lift your energy up.

(-) NEGATIVE - suppressed energy	(+) POSITIVE - uplifting energy
Angry	Calm
Anxious	Certain
Arrogance	Humble
Confused	Clear-headed
Depressed	Optimistic
Desperate	Cheerful
Dishonest	Honest
Embarrassed	Confident
Fearful	Daring
Grieving	Accepting
Hateful	Loving
Hostile	Agreeable
Jealous	Trusting
Lazy	Motivated
Lonely	Contented
Nervous	Excited
Resentful	Satisfied
Resistant	Receptive
Sad	Happy
Scared	Secure
Selfish	Generous
Thankless	Grateful
Vindictive	Forgiving

WHAT'S EMOTIONAL INTELLIGENCE?

Having emotional intelligence (or EQ) means you know and understand yourself and, therefore, can make better decisions and empathise in situations of conflict or stress.

Understanding others and sharpening your EQ is vital for strong personal and business relationships. It allows you to connect on a deeper level with those closest to you.

Some of the traits of a person with a high EQ:

- Awareness of other people's feelings.
- Command of their own thoughts and emotions.
- Empathy and compassion.
- Responsibility for their mistakes and actions.
- Forgiveness and tolerance of others.
- Acceptance of criticism as a chance to grow.
- Ability to give praise and recognise the efforts of others.
- Self-reflection and introspection.

Very Well Mind what are emotions, imposter syndrome, Tony Robbins emotion is created by motion, change your physiology, change your state, change your story, Growth Engineering The limbic brain; Psychology Today feelings and emotions, Wikipedia meaning of emotion, Meaning of emotion and emotional intelligence and gaslighting, Free assessment get your saboteur score, D. Ivan Young emotional Intelligence, TEDX improve your emotional intelligence, Positive Intelligence ways to challenge negative thoughts

Book: J. Panksepp (2005) *Affective Neuroscience: The foundations of human and animal emotions*

"Men (people) are disturbed not by things, but by the view which they take of them."

Epictetus

INTUITION - HOW TO HAVE FAITH AND FOLLOW YOUR 'GUT FEELING'

Intuition is that sixth sense when you 'just know' something. It's not conscious thinking.

It's a feeling that turns out to be right. If you pay attention and tune-in, it will guide you like a compass.

Your gut feelings will usually happen when you're in a relaxed (unstressed) state of mind, when you're not forcing your thoughts this way and that way.

8 TIPS TO FOLLOW YOUR INTUITION

- Listen and acknowledge that 'inner voice'.
- Let go of negative thought patterns that can cloud intuition.
- Meditate and be mindful. Be still and quiet. Be in the moment.
- Pay attention to your first thoughts when you wake.
- Sleep on it. Sleeping rests your mind and helps you process information.
- Have faith in the 'feeling'.
- If something 'doesn't feel right' notice that thought. Check in later to see if it WAS right.
- Do exercises to develop intuition, by getting to know when those feelings lead you down the right path.

Wikihow follow your intuition, ways to develop your intuition

"Little minds are tamed and subdued by misfortune, but great minds rise above them."

Washington Irving

ANGER - BASIC TIPS TO UNDERSTAND AND DEFUSE ANGER

WHAT IS ANGER?

Anger is a normal, healthy emotion to help us express and deal with difficult or challenging situations.

Learning to express anger appropriately is an important part of managing our mental health.

Anger can motivate us to make changes in our lives.

SOME WAYS TO DEAL WITH ANGER

- Recognise the early warning signs and triggers.
- Count to 10. Take time out. Take some deep breaths to relax and help you to think rationally.
- Step away from the situation to defuse the moment. Reframe your thinking.
- Move your body to break the cycle. Do some exercise.
- Work out what caused it. Write it down. Think about solutions and making some changes.
- Talk to a friend and/or a health professional.

Headspace how to manage anger, ReachOut 8 way to deal with anger and cognitive behavioural therapy

THE STORY OF TWO WOLVES

An old Cherokee chief was teaching his grandson about life.

"A fight is going on inside me, inside all of us," he says to the boy.

"It's a terrible fight between two wolves."

One is evil. It is jealous, angry, resentful, dishonest, greedy and selfish.

The other is good. It is loving, joyful, kind, generous, truthful and humble."

The boy thinks for a moment and asks, "Which wolf wins?"

The old man quietly replies, "The one you feed."

Cherokee wisdom

WHY FEAR IS THE ENEMY

Fear – the 'fight or flight' emotion – was once useful when we were being chased by predators in prehistoric times. It's still useful to protect us from danger. However, in the modern era, fear can keep us stuck in a self-imposed prison, preventing us from reaching our fullest potential.

It's a handy emotion to blame for hiding away in our little shell (the prison) and occasionally popping our heads out to see if it's safe (then retreating into the shell again!)

We can avoid judgement and possible failure (because we didn't try anyway); and avoid taking risks (and therefore not progress and grow) and use it as an excuse to be a tad bit lazy (to procrastinate).

"Fear is the biggest thing that holds you back!" according to world-recognised motivational coach and author of *You Were Born Rich,* Bob Proctor.

"The person who's living in fear chooses comfort."

"There's no-one who can't live the way they want to live (in the developed world). Why don't they? Because they don't know how. They don't understand themselves."

He says, "worry and fear express themselves as anxiety, and when suppressed and bottled up inside, can lead to depression."

"When fear strikes, the wall we hit is known as the terror barrier," according to Bob.

"On the other side of the terror barrier is personal freedom! Very few people get through that terror barrier. If you don't learn to go through the terror barrier, and push outside the comfort zone, you'll stay right where you are for the rest of your days."

Very Well Mind the psychology of fear, Lifehack use fear to your advantage, Bob Proctor the terror barrier, Brian Tracy why negative thoughts are an enemy

Books: The Dalai Lama *The Art of Happiness*; Eckhart Tolle *The Power of Now*

"The cave you fear to enter holds the treasure you seek."

Joseph Campbell

WORRYING IS A FEAR-BASED, UNPRODUCTIVE EMOTION AND A WASTE OF PRECIOUS TIME.

Worrying takes you out of the present moment to *dwell on past events*; or into the future to *anticipate future events*. The only moment you can control is the present.

Life coaches, like Tony Robbins, look at problems as a gift. Struggles are a chance to grow, learn and build spiritual character. Problems are a sign of life.

According to Norman Vincent Peale, "the only people who don't have problems are in the cemetery."

When you have a problem, ask yourself this ...

Is there anything you can do about it?

NO. Then *don't worry.*

YES. Then *don't worry.*

VULNERABILITY IS THE GREATEST MEASURE OF COURAGE

"Vulnerability is not weakness. That myth is profoundly dangerous. Vulnerability is the birthplace of innovation, creativity and change," according to author and social scientist, Brene Brown.

She says vulnerability is a willingness to show up and be seen, and face risk head-on, even when there are no guarantees, even when there's uncertainty and even when we might fail.

"It's our most accurate measure of courage," Brene says.

Courage is taking the risk of being imperfect... it's feeling the fear and doing it anyway.

"The trouble with perfectionism is people hide behind it to avoid criticism, blame and ridicule. But it's a shield. It keeps us from being seen. It prevents us from moving forward.

"When perfectionism is driving, shame is always riding shotgun," she said.

Why vulnerability shows strength and courage, Evan Carmichael Vulnerability and belonging, Brene Brown book *Dare to Lead,* Power of positivity 5 ways being vulnerable means you're strong, Susan Jeffers Feel the fear and do it anyway, Book - The Power of Positive Thinking

> "It's better to have tried and failed, than to live life wondering what would've happened if I had tried."
>
> *Alfred Lord Tennyson*

A FAILURE TO TAKE RISKS, IS A FAILURE TO GROW

If Thomas Edison and other inventors had strived for perfection and not risked failure, where would we be?

Edison failed 1,000 times before successfully inventing the prototype of the light bulb (as legend has it).

When he was asked how it felt to fail 1,000 times, Edison replied: "I didn't fail 1,000 times. The light bulb was an invention of 1,000 steps."

He famously said, "I am not discouraged, because every wrong attempt is another step forward."

> "The fear of being different prevents most people from seeking new ways to solve their problems."
>
> *Robert Kiyosaki*

THE SECRET TO HAPPINESS

Consistently practising gratitude boosts your happiness level by 25%, according to Dr Robert Emmons, author of the book, *Thanks! How the New Science of Gratitude Can Make You Happier*.

Gratitude has a way of creating a positive ripple of happiness from everyone it touches.

HAPPINESS IS A CHOICE

If you say, "I'll be happy when…" this makes happiness conditional. If you say, "I don't like Mondays" or "I always feel down when it's not sunny…" these are self-imposed conditions. Instead, choose to be happy regardless of external factors.

Give yourself permission to feel amazing, every day.

> "The secret of happiness is to count your blessings while others are adding up their troubles."
>
> *William Penn*

EFFORTLESS WAYS TO CRACK THE HAPPINESS CODE:

- **Spend 10 minutes a day quietly focusing on the good things in your life.** If a negative comes up, push it aside and re-focus on the good.
- **Write a gratitude journal.** Write 3-5 things you're grateful for every day.
- **Laugh more.** Laughter releases stress and lowers blood pressure.
- **Smile more.** Smiling is good for the soul, and most people will smile back.
- **Make gratitude part of your daily routine.** It will bring positivity to your life.
- **Say: "I'm fantastic, thanks!"** instead of "I'm fine"
- **Speak only kind words.** Speak nicely about others and speak kindly to yourself.
- **Tell someone you love or appreciate them.** Give a compliment or give to a charity.
- **Pay it forward.** Doing something nice for someone increases feel-good hormones.
- **Say thank you** to people in the community when you're out doing stuff in daily life.

- **Appreciate nature** and the beauty around you and what you have in your life.
- **Live in the now.** You can't change the past or predict the future. All you have is now.

Ways to practice gratitude, Positive psychology gratitude exercises, LifeHack gratitude

> "There is only one way to happiness, and that is to cease worrying about things which are beyond the power of our will."
>
> *Epictetus*

HAVE YOU NOTICED KINDNESS IS CONTAGIOUS?

IT'S COOL TO BE KIND

You may have heard of the terms 'pay it forward' and 'random acts of kindness' (RAK).

It's where a simple act of kindness, even a smile, makes a person's day and makes your day too.

Kindness comes back to you 3-fold, because, 'what you put out, you get back'.

The reward-related part of the brain that's activated when you decide to do something nice for others is called the striatum. It stimulates the feel-good hormone (dopamine) and shifts your emotions.

In the same way that collective fear around a virus can ripple through a small town, through a nation and through a global community, kindness can have the same effect. It demonstrates that we're all connected in an energetic way.

Social psychologists call it 'the law of reciprocity', which is when someone does something nice for you, you will have a deep-rooted urge to do something nice in return.

Stay Kind Movement why stay kind, Brian Tracey the law of reciprocity, RAKS kindness ideas, The good human factory

> "Everyone you meet is fighting a battle you know nothing about. Be kind. Always."
>
> *Unknown source*

MANAGING THE MIND THROUGH MINDFULNESS AND RELAXATION

MEDITATION ASSISTS WITH:

- Management of pain and stress
- Resilience and compassion
- Focus at work and in the classroom
- Creativity and collaboration

Mindfulness is a mental state achieved by focusing awareness on the present moment, while calmly accepting your feelings, thoughts and bodily sensations.

HOW CONSCIOUS BREATHING IMPROVES HEALTH

Did you know? There's a right and a wrong way to breathe, beyond sustaining life.

Learning to breathe effectively fuels the body with oxygen, helping your immunity and giving you greater mental clarity, plus improved sleep and digestion, while regulating the sympathetic nervous system (to manage stressful situations).

Research shows that long-term shallow breathing can seriously affect our health. It can "turn into panic attacks and stress," according to headspace. "Diaphragmatic breathing, on the other hand, can lower blood pressure, reduce the heart rate, relax muscles, decrease stress, and increase energy levels. Deep breathing grounds us as well."

AN EXAMPLE OF A MINDFUL BREATHING TECHNIQUE

Yogic breathing is a balancing breathing exercise that's used as an anchor for concentration and mindfulness. It stills the mind and can transform your state of mind, by reducing anxiety, stress and helping insomnia, and is regularly used in yoga practices. A longer exhalation is thought to help induce the body's relaxation response by activating the parasympathetic nervous system. For example:

- Breathe IN through the nose for 4 seconds / HOLD for 2 seconds....
- Breathe OUT through your mouth for 4 seconds / HOLD for 2 seconds. (Repeat)

TIP

Try this technique to get to sleep, while putting your attention on counting the breaths.

Headspace: how shallow breathing affects your whole body and meditation for beginners, Yogic breathing, Buteyko information, Smiling Mind what is mindfulness, Free meditation app Insight Timer Healthline: parasympathetic nervous system

STRESS MANAGEMENT – UNDERSTANDING THE BODY-MIND-RELATIONSHIP

The mind and body are intrinsically connected.

If one is out of balance, the other can react, like getting an upset stomach when stressed, or feeling scared or anxious when you've injured yourself.

IF YOU'RE FEELING DOWN, ASK YOURSELF THESE QUESTIONS. HAVE YOU:

- Eaten enough (or at all) today? Your blood sugar levels might be low.
- Drunk enough water? You might be dehydrated and not thinking clearly.
- Got enough sleep? You might be tired and run down.
- Moved your body and done something active? This will get your blood pumping and oxygenate you.
- Done a short meditation track? This will clear your mind of clutter and give it a rest.
- Considered that you may be sensitive to certain foods? Ask your GP for an IgE (allergy) and full blood test to check if that may be causing unrest.
- Talked to anyone today? You might be lonely. Call a (positive) friend and have a chat. Or call a hotline.
- Have you stayed at home all day? If so, head out for a walk and connect with nature. Or go to the shops to be around people.
- Dwelled on things in silence? Play some uplifting music or listen to some positive or humorous podcasts.
- Said some kind things to yourself lately? Show yourself love. Remind yourself how amazing and original you are, every day.

WHAT IS 'STRESS'?

Our bodies are hard-wired to react to protect us against threats. Whether the threats are real (e.g., you're about to get run over by a car) or imagined (e.g., someone might be talking behind your back), your body still produces stress hormones.

When the body encounters a stressor, it ignites a tiny region in the brain called the pituitary gland (a gland attached to the hypothalamus - the control centre at the base of the brain). This sets off an alarm for the adrenal glands to produce hormones (such as cortisol and adrenaline). The pituitary gland is also known as the 'master gland', as it plays a key role in regulating body functions such as metabolism, growth, reproduction, sex drive, blood pressure and many other functions.

Long-term activation and over-exposure to stress hormones can disrupt almost ALL of the body's processes.

"The greatest weapon against stress is our ability to choose one thought over another."

William James

STRESS (AND OTHER) HORMONES

HORMONES THAT AFFECT OUR MOODS AND BODILY FUNCTIONS

CORTISOL – The Stress Hormone: It has many functions in the human body, helping the body respond to stress or danger and regulating immunity, metabolism and inflammation. Cortisol increases sugars (glucose) and enhances the brain's use of these sugars to repair tissues. HIGH levels of cortisol can result in anxiety and other mental health issues, weight gain or loss, headaches, fatigue, increased blood pressure, low libido, slow healing and digestive problems.

ADRENALINE – The Fight or Flight Hormone: Have you heard of the term 'adrenaline rush'? Through the adrenal glands, adrenaline increases the heart rate, elevates blood pressure, increases metabolism, enlarges the lungs, dilates the pupils and boosts energy supplies to prepare the body for action or reaction (fight or flight).

It also increases the body's pain threshold, to allow it to continue running from danger or a threat, and therefore produces an increase in strength and performance.

To help control the defence system's 'fight-or-flight' hormones, some experts suggest activating the parasympathetic nervous system, also called the 'rest-and-digest' system.

OXYTOCIN – The Love Hormone: Our body has a built-in mechanism to counter stress. One of the anti-stress hormones is oxytocin. This hormone is sometimes called the 'love' or cuddle hormone as it increases feelings of trust and emotional bonding. It also promotes eye contact, touching, stroking, cuddling, cooing or mother speak, and after birth it's responsible for triggering lactation.

DOPAMINE, SEROTONIN AND ENDORPHINS: These are 'feel-good' neurotransmitters that regulate countless functions in the body, including sleep, empathy, sex, mood and metabolism. Dopamine and endorphins increase when you engage in reward-producing activities, such as affection, working out and showing kindness to other people.

SEX (STEROID) HORMONES, such as testosterone and estrogen, are produced by the testes and ovaries (respectively) and affect the growth and function of the reproductive organs.

Mayo Clinic stress management, Health Direct the role of cortisol in the body, Healthline adrenaline rush, Zenlama oxytocin versus cortisol, Atlas BioMed essential guide to serotonin and other happy hormones, Psychology Today why the stress hormone is public enemy #1, Science Daily how smiling can make people happier, Very Well Mind what is the fight or flight response

SIX STEPS TO REFIRE AND MASTER YOUR MIND

Sydney based neuroscientist, Dr Sarah McKay, is director of The Neuroscience Academy, and author of *"The Women's Brain Book"* and *REFIRE: 6 Steps to Rewire the Brain*.

Dr McKay says, "As children, our brains are like a sponge, and are shaped by every experience. This ability to change is termed neuroplasticity."

Our adult brains are still capable of learning and change, but because the capacity for neuroplasticity declines in adulthood, the (conscious) effort required to change is greater.

STEPS TO REFIRE THE BRAIN:

R – REASON is your why. Your reason needs to be clear (and in do-able, bite-size bits) to reduce uncertainty and increase motivation.

E – ENGAGE the skills of a teacher, a mentor or a coach. This helps to keep you on track and accountable and ensures you immerse yourself and take ACTION.

F – FEEL and flow. This is where we find the SWEET SPOT in the emotions, between under-emotion (frozen in fear) and over-emotion (wound up with anxiety). There needs to be some neuro-friction and tension to make things happen (i.e., slight stress to get in the flow).

I – IMAGINE is the mental rehearsal of clearly imagining and thinking of the outcome as if it has already happened. This is particularly used by competitive athletes. It can also be used to practice how to respond to an emotional situation (like with your boss or parents). If you play and rehearse all the possibilities over and over in your mind, you feel like you've done it a million times before.

R – REPEAT it over and over until it is embedded in the synapse (the junction between the nerve cells of the mind).

E – EXTEND out of your comfort zone. As you reach each new level it will become easier. But don't stop. Keep challenging yourself. "Successful people keep going until they can't get it wrong."

Dr Sarah McKay, S PhD. (October 2020) REFIRE: 6 Steps to rewire your brain.

'TAKE 5' AND TAKE A BREATHER

When you feel your negative emotions taking over, take 5 minutes to reboot your brain by focussing your attention on your 5 senses.

Sit quietly, close your eyes and take 5 slow deep breaths and exhalations, then settle your breath.

For 5 minutes tune into the 5 senses. Bring your hands together in the 'prayer position' to realign your energy and 'honour the moment'.

FEEL – Rub your fingertips of one hand against the fingertips of the other hand, and tune into the feeling as you rub over the sensitive palms of your hands.

SEE – Think of a beautiful sanctuary in your mind's eye, where you feel at pure peace. It may be a pond or a forest. See it in all its richness. Make it more bright and vivid each time.

HEAR – If you're in a quiet space, listen to all the distant sounds (the birds singing or trees rustling). Listen to your own breathing. If it's a noisy place, block out external noise and recall some music that brings you peace.

SMELL – Breathe in, smell the air and feel it coming and going. Really connect to that sensation. Imagine it cleansing your body and soul on the in-breath and removing toxins on the out-breath. Or imagine a beautiful fragrance and how it makes you feel.

TASTE – Visualise your favourite food and flavour. Vividly recall those senses and the rich textures. Maybe they were sweet or salty, or creamy or textured.

Open your eyes after 5 minutes. Write down 5 things you're grateful for today.

Your gratitude list reminds you of all the good things in your life. They could be as simple as being happy to have food on the table, or a car to drive, or the sun shining.

In your quiet moments through the day reflect on them.

THINGS I'M GRATEFUL FOR TODAY

1.
2.
3.
4.
5.

"If it's meant to be, it's up to me."

Tom Dreeson

7. TAKING CARE OF YOUR MENTAL HEALTH

MENTAL HEALTH – WHAT IS IT?

This section provides general information and support. While mental health professionals have reviewed the content, this is not intended as medical advice. If you have any mental health concerns, we recommend contacting your doctor or another health professional.

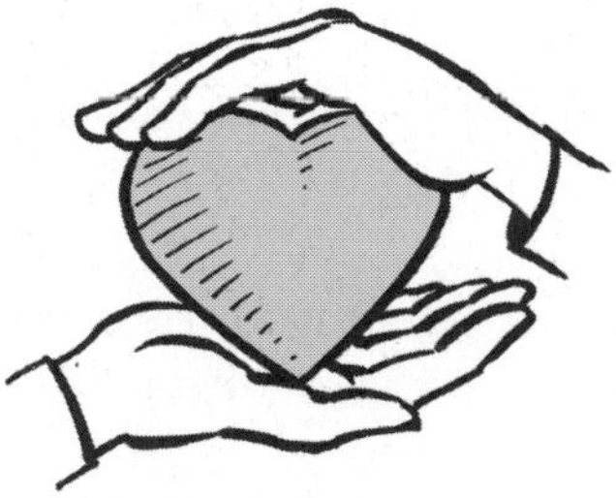

Mental health relates to our emotional and psychological well-being. It affects our mood, our physical health and how we think, feel and act. It also affects how we handle stress, relate to others and make choices.

Just as we take care of our physical health, it's important to learn to take care of our mental health too.

MENTAL ILLNESS CAN BE CAUSED BY A REACTION TO:

- Environmental stresses and life experiences, such as trauma or abuse
- Genetic (biological) factors
- Biochemical imbalances (or a combination of all three)

MENTAL HEALTH ISSUES WILL AFFECT 45% OF AUSTRALIANS

An estimated 45% of Australians will experience a mental health condition in their lifetime, according to Beyond Blue.

Anxiety is the most common mental health condition, affecting 25% of people (one in four) at some stage in life.

Beyond Blue estimates that around 3 million Australian adults have anxiety and depression.

TYPES OF MENTAL HEALTH DISORDERS ARE:

- Mood (such as depression or bipolar)
- Anxiety
- Personality
- Psychotic (such as schizophrenia)
- Eating
- Trauma-related (such as post-traumatic stress)
- Substance abuse

HERE ARE SOME EARLY WARNING SIGNS OF A POTENTIAL MENTAL HEALTH PROBLEM:

(Please note: It's normal for most people to experience these symptoms mildly, at some stage, due to life events. Seek help from professionals if any of these signs are prolonged, extreme, combined or causing you concern.)

- Severe mood swings. Extremes of emotions.
- Fighting regularly with family and friends and pushing close contacts away.
- Eating or sleeping too much or too little. Weight loss or gain.
- Reclusive and withdrawn. Not wanting to leave the house.
- Pulling away from usual activities and friends.
- Constant low energy and lethargy.
- A 'don't care' attitude, like nothing matters. Lacking confidence.
- Feeling helpless, hopeless or overwhelmed.
- Excessively drinking or using drugs.

- Forgetful, confused and preoccupied
- Overly emotional, angry, upset, guilty, scared or worried.
- Dwelling excessively on thoughts or memories.
- Hearing voices or believing things that are not true.
- Self-harm or harming others.
- Unable to cope or perform daily tasks.

UNDERSTANDING ANXIETY AND DEPRESSION

ANXIETY is your body's natural response to stress. It can occur when fearing and anticipating events that have not yet happened or when you feel under pressure.

For some people, anxious feelings don't go away and affect their ability to cope with daily life, and they may need support to recover. The sooner you get support, the more likely you can recover.

Symptoms can include increased heart rate, excess worry, restlessness, difficulty concentrating, difficulty breathing and disturbed sleep.

If the anxious feelings don't pass once the stressful situation has passed, or interfere with your daily activities, or continue for months, you may be diagnosed with an anxiety disorder.

DEPRESSION is more than a low mood. It is a severe condition that impedes functioning over a long period of time.

The World Health Organisation (WHO) estimates that 264 million people worldwide are affected by depression.

Causes include: Severe stressors and life events, genetics (runs in the family, but does not mean you will suffer from it), personality tendencies, like obsessive compulsive behaviour, chronic medical illness or acute injury, drug and alcohol abuse, traumatic stress events, inability to move on from the past. There are usually multiple causes of major depression.

Treatment: Mental health illnesses are treatable with specialist support or, in some cases, medications. Often patients think there is a quick fix, but it may take some time to find the most suitable treatments.

Who can assist with anxiety and depression?

- General practitioners (GPs)
- Psychologists
- Psychiatrists
- Mental health nurses
- Accredited mental health social workers
- Occupational therapists in mental health
- Counsellors specialised in mental health

ONLINE THERAPY TOOLS:

- MyCompass help with mild depression and anxiety
- Mindspot online assessment
- MoodGym tools for depression and anxiety
- Healthdirect's Symptom Checker
- Black Dog Institute
- Beyond Blue 1300 224 636
- World Health Organisation
- Health Direct
- (Also refer to the list of contacts at the start of this guide.)

SUICIDAL THOUGHTS – WHERE CAN I GO FOR SUPPORT?

Have you been thinking of suicide?

Wait! Don't act on those thoughts.

Talk to someone you trust, or call **Lifeline on 131 114.**

Or call the suicide call-back service on 1300 659 467.

Or if you are in distress or immediate danger, call triple zero **000.**

When suicidal thoughts are strong, it may feel like you have to act on your thoughts immediately. It's really important to postpone the decision to end your life and not act on impulse.

Sometimes people feel helpless and overwhelmed in their lives. The majority of people say that putting off their decision to die was the best decision they've ever made. They were able to get the support and coping strategies they needed.

If you're not coping, tell someone you trust.

Talking to someone you trust can help you to see alternative ways of solving or thinking about your problems or feelings.

Your family and friends may not be aware of how you're feeling because people who are feeling suicidal often withdraw inside themselves, making it hard for others to understand what they're going through.

Reach out to a family member, friend, teacher, counsellor or any person that you feel comfortable with.

There's always someone who's just a phone call away.

IT'S OK TO ASK FOR HELP #YouCanTalk #AreYouOK?

WHAT TO ASK IF YOU SUSPECT A FRIEND, COLLEAGUE OR FAMILY MEMBER IS CONSIDERING SUICIDE:

Ask them, 'are you ok?' ...and ensure you continue the conversation. For example:

'I've been worried about you lately', or

'I've noticed some differences in you lately and I'm wondering how you are,' or

'Have you been thinking of harming yourself?'

If they say 'yes', ask them more questions, such as 'How long have you felt this way?'; 'Have you thought about how you would end your life?'; 'Has anything happened recently that has made you feel worse?'

Explore their feelings and find out who else might be able to help.

For more ways to ask the right questions, visit the Conversations Matter website (resources): Conversations matter and RUOK; The #YouCanTalk program exists to encourage all Australians to have a conversation with a friend, family member or work colleague that they're concerned about.

If you're concerned for their safety, stay with them to assist them to call Lifeline 131 114. Reassure them that this is a confidential service.

Possible suicidal warning signs include withdrawal from other people, engaging in risky or self-destructive behaviour, severe mood swings, inability to sleep, extreme hopelessness and anxiety, agitation, abusing alcohol and drugs, saying goodbye or giving away possessions, talking about suicide or death, taking less care of their appearance (also refer to the previous section).

Suicide risk factors include previous suicide attempts, history of substance abuse or mental health conditions, recent death of a family member or close friend, seeking access to harmful means or weapons, ongoing exposure to bullying, a traumatic event, loss of financial security, legal or disciplinary disputes.

With the support of a health professional, you might also consider self-help tools, such as:

- Create a safety plan – highly recommended: **The BeyondNow app** or web version. Suicide safety planning
- Know your warning signs so you can put in place your safety plan.
- Journal the positives in your life. Write down things that lift your mood.
- Maintain a healthy lifestyle (regular exercise, eat well, avoid alcohol and drugs).
- Make a list of people you can spend time with or social places you could go to.
- Reach out for support from health professionals and support groups.
- Consider complementary therapies (e.g., acupuncture, meditation, yoga, massage, homeopathy, kinesiology, dietary supplements, naturopathy or hypnosis).
- Research and undertake courses on mind-wellness.
- (Also refer to SELF-CARE TIPS in this guide.)

HOW DOES THE MEDICARE REBATE WORK?

A doctor can provide a mental health treatment plan to see a psychologist, who will guide you through a program to recovery.

Under the GP mental health treatment plan, Medicare rebates are available, with a certain amount of mental health services per calendar year. This plan is available to patients with an assessed mental disorder, who are referred by a GP or psychiatrist or paediatrician.

Speak to your doctor for current rebate information and ask if you're eligible for free mental health care under the primary and community care service.

HELPLINES AND RESOURCES:

- Lifeline 131 114 – 24-hour confidential crisis counselling service
- Or text a crisis supporter on 0477 131 114 (6pm to midnight Eastern Standard Time, 7 days/week)
- EveryMind website ; eheadspace 1800 650 890 Beyond Blue 1300 224 636
- Suicide call back service 1300 659 467; Self-care guide Suicide Prevention Australia
- Mental health treatment plan
- Call triple zero **000** if you or anyone is in danger or needing an ambulance
- (Also refer to the list of contacts at the start of this guide.)

> "Keep in mind that part of growing up is dealing with difficult issues, and the benefits can be great if you have the courage to ask for help. Human beings are not designed to go through life alone. No-one has to bear the burden of tough times all by themselves."
>
> *Jack Canfield*

YOU'RE NOT ALONE. PLEASE REACH OUT

Special note from the author: I have a particular concern about the number of suicides recently.

As someone who attempted suicide at 13, I can tell you that sometimes it might seem like the answer, but it's not. You owe it to yourself to see it through, to find a solution to whatever you're worried about, to get some support, or let your head heal or your hormones catch up if you've been taking some drugs or self-medicating.

The sadness and despair might seem overwhelming at that very moment. This is a big decision. The biggest you'd ever make. And it's final. There is no room for regret and no coming back if you make that choice. It goes against every instinct to do it, so please don't do anything on impulse.

When you talk to other people, you'll find it's more common than you think for people to, at times, feel tired of this thing called life. There'll be great days and really s*** days. That's the way it rolls.

If you've lost money, it's just money which comes and goes, and you can make it back.

If you've done something wrong, forgive yourself or make amends.

If a loved one has gone, give yourself time to heal. It may not heal completely, but it will get easier.

If you're angry or you've had a big fight, take time to let it simmer down.

If you think you'll fail at an exam, it's ok, you can redo it or take a new direction in your career, which might be a better path anyhow.

If you're being bullied, tell them to ****off and mind their own business.

If you're coming down from drugs, let yourself bounce back.

Don't be too hard on yourself. Sometimes we have to hit rock-bottom to sort out a problem. Ride it out and see what your destiny has in store. Give it a day, a week, a month, or even a year, or however long it takes to find new ways to cope. If it's a chronic longer-term imbalance, it will take more time. Allow yourself that time.

Please know that you're special. You are loved. You might leave, but the pain to those you would leave (your loved ones) goes on. They would have to live with the agony and loss every single day for the rest of their lives. Whole communities can suffer when someone takes their life because they wish they could have done more to help.

If you've been feeling suicidal, please promise you'll reach out to someone. There's nothing wrong with feeling overwhelmed. We all feel it at times. There are many people who want to help you get back on the road to recovery...but you need to ask first, so they know how you're feeling.

Importantly, learn to love yourself first, over anything or anyone.

Love and hugs to you. Deb xx

THE FACTS ABOUT EATING DISORDERS – By Joanne Cohen

Joanne spent two years working in an inpatient high-dependency unit at Barts and the London Hospital in the UK, working with young people with eating disorders, among other mental health presentations.

Eating disorders are estimated to affect 9% of the Australian population between the ages of 15 to 25 years. There are lots of societal pressures on young people in today's world, via magazines pinpointing celebrities, beauty and fashion, social media platforms such as Facebook, Twitter and Instagram portraying an image of what's trendy and in fashion.

There is endless speak of diets that are good for our health including taking a pill or drinking a milkshake to help us shed the kilos.

A person with an eating disorder will invariably have a disturbed body image and intense fear of weight gain.

TYPES OF EATING DISORDERS:

- Anorexia nervosa
- Bulimia nervosa
- ARFID (avoidant restrictive food intake disorder)
- Binge eating disorder

PEOPLE WITH EATING DISORDERS CAN EXPERIENCE THE FOLLOWING:

- Being afraid of gaining weight.
- Feeling fat despite being very thin.
- Preoccupation with food such as obsessive calorie counting.
- Rapid weight loss and not wanting to eat.
- Maintaining a body weight below one's healthy resting weight.
- Obsessive weighing.
- Irregular or absent menstrual cycle.
- Feeling depressed and irritable.
- Denying that anything is wrong.

THE CAUSES OF ANOREXIA ARE STILL UNKNOWN. BELOW ARE SOME CONTRIBUTING FACTORS:

- Females are at higher risk, particularly after puberty.
- Genetics – the risk of developing anorexia increases if another family member has had it.
- Personality traits such as perfectionism, negative self-image and food obsession.
- Dieting – this is one of the main triggers for the condition.
- Traumatic events, physical, sexual or emotional abuse, bullying at school, death or illness can all be triggers and exacerbate the condition.

CURRENT EFFECTIVE TREATMENTS FOR EATING DISORDERS:

- Behavioural therapy
- Cognitive analytical therapy
- Cognitive behavioural therapy
- Adolescent-focused individual therapy
- Family interventions focusing on food disorders
- Specialist supportive clinical management

Alongside the above therapeutic treatments, the use of medication can assist, however, it should not be the primary treatment. Instead it should be used in conjunction with therapy appropriate for the treatment of anorexia and other eating disorders.

First and foremost, it's important that you seek professional support.

IN ADDITION, YOU MIGHT CONSIDER USING SOME SELF-HELP TOOLS. FOR INSTANCE:

- Keep a 'recovery' journal.
- Spend time around supportive people.
- Talk to other people who have recovered.
- Go on body-positive outings.
- Read recovery-oriented books.
- Take up a hobby.
- Do things that nourish your soul.

The Butterfly Foundation, headspace, National eating disorders collaboration helplines, Eating disorder counselling, Eating disorder helpline Australia

PLEASE NOTE: The book's author is aware that there are many types of mental health disorders and has highlighted eating disorders as they're very relevant to this age group. If you have any mental health concerns, we encourage you to contact a health professional or the helplines in this guide.

> "Be kind, for everyone you meet is fighting a hard battle."
>
> *Ian Maclaren*

GRIEF - HOW TO COPE WITH GRIEF

Grief is a natural response to loss. It's a very personal process and it can take months or years to come to terms with the loss of a loved family member or friend.

It's important to be kind to yourself during this process. Talking to a friend, a family member, or a professional about how you feel is important in understanding your emotions, which can range from shock, disbelief, sadness and guilt, through to anger and fear.

Everyone deals with loss differently, and no loss is the same. Grief is not limited to a time when someone dies, but also when you've experienced other types of losses, such as when a significant relationship ends (like a break-up or divorce) or when a pet dies, or with the loss of a job or loss of financial stability.

Dealing with loss and grief is all about processing your feelings. Try to sit with your feelings when they come up rather than stuffing them down or running away from them, tempting as that may be.

The more you acknowledge your feelings, the more you will be able to move through your grief to reach a place of acceptance.

The 5 stages of grief model (below), created by Elisabeth Kubler-Ross, defines the stages as **Denial, Anger, Bargaining, Depression and Acceptance**.

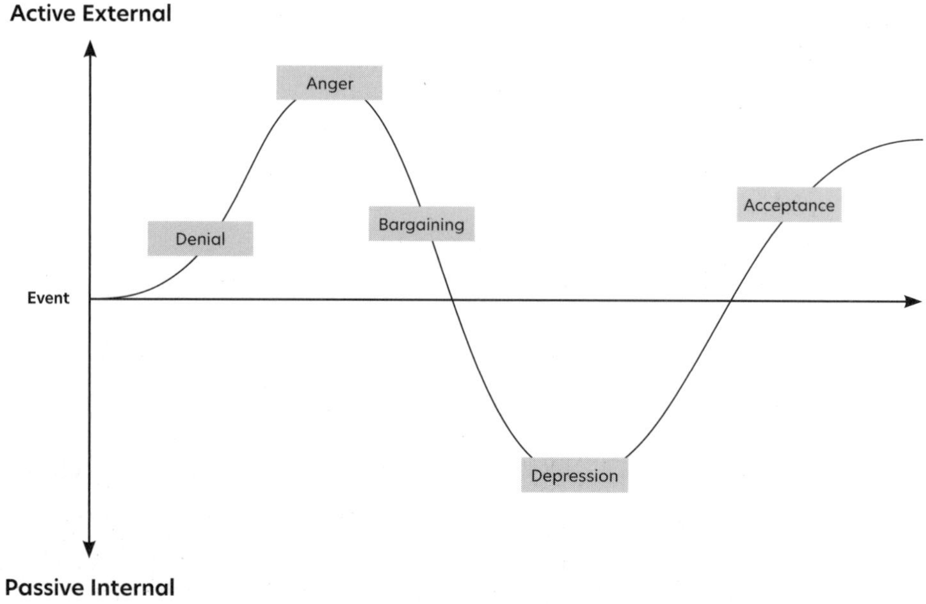

Source: Kubler-Ross model

WAYS TO TAKE CARE OF YOURSELF AS YOU GRIEVE

- **Talk to someone you trust:** Talking gives comfort and allows you to let your emotions out in a safe environment. If you bottle up your feelings, they can magnify. It is best to share them with someone you trust.
- **Grieve in your own way:** Know that sometimes your feelings will rise at unexpected times. Allow time during the day to grieve without distractions and let emotions out within your own space. Know that there will be trigger times, like anniversaries and birthdays, or times of the day when you are sad and vulnerable.

- **Write a journal:** Write down how you feel and acknowledge those emotions. You can honour the person you have lost by writing memories of them. You can light a candle or plant a special plant in the garden.
- **Let yourself cry:** Crying is a part of the healing process. Tears are the body's release valve for grief and stress.
- **Give it time:** It takes time to heal and come to terms with a loss. You might feel a rollercoaster of emotions at different stages (see 'stages of grief', above). This is normal and can happen at different times.
- **Get professional help:** Managing your grief will be much easier and faster if you have professional support.
- If you need help contact your doctor or other health professionals.

GriefLine 1300 845 745, ReachOut (grief and loss), Help Guide, Lifeline 131 114

(Also refer to the list of contacts at the start of this guide.)

> "It is better to light a candle than curse the darkness."
>
> *Eleanor Roosevelt*

30 SIMPLE WAYS TO SHOW YOURSELF SELF-CARE AND SELF-LOVE

1. **MOVE YOUR BODY** – Get physical. Do some exercise to let off steam and reboot the nervous system.
2. **TAKE TIME OUT** – Practice relaxation, yoga, meditation or read a book (*try free apps).
3. **BREATHE** – Switch your thought pattern and take long slow in-breaths and out-breaths.
4. **BE KIND TO YOURSELF** – Practice inner hospitality. Love yourself.

5. **SWITCH YOUR THOUGHTS** – Switch your thoughts to happy moments.
6. **DAILY AFFIRMATIONS** – With repetition, affirmations can reprogram your thoughts. E.g. I am enough. I believe in myself, I create my own happiness, etc.
7. **BE GRATEFUL** – for what you have, no matter how small. Keep a gratitude journal.
8. **REACH OUT** – Talk to someone you trust. Don't be alone for long stretches. Connect with friends.
9. **MEET-UP** – Meet with a friend or friends. Get involved in activities or meet-up groups.
10. **RECALL GOOD TIMES** – Take your mind back to the times you felt happy.
11. **DO FUN STUFF** – Do something you enjoy. Or find a new purpose or passion.
12. **SPOIL YOURSELF** – Have a massage, treat yourself (something small can lift your spirits).
13. **FUEL UP** – Eat healthy, nourishing meals. Maintain blood-sugar levels. Stay hydrated (drink water).
14. **DETOX** – Avoid alcohol, caffeine, non-medication drugs, junk food, social media, phone-free time.
15. **SLEEP** – Get enough sleep. Try sleep and meditation techniques and free apps.
16. **NATURE-BATHE** – Get back to nature. Sunlight and connecting with nature improve your mood.
17. **SAY 'NO'** – Learn to say 'no'. Avoid taking on extra commitments or workload.
18. **SMALL GOALS** – Set small goals. Write down your problems to help solutions come to you.
19. **FORGIVE YOURSELF** – No need to be perfect (there's no such thing). Forgive yourself and others.
20. **ACCEPTANCE** – Change the things you can and accept the things you can't change.
21. **UNDERSTAND** – 'this too shall pass' (i.e. like everything in life, events will also pass).
22. **TRAIN YOUR BRAIN** – Learn about your mind. It's like a muscle and can be trained.

23. **GP CHECK-UP** – Go to the doctor to check your general health, which can impact your mental health.
24. **LEARN WHAT TRIGGERS YOU** – Pay attention to what triggers your anxiety. Make changes.
25. **PAY IT FORWARD** – Doing something nice for others increases your 'feel-good' hormones.
26. **EXPRESS YOURSELF** – Cry, laugh, sing, dance and be silly and playful. Let your emotions out. Watch a comedy or have a go-to video that makes you laugh out loud, i.e. shift your energy.
27. **PLAY MUSIC** – Play positive music. It will lift your mood energetically.
28. **BE KIND TO YOURSELF** – Give yourself time to heal. Seek professional help for coping strategies.
29. **BE YOUR OWN BEST FRIEND** – Look after yourself in the same way you would a good friend.
30. **LIGHTEN UP** – We all screw up. Don't be too hard on yourself or take it all too seriously.

"When you decide to practice inner hospitality, the self-torment ceases."

Anam Cara (The Language of Touch)

1020

8. THE SECRETS TO SUCCESS

HERE'S THE KEY TO ATTRACTING PHENOMENAL SUCCESS IN LIFE

PSST! WANT TO KNOW A SECRET?

You have the power to attract anything you desire into your life by tapping into your subconscious mind. You can 'tell' your mind to do anything. It can bring you success and happiness or, equally, it can keep you a prisoner of your own limiting beliefs!

"The secret to obtaining anything you desire is based on the universal Law of Attraction. Anyone can access its power to bring themselves health, wealth and happiness," according to US behavioural expert, Bob Proctor, the author of the book *You Were Born Rich*.

Do you know why 1% of the population earn 96% of the wealth? "It's not luck," according to Bob. "Successful people know the rules of the mind to attract prosperity. They understand that 'whatever you think, you can become.'"

This concept was widely spread with the best-selling book by Rhonda Byrne, *The Secret,* inspired by Wallace D. Wattles book, *The Science of Getting Rich.*

It's been no secret to the world's most celebrated philosophers and influencers, like Plato, Galileo, Leonardo da Vinci and Albert Einstein. For centuries, these great minds (and hundreds of others) have been mastering the most powerful tool they possess – their minds. And, more recently, influencers such as Oprah, Bill Gates and Michael Jordan (to name a handful of well-known celebrities) have used the power of their minds to achieve phenomenal success in their lives.

They realised that whatever they repeatedly imprinted into their subconscious minds on a consistent basis, manifested into their reality.

This philosophy has been adopted and adapted by many successful entrepreneurs and behavioural experts, who travel the world sharing their learnings and changing the lives of millions of people, including John Kehoe, John Assaraf, Tony Robbins and Dr John Demartini.

Ok, here's the secret...

WHAT YOU FOCUS ON DETERMINES HOW YOU FEEL, THINK AND ACT!

- If you choose good thoughts, you'll feel positive.
- If you choose negative thoughts, you'll feel negative.
- *Whatever you practice over and over, you'll bring into your reality.*

Law of attraction, John Kehoe train your mind to manifest anything, Bob Proctor why 1% of the population earns 96% of all money

WHAT DO THE WORLD'S MOST SUCCESSFUL PEOPLE HAVE IN COMMON?

Most successful people make fast decisions and are fully committed. Top performers, like high-level sportspeople, are optimistic and know they can take the shot. There's no doubt in their minds.

THE RICH AND FAMOUS KNOW HOW TO:

- Switch-on their mojo, so they speak and stand with confidence.
- Tell the truth and are credible.
- Understand failure is the way to learn, grow and innovate.
- Manage time and not get easily distracted.
- Have a structured morning routine.
- Have vision, focus and see the big picture.
- Have a 'can-do' attitude and speak 'success' words.
- Take action. They do it! They back themselves and are decisive.
- Be thankful and grateful for what they have.
- See new opportunities and act on them.
- Be courageous and relish a challenge.
- Care about others, listen and think altruistically (for their well-being).
- Not let fear get in the way of a good thing.

> "You've always had the power my dear, you just had to learn it for yourself."
>
> *Glinda, Wizard of Oz*

SCHOOL GRADES DO NOT DEFINE YOUR LIFE

Did you know some of the world's most successful entrepreneurs and influential thinkers didn't finish school?

Therefore, it's not all about school results. There are other avenues to achieve success.

In fact, many times, the people who are most challenged at school, and in life, are 'forced' to come up with the innovative and inventive solutions.

It's also interesting to note that a large number of thought leaders have dyslexia. Many of those people have mentioned in interviews that they believe it made them more creative and able to think outside the box. They say they had to find creative ways around their challenges of attempting to fit into the rote-learning environments in our traditional school system.

Some famous reportedly dyslexic people are Richard Branson, Albert Einstein, Steve Jobs, Thomas Edison, George Washington, John F. Kennedy, Tom Cruise, Whoopi Goldberg and Cher. (Source: Psychology Degree - 50 famous people who are dyslexic)

Richard Branson says, "I was dyslexic. I had no understanding of schoolwork whatsoever. I certainly would have failed IQ tests. And it was one of the reasons I left school when I was 15 years old."

"There is nothing either good or bad, but thinking makes it so."

William Shakespeare

Did you know? David Letterman created a scholarship for the average 'C student,' recognising that it's not all about marks, as some students are extraordinary and amazing in other ways. "Many entrepreneurs didn't do well in traditional education. It says nothing of your capabilities to succeed as an entrepreneur. Let life and its experiences be your education." (Entrepreneurs HQ)

Did you know? Walt Disney, at the age of 22, was fired from a Missouri newspaper for 'not being creative enough'.

Did you know? "The trouble with school is they give you the answer, then they give you the exam. That's not life," according to the author of *Rich Dad, Poor Dad,* Robert Kiyosaki. "In the real world, the smartest people are people who make mistakes and learn. In school, the smartest people don't make mistakes."

"Winners are not afraid of losing. But losers are. Failure is part of the process of success. People who avoid failure also avoid success."

Robert Kiyosaki

VALUES – WHAT ARE YOUR DEAL BREAKERS? WHAT'S REALLY IMPORTANT TO YOU?

VALUES ARE STANDARDS OF BEHAVIOUR THAT A PERSON HOLDS IN HIGH REGARD.

Values guide you in the way you live, the decisions you make, what motivates you, the friends you keep and your ideas about what's right and wrong (your morals).Despite the importance of values, not many people choose them. Instead, they adopt the values of their parents and the dominant values of the groups in which they spend the most time.

Write down a list of things that you hold in high regard, to understand what guides and drives your decisions and choices.

SOME COMMON VALUES ARE:

- **Honesty:** being trustworthy and truthful.
- **Humility:** being modest, free of arrogance.
- **Integrity:** doing the right thing and treating others with decency.
- **Kindness:** being caring, helpful and loving.
- **Achievement:** having attention to personal-growth and being the best you can.
- **Discipline:** showing up on time and showing commitment.
- **Fairness:** being courteous, tolerant and forgiving.
- **Responsible:** showing good judgement and common sense.
- **Supportive:** having a sense of community, being a team-player and cooperative.
- **Contribution:** giving back, showing gratitude and awareness of the bigger picture.
- **Connection:** enjoying a sense of family, respect for friendships and loyalty.
- **Citizenship:** respecting the law for keeping order and being socially responsible.
- **Health-focus:** maintaining awareness of mind, body and spirit.

Your beliefs become your thoughts,
Your thoughts become your words,
Your words become your actions,
Your actions become your habits,
Your habits become your values,
Your values become your destiny.

Mahatma Gandhi

DEFINITION OF VALUES, MORALS AND ETHICS:

What is ethics? – Ethics is defined as moral principles that govern a person's behaviour or code of conduct. It is a 'set of beliefs a community lives by'. Wikipedia defines ethos as a Greek word meaning 'character', used to describe the guiding beliefs or ideals that characterise a community, nation or ideology.

What are morals? – Morals are what you believe to be right and wrong, derived from the code of behaviour that is considered right or acceptable in a particular society.

What are values? – Core values are your fundamental beliefs and the guiding principles dictating your behaviour. Values determine the degree of importance you place on something or someone, and determine what actions are best to do or what way is best to live. For example, if you place high importance on fairness, you will not treat people unfairly, or surround yourself with those who treat other people unjustly.

> "If there is a single word that could guide one's life, it is reciprocity. What you do not wish for yourself, do not do to others."
>
> *Confucius*

ALIGN YOUR ACTIONS WITH YOUR HIGHEST VALUES

"Fill your day with high priority actions that inspire you, otherwise you'll fill it with unexpected low priority distractions that devalue you," according to Dr John Demartini, who is considered one of the world's leading authorities on human behaviour and personal development.

"If you don't bring order to your day, it will turn to chaos by allowing random events to take up space."

"After you identify your top three highest values, prioritise your daily actions. Stick to (and fulfil) your highest priority actions and delegate all other lower priority actions to other people to allow you to fulfil your highest and most inspiring values each day.

When setting goals, it's first wise to determine your true highest values (i.e., those that inspire you) and stay true to those.

"Anytime you set goals that are not aligned with your true highest values, you decrease the probability of having a fulfilling life and you end up experiencing what I've termed the **ABCD's** of negativity – internally directed **A**nger and **A**ggression, **B**lame and feelings of **B**etrayal, **C**riticism and **C**hallenge and **D**espair and **D**epression," says Dr Demartini.

Psychology Today - your values, your life, Dr J. Demartini. What are values?

"We are what we repeatedly do. Excellence, therefore, is not an act, but a habit."

Aristotle

GOAL SETTING – START WITH THE END IN MIND

Think of goals as putting directions into your GPS. The goal is the target (the destination), and the directions are the action plan (the road trip to get there).

THE CHEAT-SHEET ON SETTING GOALS:

1. **What's your why?** What turns you on? If you love sales and want to win a deal, think about what drives you. If you love golf and want to be a pro-golfer, find the emotion around what motivates you.
2. **What's the target?** Be clear on precisely what it is you want to do. Be specific. Push the envelope but be realistic!
3. **What's the plan?** This is the map. What do you need to do to reach the goal post?

   What action will have the most impact to reach that goal? List those from high-to-low priority.

   Make the steps measurable, either monetary or numerical (if you're a sportsperson, it might be against your times or a fitness goal).

TIP

Be careful not to make unattainable goals, or it may demotivate you. Make sure the goals can be achieved in bite size pieces, with a bit of effort each day to make you feel like you're getting closer to your goal.

4. **Who will do it?** Check your toolkit to see if you have the attributes, resources and the team to achieve your target. If not, get them! Bring in skillsets or staff (real staff or virtual assistants).
5. **When will you do it?** A plan without times and deadlines is vague and ineffective and less likely to succeed. Give time limits and check each step's progress. Get a coach to keep you accountable.

TIP

Make sure you reward yourself when you reach each (small or big) goal. If you're not hitting goals, rejig your plan and measures to keep you motivated.

6. **Take 100% maximum action:** The only way to get results is to take action.
7. **Remember to be flexible:** You can't control some things, like external factors and market demand. Being too rigid can close you to opportunities.

Positive Psychology goal setting templates, Mind Tools 5 golden rules of goal setting

"If you don't know where you're going, any road will get you there."

Lewis Carroll

TIME MANAGEMENT – 7 NO-NONSENSE TIME MANAGEMENT HACKS

1. **Have a plan**: Set your goal or intention for the day.
2. **Visually map out your plan:** Use a wall planner or time management tool.
3. **Write a to-do list:** Writing lists (and prioritising your actions) gets your thoughts on to paper and makes them tangible. You'll feel super-organised when you tick-off action items as they're completed. Do the highest priority tasks first.
4. **Set deadlines and time limits to complete tasks**. Use a timer or put reminders in your phone and calendar.
5. **Minimise distractions:** If you want to focus on a task to get it completed faster, turn off your phone (or definitely put it on silent). i.e. do one task at a time, in order of priority.
6. **Know your productive times.** Some people are more productive in the morning, some in the evening. Also allow times to have a break, in order to reboot your thoughts.
7. **Ask for help if you don't know the answer.** Talk to other people who can give you ideas to achieve the task faster. If you're procrastinating because you're out of your depth, outsource or delegate the task.

Mind Tools what is time management, Lifehack 10 ways to improve your time management, ReachOut how to manage your time

"How do you eat an elephant?
One bite at a time."

Creighton Abrams

HABITS - HOW TO KICK A BAD HABIT

What is a habit? A habit is a routine behaviour triggered by cues that routinely lead to a reward.

WHY GOOD HABITS AND RITUALS HELP YOU:

- Be productive and focused, to make clearer decisions.
- Be in control of your life, rather than life controlling you.
- Clarify your values and establish what matters to you.
- Overcome addictive behaviour.
- Establish structure and certainty to your days.
- Increase your confidence and contentment levels.
- Improve work-life balance and relationships.

HOW DO HABITS FORM?

There are 3 steps in a self-perpetuating cycle (a Charles Duhigg concept).

1. A TRIGGER or CUE (e.g., a time, situation or emotional state).
2. AN ACTION (something that is done over and over on autopilot).
3. A REWARD (this is the 'why' of what you do. You identify a reward or benefit in your behaviour).

(Remember: The behavioural patterns we REPEAT slowly become etched into our neural pathways.)

> "We first make our habits, and then our habits make us."
>
> *John Dryden*

How to break a habit: If you write down your trigger moments, you'll see a pattern of when you get triggered, and be able to plan to adapt your behaviour at that time. It will trick the cue. You will get small wins which will build momentum to change the habit.

It takes 'at least 21 days to form a new habit' according to Dr Maxwell Maltz, who conducted a study in 1960. Some researchers suggest it's more like 66 days or longer to break a habit.

Books: Sean Covey (2004) *The Seven Habits of Highly Effective Teens*; Brendon Burchard. *High-Performance Habits;* and Dean Graziosi. *Millionaire Success Habits.*

Wikihow change a habit, Brian Tracy. 7 tips to be more effective, Charles Duhigg *The Power of Habit*

"Procrastination is the thief of time."

Edward Young

DECISIONS – 10 TIPS TO MAKE SUPER-FAST DECISIONS

Decisions, decisions...Life's a series of decisions!

Research shows adults make as many as 35,000 decisions each day (children just 3,000).

If you're indecisive, that's perfectly ok. You might simply have one of these life-restricting traits:

- Procrastination
- Perfectionism
- Over-thinking
- Over-analysing

TRY THESE 10 TIPS TO MAKE DECISIONS FASTER:

1. **Go with your gut.** Your first instinctive thought is often the right one.
2. **Give yourself a deadline** to avoid procrastination.
3. **Embrace the concept of failure.** Avoid the 'what ifs'.
4. **Forget the desire to be perfect.** Learn from mistakes and move on.
5. **Weigh up the pros and cons.** Write a list of the (+) positives and the (-) negatives.
6. **Stick with what you know:** When you're familiar with a subject, 'you just know'. If you're short on knowledge, ask advice or do your research.
7. **Emotion versus rational?** What would someone completely detached from the decision do?
8. **Do what's best for you, right now.** Seek advice and input from others but it must be right for you.
9. **Sleep on it.** If it's a big decision or could adversely affect others, don't be rash. Instead, sleep on it to give you a clearer perspective.
10. **Don't make excuses, make choices.** Cast off fear and back yourself.

Jim Kwik 5 mental hacks to end procrastination, Mel Robbins the 5 Second Rule, Brian Tracy 10 steps to solve any problem, *Tony Robbins the 4 rules for decision making, Psychology Today how many decisions do we make each day*

> "You are one decision away from a completely different life."
>
> *Mel Robbins*

"Opportunities are never lost. They just go to someone else!"

JT Foxx

'OPPORTUNITY KNOCKS BUT ONCE' - OLD PROVERB

When you sit back in 30 years' time don't be that person saying, "I wish I'd done this, or that!" Be sure you don't regret anything, especially something you didn't do!

When you chat to older people, like your parents and grandparents (which is a great way to learn stuff by the way), they'll often say their biggest regrets were the things they DIDN'T DO, not what they did do.

They wish they'd taken that job overseas, or bought that house in 1980, or told their lover how much they loved them before their lover left and married someone else. When they reached that fork in the road, and made that life-changing decision, things just might have gone differently!

If you're good at something or want someone, give it your best effort; and if it doesn't work out, you can look back and say: "I gave it my best shot and I'm happy where I'm at."

"Look, if you had one shot, one opportunity to seize everything you ever wanted; one moment, would you capture it or just let it slip?"

Eminem

RESILIENCE – HOW TO MAKE LIFE HAPPEN FOR YOU, NOT TO YOU

Resilience is 'mental endurance'.

And like all human development, you need to crawl before you walk; walk before you run...and fall over a heap of times to get good at it.

It takes training and practice to toughen up and not cave in to mental and physical pressure.

> "That which does not kill us, makes us stronger."
>
> *Friedrich Nietzsche*

RESILIENT PEOPLE DON'T DO THESE THINGS:

1. **They don't blame other people for things.** Instead, they 'own' their s***.
2. **They're not puppets to other people's comments.** They pull their own strings.
3. **They don't get angry and see the negative in everything.** They see the positive in a negative.
4. **They don't say 'poor me'.** They know everyone has crap going on. The question isn't 'why me'? It's 'why *not* me?'
5. **They don't look inwardly,** thinking they're on this ship alone. They have a bigger picture of life.
6. **They don't wallow in self-pity.** They look for solutions to problems.
7. **They don't put themselves last!** They love themselves first, so that they can give to others.
8. **They don't like setbacks.** Instead, they know setbacks help them to be resilient.
9. **They don't end a friendship over a little feud.** They see the value in keeping friendships intact.

10. **They don't accept s****y treatment from others.** They know they're worthy of respect.
11. **They don't abuse their bodies and expect it to perform the next day.** Their body is their temple.
12. **They don't see the dark side of things.** Instead, they can laugh at themselves and at life, for all its absurdity at times.
13. **They don't think twice about giving to people less fortunate.** They know a kind gesture comes back many-fold and increases feel-good serotonin levels.
14. **They don't sit in the boat without rowing and expect it to go somewhere.** They know they have to dig in the oars to get to their destination.
15. **They don't let negative people weigh their boat down.** They cast them off, so they can row their boat without excess baggage.
16. **They don't blame their parents.** They realise their parents were doing the best they could, even if they were not perfect, just like themselves.

REINVENTION – WAYS TO REINVENT YOURSELF WHEN THINGS GO TO CRAP

No-one anticipated the tough lessons that 2020 brought on. It slapped us around with a big stick to test our resilience in the face of the very scary likelihood of death if we didn't behave ourselves.

It took one deadly little, microscopic parasite infecting one patient (Patient Zero) to set off a catastrophic chain of events and demonstrate to world leaders just how connected we are as a global community and that 'we're all in this together'.

COVID-19 HAS REMINDED US OF THIS:

- Nothing is static. There's no such thing as permanence and, therefore, certainty is never guaranteed.
- We can't be too rigid in our planning. Our thinking must be agile and flexible.

- Survival is based on adapting and evolving with a changing environment.
- Creativity and ideation are massive pluses for humans when the **** hits the fan.
- The importance of hygiene and constantly washing our hands.
- Did we ever really need to kiss *everyone* hello and goodbye?
- Families and friends are the mainstay of a happy existence.
- We can't live (well) without human touch and connection. Touch is food for the soul.
- Overcoming a pandemic requires an inordinate amount of TEAM WORK on a global scale!
- 'Survival of the fittest' applies more than ever. *Charles Darwin's theory of natural selection, where organisms best adjusted to their environment are the most successful in surviving.
- We'll never take our freedom for granted again (hopefully).
- The downtime gave families some time to reconnect. While it divided some, it bonded many.
- It forced us to delve into our inner reserves and check-in on ourselves.
- We asked ourselves how could we grow our skills and expand our minds to discover new opportunities? We questioned our previous 'just the way we do things' paradigms.
- Could we find another way (or ways) to make a living?
- Could we really work from home, save on the commute and conduct business as usual via Zoom?
- Could we find other ways to entertain ourselves?
- Could we cope with the social isolation? For many the social disconnect was the hardest to accept.
- While some industries collapsed, others boomed!
- And so blossomed these businesses – ecommerce, Zoom and virtual conferencing, online courses, online streaming, online entertainment, home deliveries, logistics, home deliveries, take-away food, home renovations, healthcare, IT, personal protection and medical supplies, and many more.

Business Australia 9 industries that thrived during Covid-19, Forbes companies that did well during the pandemic

> "The only thing worse than starting something and failing is not starting something."
>
> *Seth Godin*

YOUR PERSONAL VISION – VISUAL TOOLS TO 'BRAINSTORM' YOUR DREAM LIFE

Let's pretend your life is the car and you're the driver.

You can't drive around aimlessly, hoping to get somewhere.

You'll need a goal and a vision to create the life you want.

You can do this with visual tools, such as dream boards, mind maps, journaling and collating photos and clippings of things that inspire you. Just like a business plan, the dream board is a personal plan for 'how you want your life to look'. For a pdf version go to: real-life.com.au - my dream board

You deserve to feel amazing, every day

DESIGN YOUR LIFE... LET YOUR IMAGINATION RUN FREE

Definition of vision: *the ability to think about or plan the future with imagination or wisdom*

The term 'vision statement' is variously bandied around by businesses, where they use a bunch of words to express their vision.

It's far more effective to create your 'vision' *visually,* using photos and clippings of the things you want to attract into your life.

Maybe you dream of having a new car, a boat, a bike, a house, a partner, new friends, happy situations, a lifestyle, or a health and fitness goal. Cut out those images and clip them to a vision board, to reinforce these dreams and desires in your mind.

My Dream Board

Career/Work Plan

Education/Upskilling Plan

Goals and Achievements:
My Biggest Achievements So Far

Things I Want to Achieve

My Financial Plan

1 Year

5 Years

10 Years

My Dream Purchase & Goals
(e.g: Car, House, Holiday)

Things That Make Me Happy

What Are My Strengths? What Am I Good At?

My Ideal Version of Me:
How Do I Show Up in Life?

What Drives Me? What's My Why?

Things That Inspire Me
(Podcasts, Books?)

Who Do I Look Up To?
(Role Models)

Favourite Quotes

How Do I Give Back to Society?

Things I'm Grateful For

Lifestyle Plan: How I Want My Life to Look in:

1 Year

5 Years

10 Years

Health Plan: How Do I Stay Healthy?

Physical:

Mind:

Diet:

How Do I Show Self-Love?

My Values: What's Important to Me

My Daily Routine: Best Habits That Serve Me Well

Who is Important to Me?

Family:

Friends:

Ideal Partner:

How Do I Honour Those I Care About?

Creative tools to help visualise your goals:

- COLLAGE: A collage can be made up of printed images (to stick on a board) or a digital design
- SCRAPBOOK: If you prefer, you can stick images and cut-outs in a scrapbook or folder.
- JOURNALING: Write down things that inspire you or things you want to improve in your life. Include photos, memories or little things of interest to keep them all together.

TIP

print out the digital design so you see it regularly, to remind you of your vision. Or make it your screensaver. Cut out quotes and things from magazines or the newspaper that you want to manifest in your life.

Regularly look at your dream board, collage, scrapbook and journal to remind and reinforce your vision...and to make your DREAM A REALITY.

Mind mapping the benefits of mind mapping, Filmora video montage maker, Canva photo collage maker, Mind maps mind map app, Jack Canfield the art of visualisation

YOU'RE THE WRITER, DIRECTOR AND STAR OF YOUR OWN AMAZING LIFE

If you had a blank canvas to create the exact life you dreamt about, how would it look?

When you write your dream...your life story...anything goes. *The sky's the limit!*

Movie Title: 'THIS IS MY LIFE'
Director: ______________________(add your name)
Leading actor: ______________________(add your name)

You're the director. Don't let other people direct it. This is your story!

Start by writing the script. You won't know the ending, but you can design - in rich, colourful detail - exactly how you want your life-story to unfold.

The spotlight is on you. You have the starring role as the 'protagonist'. You drive the plot forward.

How do you want your character to develop and transform?

How will you set the scenes and map out the story line?

Where will your life be filmed? What scenarios do you visualise and what timeline?

There will be unexpected setbacks, sliding door moments, dramas and highs and lows (and everything in between). Make sure you have some contingency plans and optional storylines.

Who will be the other main characters, members of the cast and the 'extras'? Your family? Your friends?

The crew will be your acquaintances and work colleagues, who support you behind the scenes.

Ensure you look after and reward the cast and crew who stick by your side. If they're not loyal, or not cooperative and not working towards your goal, sack them or put them in the back office.

You'll need to rehearse scenes over and over and do lots of 'takes' to get a particular shot just right. That's normal. They'll be lots of mis-takes too. ☺ Keep doing it until you get it just the way you like it.

You can re-cast characters, change the set and add as many special effects as you like.

Or you can rewind and freeze-frame a shot...and place new situations and scenarios in the frame.

If the story goes off track, let it evolve. Who knows where it will take you? It may become a beautiful twist of fate or a momentous date with destiny.

As the credits roll... this is what people will say about you as the curtains close.

How will that look? Did you give, did you take, did you make a difference and leave a legacy that people will talk about for years to come? Write that into the script.

Happy writing, directing and en-acting your own extraordinary life story'!

Dr Wayne Dyer the power of intention, Mind movies digital vision boards, Mindvalley how to create a vision for your life so bold, it makes you shine, Tony Robbins Change your story, change your life

"Our life is the creation of the mind."

Buddha

A PRACTICAL GUIDE TO PERSONAL FREEDOM

Based on ancient Toltec Wisdom, The Four Agreements: A Practical Guide to Personal Freedom, by Don Miguel Ruiz, provides a code of conduct to create freedom, integrity and peace in our lives.

1. BE IMPECCABLE WITH YOUR WORD

- Speak with integrity.
- Say only what you mean.

- Avoid using the word to speak against yourself or to gossip about others.
- Use the power of your word in the direction of truth and love.

2 DON'T TAKE ANYTHING PERSONALLY

- Nothing others do is because of you. What others say and do is a projection of their own dream.
- When you are immune to the opinions and actions of others, you won't be the victim of needless suffering.

3. DON'T MAKE ASSUMPTIONS

- Find the courage to ask questions and to express what you really want.
- Communicate with others as clearly as you can to avoid misunderstandings, sadness and drama.
- With just this one agreement, you can completely transform your life.

4. ALWAYS DO YOUR BEST

- Your best is going to change from moment to moment; it will be different when you are healthy as opposed to sick.
- Under any circumstance, simply do your best, and you will avoid self-judgment, self-abuse and regret.

> "God, grant me the serenity to accept the things I cannot change, the courage to change the things I can, and the wisdom to know the difference."
>
> *Dr Reinhold Niebuhr*

9. THE KEY TO QUALITY COMMUNICATION AND RELATIONSHIPS

Do you know that the quality of our communications has a direct impact on almost everything we do, especially our relationships?

Have you ever thought 'everyone talks over me' or 'people don't listen to me' or 'my boss doesn't even notice me' or 'I just upset my best friend'?

Then you'll know that communication is a powerful (and at times dangerous) tool. Once spoken, words cannot be taken back. They have the potential to make or break relationships (i.e. to build bridges OR walls!)

To be *heard* and *understood* in professional and personal relationships, it's critical to communicate clearly, honestly and openly so that you're not only understood, but so you can understand others.

THE ART OF COMMUNICATION

What is communication? It's the act of conveying information between two or more people through speaking, writing, body language and facial expressions.

You might think communicating is all about your choice of 'words'. However, words are a small part of the overall communication process.

Only 7% of communicating is through words, while 55% is via body-language (non-verbal), as Albert Mehrabian's famous communication model shows:

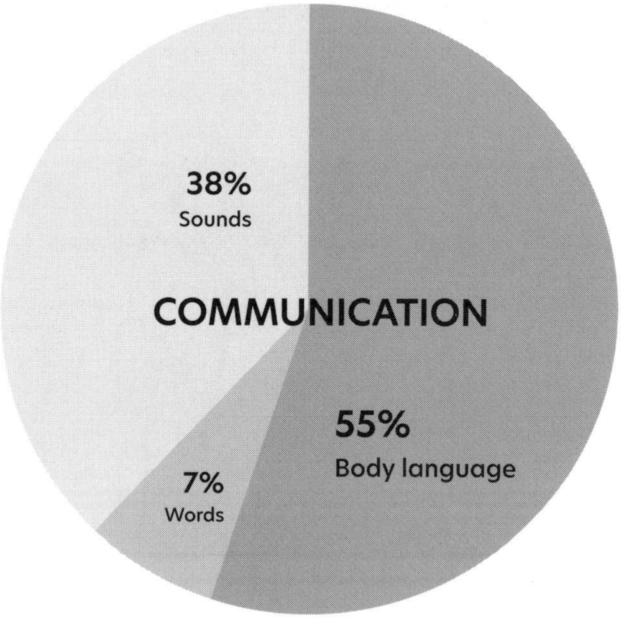

Learn to actively listen: An essential part of being a good communicator is learning to actively listen.

If you observe the top salespeople, they know the benefits of the 70/30 rule.

They actively **LISTEN 70%** of the time and **TALK 30%** of the time, according to communication experts.

WHY ARE TEXTS AN EASY WAY TO MISCOMMUNICATE?

- texts are out of context.
- texts are without inflection (i.e. tone and nuance).
- texts are abbreviated and often rushed.
- how the text is received is dependent on how the person (the receiver) is feeling or how busy they are.

TIP

If it's a complex issue, it's always better to talk on the phone, or even better to meet in person, as the face, eyes and body language are crucial communication tools.

THE 2-SECOND RULE (THINK BEFORE YOU SPEAK)

Have you ever had a moment where words spill out of your mouth, like a slow-motion movie unfolding? You may wish you could 'eat your words', but unfortunately you've already left a trail of destruction and, sadly, you can't retract those words or make it all better, unless you're a very smooth negotiator.

A good way to keep your words in check, so you don't say something you regret, is to pause for 2 seconds before you speak.

It's amazing how 2 or 3 seconds can give you a chance to 'think before you speak', to construct a comment, or consider how your words might be received.

"We have two ears and one mouth so that we can listen twice as much as we speak"

Epictetus

'EVERYTHING IN LIFE IS A NEGOTIATION'

You'd be surprised how many negotiations take place on an everyday basis. It might be to persuade a friend to come over, or a teacher or boss to extend a deadline, or win over a parent or partner, or clinch a job.

Understanding negotiation skills is a powerful tool to influence people.

The very basics of negotiation are:

- **It's not about you winning:** It's a collaboration. Aim for a win-win outcome.
- **Connection is the key:** Enter into negotiations with a desire to understand the other person's needs, concerns, fears, emotions and motivation.
- **Appear calm and unphased:** Present your views in a calm and calculated way to remain rationale and receptive.
- **Build trust and rapport:** Genuinely build a mutual understanding, empathise with the other person and defuse negative feelings or objections. Reinforce any positive emotions.
- If you have a trump card, use it for best effect. Former FBI hostage negotiator, Chris Voss, describes this as a 'black swan'. You might be trying to get a payment from a client, and you've heard they've just posted record profits. Having this knowledge makes it harder for the client to defend late payments and puts you in a stronger bargaining position.

ReachOut Australia communication skills, How to talk to anyone, Very Well Mind – Understanding Body Language, *iNLP Center – What is neuro-linguistic programming, The art of negotiating Chris Voss YouTube Podcast (source of quote)*

PUBLIC SPEAKING IS AN ESSENTIAL SKILL FOR WORK AND LIFE

Did you know some people fear public speaking more than death?

However, speaking with confidence is vital to communicate in business and in everyday life, like:

- Meetings
- Interviews
- Presentations
- Networking
- University or courses
- Special events (e.g. weddings)

11 TIPS FOR HIGH-IMPACT PRESENTATIONS:

1. **Focus all your attention on the audience.** It's not about you. Take the ego part out.
2. **Who IS your audience?** What are their needs, demographics, and what do they want to hear?
3. **Be concise and structure the content, i.e.,**
   - What is your purpose for speaking?
   - What is your take-away message and call to action?
   - How can you help the audience?
   - Tell stories to make it real and authentic. Use your character and have some fun.
4. **You need the nerves to perform!** Embrace them as part of performing. Accept that they're needed to help you think on your feet.
5. **Know the 5+1 Ps:** Prior Preparation Prevents (P**s) Poor Performance.
6. **Speak clearly.** Step up to the podium, breath and pause for effect, then speak and conduct yourself as an actor would on stage. Vary your tone and speed, and really emphasise key points.
7. **Put energy and enthusiasm behind it.** Get your physicality right. Listen to motivational music before you arrive, do effective breathing exercises, and walk up with purpose.

8. **Aim most of your attention at ONE person.** (The one who is most connected and smiling at you.) Look above the audience to project your voice wider.
9. **Don't read every word from notes.** Have palm cards with reminder words to prompt your thoughts. No need to be perfect. People listen more to natural intonation and the occasional slip-up. It's more real and relatable.
10. **How do I ignore my nerves?** When you take the focus off yourself, the nerves dissipate. Keep reminding yourself that 'it's not about you'! It's about the person or people you want to inspire and motivate.

Very Well Mind public speaking

"To err is human; To forgive, divine."

Alexander Pope

WORDS HAVE POWER

THE IMPORTANCE OF GOOD GRAMMAR

Before sending a job application or important business letter, double-check your spelling and grammar.

Poor spelling is ok when casually texting or messaging, but you lose credibility when you write poorly in formal letters and communication.

If potential employers receive 30 job applications, they're looking for reasons to ditch non-starters. Some might be hitting the circular filing cabinet (the bin) based on poor grammar alone.

Always use spell-check or a spelling application before sending an important email or document. But be careful; it might be the correct spelling, but not in context.

Check my grammar Grammarly

COMMON BASIC GRAMMATICAL MISTAKES:

- **The apostrophe** goes before the 's or after the s' to show ownership or possession – The bike belongs to ONE girl = girl's bike. The bike belongs to MANY girls = the girls' bike.
- **It's** – is short for 'it is'.
- **Its** – is possessive. It shows something belongs to something – e.g., 'the cat ate its food'.
- **Should have** – When people write 'should of', what they actually mean is 'should have'. The shortened written version of 'should have' is 'should've'.
- **There** – in, at or to a position or place (the opposite of here). e.g., 'over there' or 'there are no cakes'.
- **Their** – shows something belonging to them – e.g., 'their house'.
- **They're** – is short for 'they are'.
- **To** – used to express motion (toward a person, thing or place) – e.g., 'to walk'.
- **Too** – means 'also' or 'as well' or an excessive amount of something – e.g., 'too much'.
- **Two** – is the number '2'.
- **Your** – shows something belonging to you – e.g., 'your bike'.
- **You're** – is short for 'you are'.
- **Were** – past tense of 'are'.
- **We're** – short for 'we are'.
- **Where** – used to refer to a place or position – e.g., 'where is the chocolate'?

> "Know your s**t, or know you're s**t."
>
> *Joanne Adams*

DIMINISHING WORDS THAT POWERFUL PEOPLE DON'T USE

Successful people are aware that certain words can strengthen or, equally, diminish their message.

Here are some examples:

- **'Sorry'** – Excessive apologising implies you're insecure or submissive. (It's better to apologise once genuinely when a situation is an honest mistake.)
- **'Very' and 'Totally' and 'Really'** – These are drama words and don't add value.
- **'Just', 'I think' and 'In my opinion'** – These are protector words that downplay the meaning to protect you from potential conflict if someone has a different opinion. All thoughts are 'your opinion'.
- **'I'll try' and 'Don't worry about it'** – These are (in)ability words which make people doubt you. Trying to do something suggests you're not sure of your ability or intention to do what you say.
- **'Should'** – People using this word are thinking in the past or putting their expectations on you. It can be replaced with 'could' or 'next time'.
- **'Probably' or 'Maybe'** – These are vague and unsure words that don't instil confidence in your abilities.
- **'If'** – A hypothetical word, usually used when doubting or complaining. 'If only I had done...'
- **'Like', 'Umm' or 'Whatever' or 'You know'** – These are filler words that give people time to think.
- **'But'** – The word 'but' contradicts what was just said and diminishes the message.
- **'Never' and 'Always'** – Both are non-negotiable and final words. They give little room for change.
- **'Can't'** – Can't is a negative 'self-talk' word. Successful people don't say 'can't'. They say 'can'.
- ****** and ****** Excessive swearing reduces your credibility and increases the likelihood of offending someone.

A. Blank. Forbes common words powerful people don't use (source)

Luke has said: "All right, I'll give it a try."
Jedi Master Yoda says: "Do... or do not ...
there is no try.
i.e., The word 'try' is not a commitment.
If Luke does not fully commit, he will fail.

SOCIAL MEDIA – IS SOCIAL MEDIA MAKING US MORE UNSOCIAL THAN EVER?

Smartphones and devices now connect us to anyone, anywhere, anytime.

Yet, **never before have we been more disconnected** from real people and real contact.

If our heads are buried in our phones, texting or checking social media, we're not truly 'spending timc' togcthcr.

The FOMO (fear of missing out) via social media means we're often *missing out* on being 'in the moment' and truly connecting with the people who matter the most – our close friends and family.

It takes us away from the natural flow and inspiration that we get from relaxing in that moment. Being lost and distracted by Instagram and Facebook means your ideas are centred on others and comparisons with others.

Social media historian Allison Graham claims "We're seeing the emotional turmoil around the number of likes somehow equalling our self-esteem. If we measure our personal value on the number of 'likes' we get, we'll always be disappointed."

S. Rose and A. Graham Is social media making us less social? (source), Indestractable: Nir Eyal How to control your attention and choose your life

HOW TO AVOID SENDING MESSAGES OR EMAILS YOU MIGHT REGRET THE NEXT DAY

1. **Write (but don't send) the email or text.** Let it all out in a draft. This will help release your negative emotions and reduce your anger.
2. **Walk away and think, or 'sleep on it'.** Give yourself some time to calm down and see if you feel differently in half an hour or the next day.
3. **Don't make assumptions.** You don't know what's going on in other people's lives.
4. **Make a decision later.** After you've cooled down, decide if you still want to press 'send'.
5. When fighting by text or over social media, **never say anything you wouldn't say in person**.
6. **Avoid swearing, anger and nastiness,** which make you appear irrational and out of control.
7. **Avoid 'you' words**, so your message is less personal.
8. **Consider if you want that relationship to end**. Be aware your words can't be 'taken back' and could harm that relationship.

> "If you can't say somethin' nice, don't say nothin' at all."
>
> *Thumper*

HOW TO NOT GIVE A **** ABOUT MEANINGLESS S***

In his book, *The Subtle Art of Not Giving a* ****, Mark Manson, talks about finding what's truly important to you and letting go of everything else.

This cool book encourages limiting exposure to 'mindless distractions' such as social media, TV and technology... and limiting your concern over things that have little to no meaning or value in your life.

Mark says, "If seeing things online or hearing things your co-workers say is really affecting you that much then you need to look at the values in your life. If your emotions are constantly being pushed this way or that way, and you feel like you're never in control, it's probably because you're valuing a lot of the wrong things."

> "When you compare your life to what you see on social media, you're comparing your 'behind the scenes' to every else's highlight reel."
>
> *Dayna Lingard*

RELATIONSHIPS – THE IMPORTANCE OF HEALTHY RELATIONSHIPS

Some of the most important things we do in life are centred around family, friends, workmates... and the many other relations we have on a daily basis.

In fact, research shows that having healthy relationships and close connections are vital to our happiness and sense of belonging.

Tips for building strong relationships:

- Clear and respectful communication
- Active listening
- Respect for each other's opinions
- Fair and consistent boundaries
- Trust and loyalty

> "Assumptions are the termites of relationships."
>
> *Henry Winkler*

8 STEPS TO TACKLE RELATIONSHIP CONFLICT AND DIFFICULT CONVERSATIONS:

1. Talk instead of text.
2. Listen and consider the issue from their perspective. Show empathy.
3. Avoid assumptions. Respect their opinion.
4. Be clear about how you feel and what you want.
5. If you get upset, take time and look after yourself. Agree to come back later if there's more to discuss.
6. Talk it over with someone else, in order to get a new, more objective perspective.
7. If things aren't going to plan, take a break. Count to 10.
8. Compromise and reach a common ground. If you need to, agree to disagree.

Headspace headspace – Why are relationships important, ReachOut how to have difficult conversations, Compassionate Communication language, Tony Robbins how to have the best relationships, Jim Rohn why attitude matters

"People come into your life for a reason, a season, or a lifetime."

Michelle Ventor

FRIENDSHIPS – WHY LESS IS MORE!

While our lives are fixated on social media and how many 'friends' and 'likes' we have, we often forget one important point – the value of **quality over quantity**.

We *can't* have 500 quality, close friends.

Friendship is not a number's game. It takes time to develop a strong connection, just like building a home with foundations, bricks and concrete, then decorating it with the little sweet extras.

BFF friends are: People who are close to you and know your s*** but love you anyway (regardless of your ups and downs and your funny, loco or offbeat ways).

Close (good) friends are: The friends who are happy to arrive on your doorstep or pick up the phone to counsel you when you're in trouble or need support. (PS, It's always two-way if you want to keep that friend.)

General friends are: A big clump of people who you see at school, work or going out, who like you and 'like' your posts, but they don't engage with you on a deeper or personal level. Yep, it's a bit superficial.

Acquaintances are: These are your work colleagues or third-tier contacts, who you don't see out and don't even 'like' your posts. They're the ones who sent you a random friend-request and you felt obliged to accept it.

"You're the average of the five closest friends you spend the most time with."

Jim Rohn

"Be who you are and say what you feel, because those who mind don't matter, and those who matter don't mind."

Dr Seuss

WHAT TO DO WHEN FRIENDS VANISH:

If you find you're losing a few friends, who have suddenly got boyfriends or girlfriends, or have moved away or moved on, then focus on the handful of good people and do things you enjoy. Once you start doing stuff (like courses or meetup groups) and being friendly, and smiling, you'll attract new people into your circle.

HOW TO WEED OUT AND CULTIVATE NEW FRIENDS:

It's better to have a handful of good friends, than a heap of bad ones. The best way to do this is to 'water' the good ones and 'weed out' the bad ones.

The bad ones talk about themselves all the time, turn the conversation back to them, think they're the only ones with problems, think the world revolves around them, project their s*** onto you, make their problems your problems, hate on everyone and everything, mega-burn their mates and are generally toxic to be around. PS: Don't let that 'bad' person be you. If it is, it's time to reinvent yourself. Do some self-reflection and think about how you can cultivate a 'new you', to attract good people back in.

Trick to eliminate toxic friends: If a 'friend' repeatedly knocks you or treats you like crap, get rid of them. Cut them from your thoughts entirely. Be ruthless. Don't waste any further mind-space on them. Bundle them into an imaginary helium balloon and visualise releasing it, cutting the cord and letting them float away. This can be a very cathartic (cleansing) process.

> "Surround yourself by optimistic people. Don't allow people to dump their garbage on the most powerful house in your life (your brain). It's the most important thing you have."
>
> *JT Foxx*

BOUNDARIES - NIFTY WAYS TO SET PERSONAL BOUNDARIES

Being clear about what's important to you, and what you will and won't accept, is the first step to creating your personal boundaries. What makes you feel good or bad?

Most people will respect your boundaries when you firmly, but kindly, explain what they are.

THERE ARE 3 TYPES OF BOUNDARY VIOLATIONS:

1. **Emotional:** e.g., manipulating, undermining, criticising, judging, bullying, guilt-tripping you, or making you feel inferior, making

unfair demands, or demeaning or excluding you.

2. **Verbal:** e.g., being derogatory, gossiping, spreading rumours, cutting you off, projecting their issues onto you and accusing you of things they did, and raising their voices to intimidate you.
3. **Physical:** e.g., touching you inappropriately, being too familiar sexually and physically, invading your space, threatening you, stalking you, taking your possessions or looking through your phone, or taking liberties (i.e., acting in a way that's too 'free' and not showing respect).

8 TIPS TO HELP YOU ESTABLISH HEALTHY BOUNDARIES:

- Get clear on your values and what's important to you. Become aware of what you will and won't accept, and who does or doesn't make you feel good.
- Surround yourself with people who fit your values and your life.
- Be prepared to stand up for yourself in a firm, healthy way and to say: "Please don't treat me that way," or "can you speak to me respectfully, please."
- Using actions and words, show people how you want to be treated. Give them a chance to alter their behaviour by explaining how the things they do and say affect you.
- Love and respect yourself first, so that other people will do the same in return.
- Know that you can't change others. You can only change yourself.
- You don't need other people to control you. You control your life. The controlling people are often the ones who don't feel in control of their own lives.
- Walk away from (or unfriend) people who have their own agenda and don't respect you.

WATCH OUT FOR GASLIGHTING AND NARCISSISM?

This is a form of psychological manipulation in which a person or a group covertly (secretly) sows seeds of doubt in a person, making them question their own memory, perception or judgment. The intention of gaslighting is to cunningly deflect blame onto the targeted person. (Source: Wikipedia).

Another condition to keep on your 'boundaries' radar is narcissism, where a person has an excessive sense of self-importance and personal power.

Psychology Today personal boundaries, Mind Body Green 6 steps to set good boundaries, Mayo Clinic Narcissistic Personality Disorder

> "The key to valuing differences is to realise that all people see the world, not as it is, but as they are."
>
> *Stephen Covey*

BULLIES - HOW TO STOP BULLIES IN THEIR TRACKS

Bullying happens everywhere – at school, at work, in sport and in friendship circles.

It doesn't matter if you're big or small, blonde or red-haired, people can pick on you for any reason.

Usually, bullies are jealous and bring you down to make themselves feel more empowered and get some control back in their hands. If they were secure, they wouldn't worry or talk about you.

See: bullyingnoway.gov.au

> "What you think of me is none of my business"
>
> *Terry Cole Whittaker*

TIPS TO DEAL EFFECTIVELY WITH BULLIES:

- **BULLIES ARE USUALLY INSECURE:** Don't take it personally. They might have been victims of bullying and they're taking their anger out on you.
- **DON'T REACT:** Bullies want a reaction. The game's over (or not as effective) if you don't react.
- **SEE IT AS A COMPLIMENT:** They're taking the time to talk about you, which is a back-handed compliment.
- **DON'T BUY INTO THEIR BS:** Tune-out of their stuff and do your own thing.
- **FIND YOUR TRIBE:** Be around people who support you.
- **TALK TO PEOPLE YOU TRUST:** Make a plan to deal with bullies.
- **TAKE SOME TIME OUT FROM SOCIAL MEDIA:** Talk to real people (family and friends).
- **BLOCK THE BULLIES:** Check your privacy settings online and on your phone. Block bullies.
- **HAVE A **** OFF ATTITUDE:** Physicality and posture are important when dealing face-to-face with bullies. If you're timid and withdrawn, bullies feel they're winning. Walk with purpose and pretend you're walking on to a stage. If you rehearse it in your mind enough, you might even walk confidently past your aggressors with a smile, and chirpily say, 'good morning' (and keep walking with a don't-care attitude). It will catch them off guard and will make you feel (and be) more in control.
- **BE YOUR OWN BEST FRIEND:** Don't worry about how other people see you. It doesn't matter, because 10 people will perceive you in 10 different ways.
- **TELL SOMEONE IN AUTHORITY:** If it becomes too much, make a formal complaint to school, uni, work or wherever the bullying is happening. Physical assault or harassment can be reported to the police.

> "Every bully I've counselled has had serious insecurity issues. Many times, it's because they were mistreated or made to feel inadequate in some way and the easiest way to feel empowered is to pick on someone that they perceive as weaker."
>
> *Patrick Allen*

WAYS TO PROTECT YOURSELF ONLINE:

- Don't react, retaliate and respond (especially when you're upset).
- Don't give your phone number to strangers. Block unwelcome callers.
- Use ID blocking on your phone to hide your number when you call others.
- Keep records of calls or messages that are offensive or hurtful (but don't keep reading them otherwise it only reinforces the negativity).
- Don't share your passwords, not even with friends. Things can change, even with good friendships.
- Social media is a public space. Don't post anything you don't want the newspapers to know about you, or don't want to see on search engines in years to come.
- Treat others how you like to be treated.

WHAT'S PASSIVE BULLYING?

Passive bullying is when a person excludes you or uses subtle demeaning comments and gestures intended to demoralise and bring you down.

If it's mean girl/guy stuff, it's usually jealousy. Talk to them, as they may not be aware they're doing it.

If that doesn't help, distance yourself from that person and focus on widening your circle of friends.

Have you heard of tall poppy syndrome?

Tall poppy syndrome is where people who feel inferior to you say and do awful things to CUT YOU DOWN to their level, which makes them feel better about themselves.

It's what bullies do.

Be aware it's not about you but about their insecurities. Know that they're jealous. Treat it as a compliment. Instead, block them and hang out with real friends who bring you up, not cut you down.

Bullying No Way understanding bullying, eSafety how to protect yourself, Lifehacker. P. Allan how to handle being bullied

"Resentment is like drinking poison and expecting the other person to die."

Source unknown

DOMESTIC VIOLENCE – WHERE YOU CAN GO FOR SUPPORT

Domestic violence is intimidating or threatening behaviour within a relationship, typically involving a partner or a family member.

There are many types of domestic violence, including social, physical, sexual and emotional.

If you've been subjected to domestic violence, there are organisations offering help and support.

FOR WAYS TO KEEP YOURSELF SAFE, VISIT:

- ReachOut Domestic violence and what you can do about it
- Lifeline 131 114 – Domestic violence support
- 1800respect 1800 737 732

(Also refer to the list of contacts at the start of this guide.)

OTHER SUPPORT SERVICES:

- **Financial support** – Centrelink has payments and support to help in crisis situations,
- e.g., via the Department of Human Services crisis and special help
- **Know your rights** – Check your legal rights at the Lawstuff website
- Each state has laws to protect against all forms of domestic violence.
- **Medical help** – If you've been injured or sexually assaulted, talk to the police and contact emergency services. Visit your nearest hospital emergency department.
- **Legal aid** – Legal Aid – what we do, Community Legal Centres Australia,
- **Extra resources** – servicesaustralia.gov.au/individuals/subjects/family-and-domestic-violence
- **Practical support** – Go to a family or friend. Or seek shelter at a refuge (where they can offer legal, practical and emotional help), such as the Salvation Army salvationarmy.org.au (Also search domestic violence support in your state.)

WHAT'S AN AVO (APPREHENDED VIOLENCE ORDER)

An Apprehended Violence Order (AVO) is an order to protect victims of domestic violence when they're fearful of threats to their safety. AVOs are sometimes called 'restraining orders' or 'protection orders.'

An AVO is not a criminal charge but an order for your future protection.

The AVO sets out restrictions on the other person's behaviour so that you can feel safe.

If you have children, the order will also protect them.

There are 2 types of AVO:

- **Apprehended Domestic Violence Order (ADVO):** When the people involved are related or have had a domestic or intimate relationship.
- **Apprehended Personal Violence Order (APVO):** When the people involved are NOT related or don't have a domestic or intimate relationship. e.g. neighbours, stalkers or colleagues.

SUBTLE WAYS TO BUILD CLOSER INTIMATE RELATIONSHIPS

ALL RELATIONSHIPS ARE ABOUT GIVE AND TAKE.

An intimate relationship is no different to a business relationship (other than the intimacy part). ☺

The same principles apply. The foundations of good relations are *respect, honesty and integrity.*

We wouldn't go to work, or run a business, and not value the needs of the customer or client. Showing respect and being attentive to your clients is fundamental to business, and in return, they're more likely to remain loyal and support you.

The same goes for close relationships.

Think of it as a bank balance, with debits and credits. When relationships are out of balance and tilted drastically in favour of one person, it leaves the giver feeling unappreciated and can lead to resentment and the slow demise of a relationship.

TIP

It's not tit-for-tat... or 'I did this, so you do that'. It's about a joint effort.

The best thing to do is to talk about what makes you happy and unhappy, and to strike a balance. If intimacy starts to wane, there are ways to keep it fun, even when children seem to be the new dominant factor in the relationship. Remember that your relationship is the foundation of the family, and so it needs to be solid and it will need some extra care when external factors seem to take over. Make sure you have one night a week for the two of you (if you can juggle it) as a 'date night'.

If a relationship goes off track, there are plenty of relationship counsellors available to help guide it back. (Also refer to the list of contacts at the start of this guide.)

HAVE YOU HEARD OF THE 5 LANGUAGES OF LOVE?

This is an awesome book that many couples refer to in order to understand what's important to them in an intimate relationship. You're likely to have a couple of these 'languages', but one or two might be stand-outs.

The 5 languages are:

1. Words of affirmation
2. Quality time
3. Receiving gifts (or signs of acknowledgement)
4. Acts of service
5. Physical touch

Dr Demartini relationship magic, Matthew Hussey 6 behaviours that kill relationships, John Gray *website and book - 5 Languages of Love*

> "How you do anything, is how you do everything."
>
> *T. Harv Eker*

HOW TO PLAY THE DATING GAME

Note: This article is aimed at people in the early stages of dating. It applies to heterosexual and LGBTQIA+ couples.

Have you heard of the saying; 'playing hard to get?' There's a reason for this phenomenon. It's the law of scarcity, which is a term used in business when you tell a customer "there's only one left in stock, so you'll need to hurry in." People often find something that's scarce more desirable.

You'll notice the law of scarcity play out on reality TV shows, such as *The Bachelor*, where one guy is the limited choice in a competitive environment, increasing the contestants' appetite for the one man. You'll rarely hear the women saying 'he's not my type' because their diminished options have created the collective desire for him.

Although *The Bachelor* is a highly unusual dating scenario, you'll see how the girls who are more secure and self-assured are more appealing to *The Bachelor* because they know (and exude a sense that) they're worth the effort. The needy, insecure, desperate ones come across as needy, insecure and desperate.

Playing it cool means keeping an element of mystery or doubt, making the person want you more, which is not 'playing games' in the manipulative sense of the term. It's working with human nature and the push-pull magnetism that goes on between two people.

For example, if a person calls incessantly (i.e., is pushy and needy), it can cause the other to pull away.

If you're too aloof, however, you may appear to be disinterested and not worth chasing.

Let the game play out equally, so you're drawn together on an equal playing field.

In the early stages, it's better to gradually get to know each other, away from the (at times) complex dynamics that sex can bring with it, such as possessiveness, jealousy and demands on time.

In the same way as you expect personal boundaries with strangers, be aware that *your body is your sanctuary, and it's better to only share intimacy with those who are worthy and have earned it.*

HOT TIPS (IN THE INITIAL STAGES OF DATING)

- Hold some cards close. Leave them wanting more. Hold the trump card (intimacy) close, which will 'qualify' them and show you if they're after a relationship, or just sex.
- Find the 'attention sweet spot' – the midpoint between giving too much and too little attention
- Have you heard of the saying 'love is blind'? It means rational thinking goes out the window once you've got an emotional buy-in. Be mindful who you fall for too quickly. If you suspect something is not quite right, listen to your instincts. Bide your time to get to know them a little better before you go in head-first.
- You'll never be too busy for someone you're 'into'!

TIPS TO STAY SAFE ON TINDER (OR OTHER APP) DATES

- If you're meeting up on a date, meet in a public place.
- Don't give your address out or meet at each other's homes (until you know each other better).
- Do not get in their car or get a lift with them. There are many predators on apps and social media.
- Be careful if they ask you for sexy photos or start talking about sex too early (see risks of 'sexting' in this guide).
- When meeting up, keep a close eye out for signs they're only after sex (like touching too quickly or excessive flattery). They might put in a lot of effort with compliments and enthusiasm, then vanish once they've achieved their goal (i.e., sex). If they're not genuinely keen on you as a person, the ones who are just after sex will move on to the next person who might be 'easier to win-over'.
- If you meet in a bar, don't drink too much or leave your drink unattended, as it could get spiked.

- If possible, meet people 'organically' (instead of on dating apps) and try to date within your circle or wider circle of friends.
- If you don't wish to see a person again, be careful how you reject them, as some people don't take rejection well and might get angry or vengeful. Say something like, "You're a great person, but I don't think I'm the one for you." (If you've ever been dumped before, you'll know to be kind.)
- Accept that sometimes 'they're just not that into you'. During dating, there's *not* always a two-way click. You're working out what you 'don't want' as much as what you 'do want'. If you get ghosted, think of it this way, 'it's not a rejection, but a re-direction'.
- Don't give 100% of yourself to someone who gives you 50% of themselves. That's a waste of your time and energy. Instead, find a mutual attraction.

10. CHOOSING YOUR IDEAL CAREER AND STUDY PATHS

YEAR 12... AND BEYOND

Even if you don't progress to tertiary education, finishing Year 12 is an accomplishment to have under your belt and sets you up for more options (now or down the track).

However, if you don't get a top ATAR result, or get into the course you'd set your sights on, there are other avenues to get there.

And while you may not want to continue studies, or need a Year 12 qualification right now, you may require it in the future if you plan to continue your education.

The other benefit to finishing secondary school is it bides time to mature a little and decide what you'd like to do in life and what really inspires you. Plus school gives you some structure, discipline and (usually) a sense of security and community until you decide.

GAP YEAR OR STUDY?

A lot of school leavers question whether to take a gap year before starting university or further studies.

THE PROS TO A GAP YEAR:

- You've worked hard studying, especially in the past two years, and you might feel you need a breather.
- If you've been accepted into a course, you may have reservations about your choice (especially if it was made hastily) and need time to think about what you really want to do. A gap year could give you time to get your act together and do trial work or work experience in the industry first.
- You'll have a chance to experience real life a bit more to see what it is you really like to do.
- A gap year doesn't have to mean doing nothing. You can save some money and see what it's like to manage your finances and save for future courses and your personal development. Or you might travel to experience life, pick up some life lessons, or go on a volunteer program.

THE CONS TO A GAP YEAR:

- You could get out of the groove of studying and lose that momentum.
- If you begin full time work and get used to a steady income, it can be hard reducing that income to juggle studies.
- If you decide to travel, you may have underestimated the high costs of travelling or the logistics around it.
- If you've bludged on your gap year, it will be hard to convince potential employers on your resume that you used the year for self-growth and self-discovery.
- If all your other friends start uni and you don't, you might feel separated from them. It may seem like they're getting ahead of you and you've lagged behind (while they might be envious of your freedom; there are two sides to every coin).

Write down (and weigh up) your own pros and cons. In the end do what's best for you, as the buck stops with you.

WHAT ARE MY CAREER OPTIONS? WHAT JOBS WILL BE IN DEMAND IN 2030?

On average, people will spend 1/3 of their lives (or 90,000 hours in a lifetime) at work, according to a report by Andrew Naber (2007) from Gettysburg College.

It's fair to say your job can have a huge impact on your life, so it's important to do what you love.

After 12 years in school, you may not know what you want for your future.

If you have a clear passion or personal strength, it's easier. If you don't, you might want to try a few jobs and do work experience. Or if you're considering university and not clear on what interests you, you can choose a course that's more generic, or have a gap year to identify what you enjoy.

If your first career choice doesn't work out, that's normal. There's no rush. Research suggests that today's young people will hold 10 to 15 jobs in their lifetime.

Plus, there are more pathways to careers than ever before, and more options than progressing to university, which is why HSC results are not the 'be-all and end-all' that they were once perceived to be.

If you're unclear about your career choices, Morrisby is a platform that helps students make better decisions on work pathways. Go to Morrisby.com

Gettysburg College - % of your life spent at work; The Balance Careers – How often people change jobs; Morrisby.com

Youth Central website is a great resource for jobs and career advice on: Career profiles, Industry profiles, Planning your career, How to find a job, Applying for jobs, Job interviews, Employment rights and Apprenticeships & traineeships

JOBS OF THE FUTURE

When choosing a career it's important to understand the changing environment and consider what jobs will be in demand (and decline) in the future.

Do your own research, but here are some examples of jobs that are expected to grow in the future:

- Healthcare
- Education and training
- Construction
- Professional, scientific and technology industries (e.g. engineering, cloud computing, content production, data and digital specialists, marketing, product and business development, etc.)

Examples of jobs that are likely to disappear by 2030 (mostly jobs that can be automated):

- Printing press operator
- Bank teller
- Cashier
- Mail (letter) services
- Travel agent
- Jeweller
- Telephone operator
- Word processor/ typist
- Train driver
- Assembler/ fabricator

Jobs of the future, Most in demand, Disappearing jobs

CAREER OPTIONS (OUTSIDE OF HIGHER EDUCATION) INCLUDE:

- Business owner
- Online business
- Real estate (residential or commercial)
- Investing
- Stocks
- Retail, wholesale or importer
- Network marketing, multi-level marketing
- Passive income, residual income streams
- Entrepreneur

WHAT SKILLS DO EMPLOYERS REALLY WANT?

Enterprise skills are 'transferable' skills required in many jobs, that employers want you to have, no matter what industry you're working in.

The demand for enterprise skills is rising, however, there is still a significant gap between what employers are seeking and current proficiency levels, according to the Foundation for Youth Australians (FYA) report.

There is a big opportunity to improve these skills' deficiencies identified in the report.

For example, 90% of future jobs will involve digital literacy. However, there's a wide gap in these skills, given that 35% of year 10 students did not meet the Australian baseline proficiency.

HOW DO YOU RATE YOUR ENTERPRISE SKILLS?

If you believe you're lacking in any of the skills listed below, you might consider taking further courses to refine those skills to give yourself a competitive edge in job applications.

HERE'S THE LIST OF SKILLS THAT EMPLOYERS WANT FOR THE FUTURE:

- Digital literacy
- Financial literacy
- Problem-solving
- Maths

EXAMPLES OF ENTERPRISE SKILLS

- Communication
- Teamwork
- Problem-solving
- Initiative and enterprise
- Planning and organising
- Self-management
- Learning
- Technology

FYA The skills young people need for the future (2016), Youth Central 8 job skills you should have, Career FAQs future jobs in demand in Australia

"90% of future jobs will involve digital literacy"

FYA report

HOW COVID-19 FORCED JOBSEEKERS TO THINK LATERALLY AND UPSKILL

The 2020 pandemic reminded the workforce of the need to be adaptable to outside influences, to be innovative and identify new opportunities in the face of a crisis. While it turned business as we knew it upside down, some industries evolved and grew, such as: ecommerce, home delivery, e-learning courses and resources, Zoom and virtual conferencing, personal protection gear and equipment, cybersecurity, online fitness, entertainment services and many more.

Industries that boomed after Covid-19

> "You have brains in your head. You have feet in your shoes. You can steer yourself in any direction you choose."
>
> *Dr Seuss*

WHY A GOOD WORK ETHIC PAYS OFF!

Your work ethic is a personal reflection of your character and commitment to the job.

The effort you put into a job is what you'll get back. You might have to start with the **** jobs, but that's normal. It's a hierarchy (like a pecking order), and you're learning. By having a 'can-do' attitude, you'll show your commitment to the job and earn brownie points with the boss (and have more chance of standing out for future promotions).

WORK ETHIC TIPS:

- Be punctual (on time).
- Be reliable (don't chuck sickies).
- Be agreeable and enthusiastic.
- Do what the boss asks, since he/she pays you (within the job specifications).
- Help out others and show team spirit.
- Do your best.
- The more you give, the more you get back (= job satisfaction).
- Think about getting a good reference at the completion of that job.

"When the going gets tough,
the tough get going."

American proverb

PERSONAL STRENGTHS – TOOLS TO IDENTIFY YOUR UNIQUE SKILLS

WHAT ARE YOUR PERSONAL STRENGTHS? WHAT IS YOUR PERFECT JOB?

Since you spend a third of your life at work, it's important to do what you love.

People who play to their strengths are the best version of themselves.

If you're NOT doing what you love, it's going to be a chore. When you work in a job that matches your 'natural style' you'll be happier, more productive and motivated to build an ongoing career pathway and have a better quality of life.

EXAMPLES OF PERSONALITY PROFILING TO HELP YOU UNDERSTAND YOUR PERSONALITY

1. **CliftonStrengths:** Developed by Don Clifton to help people discover their management style and strengths and chose the job that best suits them.
2. **Myers-Briggs Type Indicator:** A widely-used test which categorises people into 16 personality types.
3. **DISC Behaviour Test:** A behaviour-assessment tool created by psychologist William Moulton Marston, centring on four different behavioural traits: Dominance, Influence, Steadiness and Conscientiousness.

Personality test: Top resume personality test

HOW TO FIND YOUR PASSION. WHAT GETS YOU OUT OF BED IN THE MORNING?

People who say; "You'll never make a living from that" are imposing their values on you. It's not other people's responsibility to decide what you enjoy or what you'll do in life.

Yes, take on advice from different sources, but in the end, you'll run your own race.

ASK YOURSELF...

1. What can I do for hours at a time without getting bored?
2. If I had complete financial freedom, what would I choose to do?
3. What does my internet browser look like? What do I read about a lot?
4. What motivates me to get out of bed? What occupies my thoughts (other than a girlfriend or boyfriend)?
5. If today were the last day of my life, what would I be doing?

If you happen to be working in a job that doesn't *really* inspire you, then create some fun in the workplace with your colleagues or fulfil your 'passion' as an outside interest.

"If today were the last day of my life, would I want to do what I'm about to do today?"

Steve Jobs

WHAT'S YOUR PERSONAL BRAND?

Your personal brand is how you show up in the world. It's your unique signature.

When you were really young you probably practised your written signature dozens of times, to get it just the way you liked it.

You can also practise and refine your personal signature. It's a 'look'. It's a way of talking and being. Maybe you like to show up strong and powerful, or maybe you have a gentle strength?

When do you feel the most confident and at ease? What things do you value about yourself that you can nurture and develop as your own?

Pretend you're looking in the mirror for the first time. What impression do you give? Are you well-groomed? (I.e. your hands, hair, skin, teeth, clothes and perfume? People notice these things first.)

Are your clothes suitable for the situation?

Is your voice and speech congruent with your looks?

Do you use a swear word every second word, use excessive cliches, or talk only about yourself; or are you thoughtful and attentive to others?

You can model yourself on people you admire. Pay attention to people in the media (or in your life) and style yourself on them. What can you emulate about them? Do they speak and dress a certain way, or do they have values you look up to?

Sometimes people downplay their strengths to fit in or avoid being a threat to others (but, that's their problem).

TIP

Be authentic! Be your own unique brand.

HAVE YOU GOOGLED YOURSELF LATELY? WOULD YOU EMPLOY YOURSELF?

Potential employers will Google you. If you're going for a role of responsibility, like working with children or in a legal profession, your history will be visible to the public and needs to be squeaky clean.

Your Facebook profile photo is accessible to everyone, so ensure it promotes a good image (i.e., no boozy party photos, no sexy angles and preferably no selfies).

If you're on LinkedIn or other professional social media platforms, do a self-image review of those photos. Do they represent you well? It's advisable to have a professionally taken photo on LinkedIn, which can also be used to personalise your resume.

SKILLSROAD IS A FREE PORTAL to map your career journey in 5 steps:

1. Take the Career Quiz to find out your personality style
2. Research over 350 career profiles to see what interests you
3. Take the Job Fit Test to see how you stack up against chosen careers
4. Build a resume – Resume builder application
5. Jobs board – How to apply for local apprenticeships and traineeship jobs

> "Be yourself. Everyone else is already taken."
>
> *Oscar Wilde*

THE 6 SKILLS OF BRILLIANT LEADERS

Leadership skills are characteristics employed when organising a team of people to achieve a goal. They can be helpful in work and also in sports or personal pursuits. Smart leaders surround themselves with people who complement them and fill the gaps for their (known) deficiencies. They have vision and can see the bigger picture, rather than focussing on the minutiae (small things).

EXAMPLES OF AWESOME LEADERSHIP SKILLS:

1. COMMUNICATION – Strong communicator and active listener, who is approachable, empathetic and accepts constructive feedback.
2. PEOPLE SKILLS – Team builder, who is persuasive and influential. A leader who acts as a mentor, leads by example, creates a cohesive team and allows autonomy.
3. INSPIRING – Unshakeable confidence and backs themselves. A leader who is inspirational, optimistic, positive and dependable.
4. STRATEGIC – Decisive, results-driven, adaptable to change and enjoys a challenge.
5. VISIONARY – A "big picture" person, who thinks outside the box and is an insightful, progressive risk-taker.
6. ETHICAL – Shows integrity, humility, fairness, respect, solid values, gives acknowledgement and accepts responsibility.

A GUIDE TO HIGHER EDUCATION: UNIVERSITY AND VET

This section will give you general information and background on the differences between vocational education and training (VET) and university education.

There are, essentially, two types of tertiary (third level) education qualifications in Australia – **vocational educational training (VET) and university education**.

Both offer qualifications that are nationally, and often internationally, recognised.

1. UNIVERSITY QUALIFICATIONS

University courses are usually more heavily grounded in theory and are generally considered more academic than their vocational counterparts. They include:

- **Associate degree** (Usually 2 years) – An associate degree is an undergraduate qualification that offers broad-based competency in a given field. In Australia, associate degrees are similar to advanced diplomas.

- **Bachelor's degree** (Usually 3 to 4 years full time) – A bachelor's degree is the standard university degree and is the main gateway to professional occupations.
- **Graduate certificate and graduate diploma** (Usually 6 to 12 months) – These are undertaken after completing your undergraduate study (offered through both universities and private providers).
- **Master's degree** (Usually an additional: 1 to 2 years) – A master's degree is designed to enhance specific professional or vocational skills.
- **Doctorate** (Usually at least 3 years) – A doctorate, even in a non-medical subject, gives the title of 'Dr' and is the highest qualification attainable in Australia.

Career FAQs M. Kermode. guide to tertiary qualifications (source adapted)

2. VOCATIONAL EDUCATION AND TRAINING (VET) AND APPRENTICESHIPS (E.G. TAFE)

Vocational courses are practical, skills-based courses aimed at preparing you for employment in an extensive range of vocational occupations and apprenticeships.

TAFE is the leading vocational training provider in Australia, with 1,200 courses available.

Courses include:

- **Certificate I and II** (Usually 4 to 8 months) – Basic tertiary qualifications to prepare you for relatively standard and defined activities and tasks.
- **Certificate III and IV** (Usually 12 to 18 months) – Ideal for people wishing to change occupations, or to move out of entry-level positions.
- **Diploma/Advanced diploma** (Usually 2 to 3 years) – Both diplomas and advanced diplomas offer broader and more in-depth knowledge than those facilitated by a certificate III or IV.

- Certificate courses and diplomas are usually delivered by TAFE colleges, community education centres, registered training organisations (RTOs) and private colleges.

An apprenticeship offers hands-on training that leads to a nationally-recognised qualification, such as carpentry, hairdressing, plumbing, building, agriculture, engineering and community services, etc.

WAYS TO TRANSITION INTO AN APPRENTICESHIP WHILE AT SCHOOL:

- You can get a head start on your apprenticeship by selecting a school-based apprenticeship, which allows you to enter the workforce while completing secondary school.
- Pre-apprenticeships blend hands-on experience and theory and provide a steppingstone to an apprenticeship in the industry of your choice.
- You can also undertake VET courses as part of your school studies.
- In a traditional apprenticeship, you combine hands-on workplace learning with trade school.

TO HELP FIND AN APPRENTICESHIP TO SUIT YOU, THERE ARE SERVICES SUCH AS:

- Youth Transitions
- Apprenticeship support Australia
- Skills Invest

WHAT HAPPENS IF YOU DECIDE TO STUDY LATER AS A MATURE AGE STUDENT?

If you decide to defer your studies, you can always apply later as a mature age student. Speak to the university you're interested in to confirm its entry requirements. In some tertiary institutions there's no age limit, and in many cases a mature age student must be over the age of 21 and have no formal qualifications (such as HSC, TAFE certificate or similar).

WHAT ABOUT ONLINE STUDIES?

There are other options available to study, online with many leading universities and other online providers. e.g. Open Universities Australia (OUA) open.edu.au.

You can enrol in many courses with OUA from the age of 13, with your parent's or guardian's permission.

The benefit of online study is that it gives you the freedom to study in your time or allow you to continue to work.

For instance, at OUA the courses offered are provided by Australian Universities, so you'll study and graduate in the same way as on-campus students. You're able to study a full degree, at undergraduate or postgraduate levels, or a single subject to upskill.

REPORT SHOWS VET GRADUATES HAVE A 10% HIGHER RATE OF EMPLOYMENT THAN UNIVERSITY GRADUATES

A recent report dispels the myth that university is the most popular choice for education among school-leavers. It shows that VET provides education to four-times more students than the universities.

Statistics from the SAF report:

- VET graduates have a 10% higher employment rate than university graduates.
- VET graduates have a higher median full-time salary ($56,000) than university graduates ($54,000).
- 22% of HECS-HELP debts will never be re-payed every year due to poor university completion.
- 90% of highest growth jobs in the next five years only need a VET qualification.

Study in Australia high education, *TAFE courses Amber Kirkwood. TAFE versus university,* SAF Perceptions are not Reality; Year 13 website; Skillsroad website, Upskilled differences between vocational and university education? OUA Open Universities Australia

WHAT CAN I EXPECT WHEN STARTING UNIVERSITY AND VET?

Starting university and vocational courses can be a daunting experience, whether you're 18 or a mature student.

Not only are you finding your way around an unknown campus and meeting new friends, but you're adapting to a new way of learning without a teacher guiding you.

Now you're learning independently and attending lectures and tutorials where you need to be up to speed on what's expected of you.

HERE ARE SOME TIPS ON HOW TO MINIMISE YOUR NERVES:

- **Orientation week (usually specific to university students):** Orientation week, or 'O-week', is a good opportunity to get to know the uni campus and classrooms and meet new people who are on the same learning curve as you. The uni often does some fun things to help you appreciate and get familiar with the uni way of life.
- **Making new friends:** Uni and VET courses have a melting pot of people from all walks of life, age groups and different geographical areas. It's an ideal chance to make new friends and set-up learning groups to support each other. Everyone is there for the same reason – to learn and grow.
- **Lectures and tutorials:** Lectures are necessary to attend, as most of the work gets covered there. Generally, lectures are in a large theatre and can have dozens (or hundreds) of people attending, so there's not much interaction. Uni tutorials are interactive, smaller break-out groups, providing a chance to ask questions and do group work or activities.
- **Time management:** You'll need to be organised and manage your own schedule and learning program. It will take some time to adapt and get into a routine. In particular, get into the habit of keeping a diary and recording your commitments (and using phone reminders for due dates).

BEST TIPS

1. No-one will check up on your homework like the teachers did in high school.
2. If you don't attend lectures and tutorials, it will reflect on your results because that's where you get the content and interaction.
3. Study groups and friends are helpful to keep you in-check with assignments and due dates.

Career FAQs E. Collier. What to expect when starting university

6 HIGHLY EFFECTIVE STUDY HABITS

1. **Create a daily study routine and stick to it.** Know your best time to study. (Some people are better in the morning, some at night). Work to the schedule and be disciplined. Make sure you keep that time so that you avoid the habit of excuses and procrastination.
2. **Find a quiet space to study.** Turn off phones, TV and other distractions in that time to allow you to have 100% focus. You'll get tasks done faster.
3. **Set a goal at the start of the study session.** Write a checklist of things to achieve overall and break it down into allocated times for each session. (Tick them off when completed, if that's what you like doing.) Don't over-cram and go into burn-out. Space your work over sessions and take breaks to stay fresh.
4. **Tackle the hardest questions first,** so the ones that follow seem so much easier and faster to achieve.
5. **Google:** memory techniques
6. **Check-in on your mindset.** Keep a 'can-do' approach and reward yourself when you complete an assignment or task well. If you're running behind schedule, do the best you can in the time you have. Avoid comparing yourself to other students, as you'll all learn at different paces.

EXAMPLES OF MEMORY AND STUDY TECHNIQUES:

- Chunking: chunking puts large pieces of information into shorter meaningful groups or units.
- Memory tools: such as mnemonic systems, like using the first letter of each word to create a nonsense sentence that's easy to remember. (E.g., The mnemonic system to remember the order of the planets orbiting the Sun is. 'My Very Educated Mother Just Served Us Nine Pizzas'.)
- 'Practice makes perfect': Outline and rewrite notes in your own words (repetition, recall and re-writing). You can review with friends or a study group. Test yourself with practice exams.

TIPS

- Exercise regularly to oxygenate the body and refresh the mind.
- Eat healthily to keep up vitamins and minerals you need for brain function and energy levels.

Mind mapping useful tool to map and recall, Photo reading mental photographing, Jim Kwik speed-learning techniques, Super Brain tips, Education Corner habits of successful students, Mind Tools Mind Tools: Introduction to Memory Techniques, Academic Tips memory skills, Psychcentral Dr J.M. Grohol. 10 most effective study habits

"As your body moves, your brain grooves."

Jim Kwik

RESUMES - TIPS TO MAKE YOUR RESUME STAND OUT

NOTE: A resume can also be called a curriculum vitae (CV)

THINGS TO INCLUDE:

1. Full name, contact details, address, LinkedIn name
2. Brief summary of background, skills and strengths
3. Education summary
4. Work experience and short descriptions
5. Other skills, interests and achievements
6. List each referee, including their name, job title and contact details
7. Optional: Include a recent, professionally-taken photo to personalise your resume

TIPS

- Resumes do NOT need to include marital status, age, current address or ethnicity.
- Be concise and use bullet points where possible. Adapt the resume to the job if required.
- Select a format and design fitting to your industry, including the cover letter.
- Don't be bashful. Ensure you promote yourself and come across as confident in your abilities.
- Try to keep your resume concise and no more than two pages long.

Canva resume templates, Seek.com templates, Shutterstock templates (that can be edited)

COVER LETTERS - HOW TO SELL YOURSELF IN YOUR COVER LETTER

A cover letter is your chance to spruik (promote) your attributes relating to the job advertised.

This is where you explain why you're the perfect candidate for the job. It's not about regurgitating your resume.

It's your first communication with a potential employer, so you'll want to sell yourself here.

There could be dozens, or hundreds, of other applicants you're up against. They want to know why they should employ you. Be a standout!

If you feel confident enough, record a video to show your personality and interest in the position. They key is to cut through all the other applications.

Also research the 'dos and don'ts of cover letters'. (Note: Email cover letters need a slightly less formal approach. Search: 'how to write an email cover letter'.)

The Youth Central site has a range of sample resumes and cover letters from first jobs through to people who have work experience and had previous jobs. There are other suggestions, below.

Youth Central sample resumes and cover letters, Seek.com good and bad cover letters, Hudson cover letter templates, Career One Career one - Cover letters, Career FAQs templates, The Balance Careers cover letter examples, Jobsearch. Jobactive, Defence jobs

A SAMPLE OF A FORMAL COVER LETTER

NOTE: Remember to include your resume

YOUR NAME

Date (Day/Month/Year)

Address

Mobile number

Email address

Dear (Client Name) or Dear Sir, Madam,

I would like apply for the role of..."
(add job title)

"I'm currently..." (add where you're working).
Describe any work history, experience and qualifications relating to the position.

Explain your key strengths and why you're suited to the position.e.g. "I have excellent..." (add your skills) or "I am..." (add your strengths, such as self-motivated, hardworking).

Be sure to talk yourself up and sell yourself.
If the employer has asked for specific qualifications or licences, make sure you list them.

The last paragraph is the 'call to action'. e.g. "Thankyou for your time. I look forward to hearing from you and the opportunity of an interview."

Yours sincerely,

Your Name

A SAMPLE OF A RESUME (CV)

JOHN SMITH

Mobile: 0412 345 678
Email: johnsmith@mail.com

No Experience Resume

Describe your career objective in two or three short sentences. It's handy to read the job description from the position you are applying to and add a couple of relevant keywords to this section.

Key Skills

- List relevant skills here
- i.e. Strong organizational skills
- i.e. Microsoft Word
- i.e. Creative
- i.e. Great communication skills
- i.e. Honest and reliable

Experience

DATES FROM – TO

Job Title | Company, Location

Here you can write about any work experience roles or volunteer positions in a brief sentence - describe your responsibilities in this role and the skills you developed. If you haven't done either, don't worry, just delete this part and move on to the next.

Education

MONTH YEAR

Degree Title | School, Location

Just stating the name of your school is sufficient, but if you have any relevant achievements, list them underneath

- i.e. **2017:** Class Captain

Activities

In this area, you can write about any extracurricular activities that you enjoy doing, or any passions or interests you have.

Referees

Anna Wood
Principal
Mob: XXXX XXX XXX

Harvey Dent
English Teacher
Mob: XXXX XXX XXX

JOHN SMITH | **Email:** john.smith@mail.com | **Mobile:** 0412 345 678

DO'S AND DON'TS WHEN JOB HUNTING - by Joanne Esposito

Joanne Esposito has 17 years of experience as a recruitment consultant. She is a career, culture and life coach and is also the no. 1 best-selling author of 'Confessions of a Recruiter'.

TAILOR YOUR RESUME TO SUIT THE JOB

For a resume to stand out, you need to show your compatibility to the job and not waffle on. Bullet points prompt you to keep your work history short and concise. You get to list your achievements and suitability, while also demonstrating your point of difference.

Tailoring your resume isn't copying the job description. It's about including your strengths, removing any irrelevant information and using key words relating to the advertisement.

WHAT ABOUT USING VIDEO TO SUPPORT MY RESUME?

To stand out from the crowd, why not send a video of yourself to support your resume?

A video is an excellent way for a company to get an insight into who you are and why you're passionate about this opportunity. A lot of large companies are now asking for this, especially in graduate programs. It may seem daunting at first, but practice with a friend and make it fun, as your personality on video could be the very reason why you land that job. The more you practice, the more you will come across as confident and camera-ready.

A COVERING LETTER IS YOUR CHANCE TO SHINE

A covering note or letter shows why you're applying for the role. Be sure to include your key strengths, especially when your work experience does not entirely match the job. Your covering letter allows you to show why you could be the right person for the job. It shouldn't be longer than one page, and a good cover letter has a call to action at the end where you can follow up on your application and track your progress.

WHAT ARE THE BIGGEST MISTAKES YOUNG JOB SEEKERS MAKE?

Young job seekers don't always have a lot of work experience, but NOT having a 'can-do' attitude or getting 'hands dirty' at the start of your career is a big mistake as it shows you may not be adaptable and trainable.

Employers are looking for a positive attitude and a willingness to learn, more so than technical skills and academic ability. The more you show your adaptability, the more you will be noticed for other opportunities.

Other common mistakes young job seekers make include being distracted, coming across as impatient and giving up too soon. Instead of applying for everything, do your research with companies you want to work for and get familiar with LinkedIn or Meetup groups. And take social media offline, learn to network (face-to-face meetings are like practice interviews), as more than 50% of all jobs are not advertised.

Not having clarity is the number one mistake most job seekers make. Your job search is not a quick fix, so stay focused, develop patience and learn to adjust and adapt; and you will learn to move closer to attracting the role that's right for you.

Suggested watch: Everyday interview tips – 5 TED talks to watch before your next interview.

HOW TO MAKE A GOOD FIRST IMPRESSION AT AN INTERVIEW?

Master the art of small talk, as this helps brush off your nerves. Being prepared for an interview and arriving early gives you time to relax and to be present. Having a firm handshake, good eye contact and a genuine smile always make a good first impression. Try doing the wonder woman or superman pose in the bathroom for two minutes before the meeting. It calms your nerves, straightens your posture and gives you a quick dose of self-confidence.

SOME OF THE BIGGEST MISTAKES MADE DURING AN INTERVIEW INCLUDE

- Having to build instant rapport for an interview isn't easy, and some of the biggest mistakes made during an interview are not making eye contact and forgetting to smile.

- Not dressing appropriately, chewing gum and swearing are no-no's for interviews. When you're not prepared, or you arrive late, you're likely to get nervous and ramble on, and then you forget to sell yourself during the interview.
- Using filler words such as 'umm' bring out your insecurities, while fidgeting, a weak handshake and bad body language are also common mistakes.
- Learn to listen more and talk less. A simple pause will help you to come across as more intelligent.
- Believe it or not, your mannerisms and eye movements are being judged more than your skills and work history on your resume.

MY 5 POTENTIAL FUTURE CAREER TRENDS ARE:

1. Healthcare – we are an ageing population; therefore, nurses, doctors, dentists and aged-care workers will be in high demand, and also expect medical research to grow.
2. Alternative energy – this includes scientists, engineers and mechanics.
3. Education and training – professional and personal development will grow exponentially.
4. Content-creation marketing – we're moving away from sales to educational-based focus.
5. Information technology, coding and software – machines are taking over repetitive tasks. It's important to become a specialist otherwise our skills will become redundant.

WHAT ARE GEN Y AND MILLENNIALS LOOKING FOR?

Gen Y and millennials want a sense of belonging and are looking for environments that have a community feel. Security isn't as important as it was for baby boomers and Gen X but being part of a tribe and the culture is. Flexibility and work-life balance is key. They also want the ability to develop and succeed, plus company benefits and a great salary to match their credentials.

HOW LONG SHOULD PEOPLE STAY IN A JOB TO GET A GOOD REFERENCE?

About 2-3 years is acceptable to move around and having a good attitude will make it easier to ask for a reference. Unless you are in a contract or intern role, always ask for a reference when you finish up.

Try not to burn your bridges at work, even in toxic environments, so that you can ask for a good reference. Don't be afraid to ask for a character or personal reference if you work for a large company as some companies have a no reference policy.

IF A WORKER IS UNHAPPY, DO YOU RECOMMEND JUST LEAVING OR FINDING ANOTHER JOB FIRST?

It's usually best to find a job when you're in a job because you're more confident and you interview stronger. Communication is key, and if you can speak to your current manager, they may be able to make some changes to your current work situation, especially if they don't want to lose you. However, if it's not a great environment and you can't see it changing, you won't interview well if you're unhappy, and staying there will affect your self-esteem.

LOOKING BACK TO WHEN YOU WERE 16, ARE THERE ANY REALISATIONS OR REGRETS YOU HAVE?

I personally wish I had thought about my career even at 16. When you're young, one year feels like an eternity, but it really isn't because life just flies right past you. I regret not having a mentor to steer me in the right direction, and I've learnt that self-education doesn't end when you finish school.

I regret not believing in myself more so that I could have developed my true potential faster.

I also wish I hadn't taken things personally because you can't please everyone, and you learn to develop a 'thick' skin as you get older.

JOANNE'S 3 TIPS FOR JOB SEARCHING ARE:

1. Adaptability – gives you resilience and the energy that's needed for your job search.
2. Curiosity – helps you break away from routine, boredom or repetitive daily tasks and studies.
3. Be kind to yourself – maintain healthy boundaries and have the right people around in order to stay positive.

The final tip: If you only accept a job for the $$$, you will never be happy. And lastly, it's important to really love what you do and to feel comfortable with your environment because when you get into the workforce, you'll spend over one third of your life at work.

Suggested watch: Carol Dweck. TEDX talk The power of believing that you can improve

> "Get great at what you're good at!"
>
> *Dean Graziosi*

WORK CONNECTIONS - HOW LINKEDIN HELPS YOU GET CONNECTED

LinkedIn is a free online professional network used by more than 300 million business professionals worldwide to connect and build relationships.

Your professional profile links you to work and business connections and potential jobs.

It acts as an online version of your resume for potential employers to check your skills, interests, accomplishments, testimonials and any work experience.

As a school leaver, it's a good idea to set up a profile and start making connections in your desired field of work, as a lot of positions are filled through connections and referrals.

It's also a way to stay up-to-speed with news and changes in your industry and engage with people who may be able to assist you in your career growth.

SIMPLE STEPS TO SET-UP A LINKEDIN PROFILE:

- Upload a professional image of yourself (no selfies). This is the chance to make a first impression on potential business contacts and future employers.
- Write a profile heading.
- Write a description of yourself and your career goals.
- Complete the education section, volunteer work, skills, courses completed and any further achievements.
- Complete the 'jobs search' section if you are seeking work.
- LinkedIn will advise you of jobs that might suit you based on your interests.
- Start connecting with people and build a 'network'.
- 'Engage' with your feed to remain visible and relevant to your connections.
- Ask for recommendations from people with whom you've worked.

TOP TIPS

- It's not always what you know, but who you know!
- Get connected. Networking with friends and colleagues can lead to referrals for work.
- A personal recommendation is regarded highly by many employers.
- Remember, you only get one chance to make a first impression.

> "Show me a successful individual, and I'll show you someone who had real positive influences in his or her life."
>
> *Denzel Washington*

WHY MENTORS HELP YOU BECOME THE BEST VERSION OF YOURSELF

A mentor can be helpful to bounce ideas off and get unbiased work and life advice. Mentors are usually older and have experience they can share to help you make important decisions.

A good start is to find someone you trust, respect and get along with, and see how receptive they are to mentoring you. This might be a family member or a **family friend, or a work friend or teacher.**

Sometimes a mentor can be a role model that you look up to and want to be like. If someone is super-successful, it makes sense to want to emulate what they do.

In the workplace, you may talk with someone who has a lot of experience in your industry, or you think is streetwise and savvy. They can be a valuable source of information and wisdom to help you build your career. Usually they've 'been there, done that', so they can give you the heads up on how to handle potential challenges. They can also refer you to their connections. Networking is a large part of progressing through the ranks in the workplace.

If you're lucky enough to still have a grandparent (or parent) alive, pick their brains on their past and ask how they'd do things differently (or the same) if they had their time over.

If you cannot find a mentor, find a life-coach or mind-coach to keep your personal and professional goals on track.

LINKS TO MENTORING ADVICE AND WEBSITES:

- Mentoring Australia
- Big Brothers Big Sisters
- Youth Mentoring
- Imvc
- Try Mentoring
- Wesley Mission
- Youth off the streets
- Yfoundations

Youth Central Finding a mentor ; Foundations for young Australians How to find a mentor and also contact your local council.

"I don't care what you do for a living – if you do it well, I'm sure there was someone cheering you on or showing the way. A mentor."

Denzel Washington

BUSINESS START-UP

While employment has its benefits and provides a steady source income, when you work for other people, you're trading your time for pay. You can only work so many hours for so much money.

In contrast, if you employ staff, they're earning for you (known as leveraging). If you have a business which runs automatically, where business ticks over without you lifting a finger, it's called 'passive income' or 'residual income'.

If you've been thinking of starting a business, then having a 'great idea' is a good start, as it was most likely born out of identifying a gap in the market ('Necessity is the mother of invention', right?)

Firstly, do your research. You might identify a unique niche market, then specialise in that market.

A SIMPLE CHECKLIST TO START YOUR OWN BUSINESS:

- **Register the business name** through ASIC's website. Seek advice from your accountant or lawyer if you're not sure.
- **Do a SWOT Analysis**, not only your business's Strengths, Weaknesses, Opportunities and Threats, but also those of your competition.
- **Be clear what you're offering and how you'll be different.** Google: marketing a business and how to identify new business opportunities.
- **Decide on your exact target market.** Don't be all things to all people. A niche market is more effective.
- **Create a business plan** (vision and goals), so you know where you're going and how to get there.
- **Create a promotional plan** with an advertising plan, setting out how you will reach your audience most effectively. Use online and/or direct marketing methods.
- **Engage a graphic designer** to create a brand and logo that fits your identity **and your USP (unique selling proposition).**
- **Decide if you need staff and what they will do.** Create job descriptions. Involve a human resources agency if needed.
- **Have an online presence,** e.g. Facebook, Instagram, Twitter and LinkedIn. Create a website.
- **Set up an accounting system** to manage outgoings and incomings, e.g. Xero or Quickbooks.
- **Create a business community** of support people, e.g., an electrician and handyman if you're a plumber.
- **Involve a business coach** to help keep you accountable to your goals and plans.
- **Keep learning and doing seminars and courses**, e.g., small business, marketing, trends and follow thought-leaders on social media.

THE 4 MOST COMMON TYPES OF BUSINESS STRUCTURES IN AUSTRALIA ARE:

- Sole Trader
- Company
- Partnership
- Trust

WHAT'S MARKETING?

Marketing refers to all the processes involved in promoting, selling and distributing products or services from the manufacturer to the ultimate consumer.

It makes use of the 'marketing mix', which is also known as the 4Ps – product, price, place and promotion. It identifies the ideal customer for the product or service and draws attention to the product or service through sales, advertising, promotion, direct marketing, branding, price positioning, point-of-sale, merchandising and distribution.

What's Outsourcing (virtual assistance)?

Outsourcing is virtual assistance. These online services help with websites, marketing, telemarketing, bookkeeping, graphic design, copywriting and many other services.

e.g. Upwork ; Freelancer ; Fiverr

Marketing, setting up websites, outsourcing, virtual assistance, ASIC's business structure, Success Insider Dean Graziosi. Millionaire success habits, Seth Godin TED talk, The Balance what is marketing?

"People who are crazy enough to think they can change the world are the ones who do."

Steve Jobs

UPSKILLING - LEARNING NEVER ENDS

KNOWLEDGE IS POWER.

Knowledge is the primary source of value in our world today.

"Your ability to expand your mind and devote yourself to lifelong learning is the key to breaking any success barriers," according to self-development expert and author, Brian Tracy.

THERE ARE 3 TYPES OF LEARNING (BASED ON BRIAN TRACY'S THEORY):

1. **Maintenance Learning:** Maintenance learning refers to you keeping current in your field.
2. **Growth Learning:** This is the kind of learning that adds new knowledge and skills to your repertoire. Growth learning helps you expand your mind. You're acquiring information that you didn't have that enables you to do things that you could not do previously.
3. **Shock Learning:** Shock learning is learning that contradicts or reverses a piece of knowledge or understanding that you already have. Shock learning can be extremely valuable if you act on it.

Brian Tracy importance of lifelong learning, Book - Eat that Frog, Khan Academy Khan Academy free online courses, Videos You can learn anything and Brain Tricks. AsapScience, and Kwik learning

> "How we spend our days is, of course, how we spend our lives."
>
> *Annie Dillard*

11. TIPS TO OPTIMISE YOUR PHYSICAL HEALTH

Please note: This guide raises health concepts and social issues for consideration and debate. You should always seek advice from a doctor on health issues.

Your health is your greatest asset, both physically and mentally.

This chapter helps you to understand what older people regret most when they've been neglectful and ill-health crashes down on them. And that is... "they wished they'd taken care of their bodies better and now they're paying the pricc."

THE 4 SECRETS TO MAXIMISING YOUR HEALTH

1. PUT GOOD STUFF IN

- Eat a balanced, healthy, chemical-free diet.
- Eat fresh foods and wholefoods, not processed 'dead' food in cans or packets.
- Eat mindfully, as digestion starts in the mouth and is more efficient when you're relaxed.
- Avoid processed foods and trans-fats (retain some unsaturated fats, like avocado and nuts).
- Limit sugars, alcohol and caffeine.

- Have a high alkaline diet (fruit/veg) and reduce acidic foods (e.g. meat/dairy/grains/alcohol/sugars).
- Don't smoke or take recreational drugs.
- Drink filtered alkaline water (the human body is composed of up to 70% water).

2. DO GOOD STUFF

- Exercise daily (cardio and/or mindful exercise, like yoga and walking).
- Get a daily dose of sunlight (a moderate amount to stimulate production of vitamin D).
- Detox regularly (to eliminate toxins).
- Maintain good digestion and gut health (e.g., probiotics).
  Keep a healthy mind (involve a life coach, counsellor or therapist).

3. BE PROACTIVE, NOT REACTIVE

- Treat the cause of the problem, not the symptom.
- Boost and take care of your immunity.
- Take vitamins and supplements if needed (check with a doctor to see if you're deficient).
- Monitor your body mass index (BMI) to stay in a healthy range.
- Know your body (consider the effects of food on your body. Do you have allergies or intolerances?)
- Stay hydrated (when you're feeling tired, you're often dehydrated).

4. MAKE TIME FOR DOWNTIME

- Get a good night's sleep, to heal, recover, reboot and recuperate (to 'fill your cup').
- Maintain balance in life. Take time-out and de-stress.
- Spend time with family and friends.
- Keep passion, purpose and positivity.
- Practice calming exercises for the mind, like meditation.
- Treat yourself to massages, self-love treats and self-care sessions.
- "Eat your food as your medicine, otherwise you'll end up
- eating medicines as your food." – Source unknown

WHY SHOULD I KEEP FIT AND ACTIVE?

EXERCISE HELPS TO:

1. Raise energy levels and improve your state of mind.
2. Increase oxygen and strengthen the lungs.
3. Boost blood flow, lower blood pressure and improve circulation.
4. Control weight.
5. Maintain stronger muscles, bones, joints and balance.
6. Make you feel good.
7. Improve sleep and relaxation.
8. Reduce the likelihood and/or severity of chronic diseases.

NOTE: If you have an existing or underlying condition/s, speak to your doctor before starting an exercise program.

THE IMPORTANCE OF HYDRATION

Some research suggests we're comprised of as much as 70% water (some say 50%).

Regardless, if your body is in a state of constant dehydration, you're not functioning at your optimum. Good hydration helps to:

- Regulate blood pressure (blood volume) to allow proper circulation.
- Regulate body temperature (to cool your body down).
- Transport nutrients and remove waste.
- Act as a shock absorber for our joints.
- Think clearly, and avoid tiredness and headaches.

Home Doctor importance of hydration in fitness, Kids Health teens exercise, ReachOut Australia how to exercise when you're not motivated, Mayo Clinic dehydration symptoms, Healthline body/water percentage

> "It's true that we don't know what we've got until we lose it, but it's also true that we don't know what we've been missing until it arrives."
>
> *Bette Davis*

THE 5 BIGGEST HEALTH MISTAKES UNDER 25s MAKE – BY STEVE GRANT

Steve Grant played rugby league for the Cronulla Sharks, studied at Wollongong Uni and has over 20 years' experience working in the fitness industry. He's co-owner of Rushcutters Health: Gym Hub

1. EATING TOO MUCH SUGAR

Consuming too much sugar can make you put on weight and lead to weight-related illnesses. With this condition, your body either becomes resistant to the effects of insulin, which regulates sugar metabolism in your cells, or it becomes incapable of producing enough insulin to maintain normal glucose levels, which requires daily insulin injections and regular doctor check-ups.

The benefits of getting it right – The less sugar you eat, the healthier you'll be. If you maintain optimum sugar levels in your body, you will:

1. Avoid diabetes and weight gain (and related illnesses).
2. Have fewer tooth cavities and trips to the dentist.

2. LACK OF EXERCISE

I use my iPhone and laptop for hours every day – I love them! But I also understand I need to move a bit each day as well. The best types of exercise are everyday things like walking to school or work, or fun stuff like basketball and surfing. You don't need hours – just 30 minutes most days will keep you super healthy.

The benefits of getting it right – Getting proper exercise early on reduces the risk of developing major illnesses. It increases muscle tone and improves the quality of your sleep, so you have more energy each day. It gives you better muscle coordination, and if you exercise with other people, it's social and fun!

3. POOR PERSONAL HYGIENE

Poor hygiene can be a sign of self-neglect or an inability or unwillingness to attend to one's personal needs. When left unchecked, poor hygiene could produce serious conditions, ranging from social problems to potentially more serious diseases.

The benefits of getting it right – Habits such as showering daily, brushing your teeth in the morning and night and even the use of deodorant can all make you feel better about yourself and therefore improve your overall wellbeing. You'll have healthy hair, healthy nails and skin, less acne — and no physical reason for people to talk about you behind your back.

4. HEADPHONES ARE TOO LOUD

Frequently listening to extremely loud music with your headphones can result in hearing loss or tinnitus (a ringing noise in one or both ears), which is common in the music industry and high-noise industries.

The benefits of getting it right – The good news is you don't need to swear off headphones altogether to avoid this condition. But if you do use headphones, learn to regulate the volume, length and frequency of your listening to help preserve and protect your hearing.

5. UNNECESSARY RISKS – UNPROTECTED SEX AND EXPERIMENTING WITH DRUGS

It's common in your teenage years or early 20s to face tough decisions about unprotected sex and experimenting with drugs. The key here is to get proper education and surround yourself with friends and a support network who have your best interests (and their own) at heart.

THE BENEFITS OF GETTING THIS RIGHT

You can avoid nasty STIs (sexually transmitted infections) like chlamydia and herpes that can be extremely painful and potentially leave you infertile in later life. Plus, you can avoid the emotional and financial stress of raising a child before you're ready. You can also avoid the negative effects of drug addiction such as violence, unemployment, damaged relationships and serious health conditions.

EATING WELL – WHY IS EATING HEALTHILY SO IMPORTANT?

Your body is your sanctuary. If you treat it well, it will serve you well in return.

We often underestimate how crucial our health is to our quality of life until we're older and we no longer have good health (and we might wish we'd paid heed earlier).

When the damage is done, you can spend most of your money and time rectifying all your mistakes.

Interestingly, most of us don't think twice about maintaining our cars regularly, so why not have a maintenance schedule for our health? This starts with eating a balanced diet.

Also see 'Eat for Health' calculators to calculate your daily energy and nutrient requirements.

> "When we provide the body with all its nutrients we need, we remove over-eating and food cravings."
>
> *Galit Goldfarb*

THE BENEFITS OF EATING WELL

- High energy levels
- Strong immune system and general good health
- Clear thinking and handling stress better
- Less illness (healthy eating reduces the chances of developing diabetes, cancer and cardiovascular disease)
- Balanced weight and hormones
- Sleeping well
- Improved self-esteem and mental wellbeing

WHAT ARE THE RISKS IF YOU DON'T EAT HEALTHILY?

- Becoming overweight and/or obese
- Aging prematurely
- Onset of chronic diseases
- Decline in mental health
- General ill-health and lack of energy
- Poor sleep and digestion
- Hormone imbalances

> "Something that comes out of a can has no life energy, it's dead. Eat live food."
>
> *Deepak Chopra*

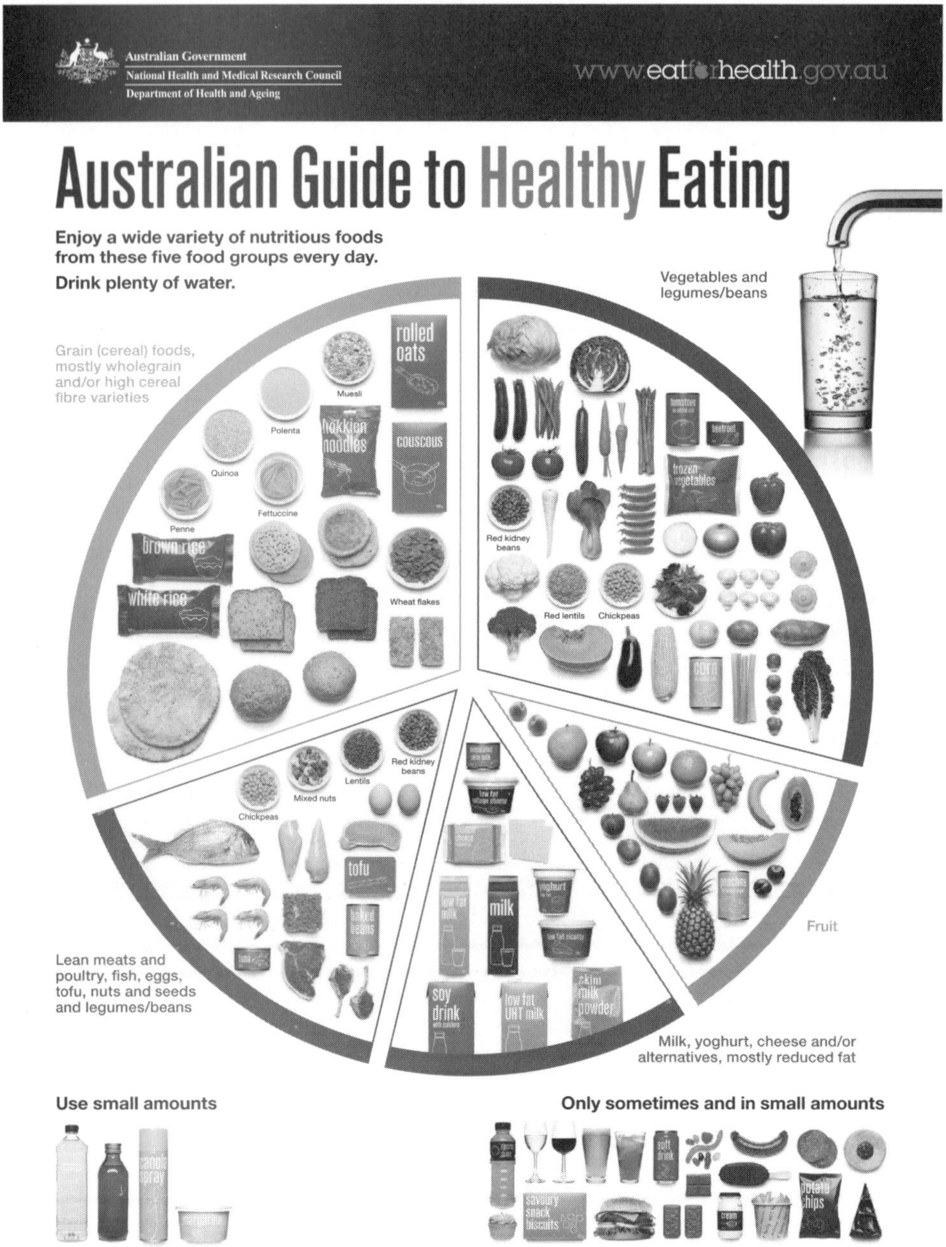

(Source: National Health and Medical Research Council) *The Australian Dietary Guidelines*
Eatforhealth.gov.au

STRESS EATING – 9 MISTAKES STRESSED PEOPLE CAN MAKE

STRESSED AND SUPER BUSY PEOPLE OFTEN:

1. **Eat too quickly** – The digestive process begins in the mouth. In a mindful state the body resets the homeostasis for weight loss and regulates your weight levels.
2. **Overeat** because they're not eating consciously and don't know when they're full.
3. **Worry too much,** which can increase the hunger hormone (ghrelin) and cortisol levels.
4. **Forget to eat**, which can slow your metabolism and muck with blood sugar levels.
5. **Binge or eat emotionally**, which can make you more emotional and feel like eating more.
6. **Make unhealthy (fast) food choices**, instead of preparing nutritious whole foods.
7. **Sleep poorly** – A good night's sleep promotes healthy metabolism and allows the body to heal.
8. **Have too much coffee, alcohol and sweets**, which promote weight gain and insulin problems.
9. **Skip exercise** – Exercise helps to increase blood flow and oxygenation and burns calories.

The effects of stress eating, J. Folk, M. Folk. Anxiety Centre. Anxiety symptoms

HOW TO BE AN INFORMED CONSUMER:

Read up on subjects such as good and bad fats, sugar content, additives in food and possible foods you may be allergic or sensitive to. Elimination diets (i.e., eliminating foods, then reintroducing them) are good to work out if you react to certain food types.

THE DANGERS OF EATING TOO MUCH SUGAR

The obsession with sugar has led the majority of the population to ignore the overwhelming evidence that eating too much sugar can cause fat build-up in the liver, which can lead to sickness and chronic diseases. The World Health Organisation (WHO) recommends reduced intake of free sugars. In both adults and children, the intake of free sugars should be reduced to less than 10% of total energy intake.

As an example: 1 can of cola = 30g, or 7.5 teaspoons, of sugar (4 grams of sugar = 1 teaspoon).

Sugar intake stats

> "The definition of insanity is doing the same thing over and over and expecting different results."
>
> *Albert Einstein*

LIFESTYLE RISKS - DON'T ASSUME EVERYTHING IS SAFE. BE 'IN THE KNOW'

The use of mobile phones to the ear and head area increases your risk of exposure to radio frequency (RF) radiation, which is high-frequency electromagnetic radiation from wireless equipment, devices and data transmission.

Note: When purchasing a mobile phone, manufacturers provide RF exposure legal disclaimers. Read these warnings. Example: Apple RF Exposure Legal Disclaimer

HOW TO AVOID CHEMICALS IN DAILY LIFE:

Chemicals are in almost every product on our supermarket shelves, as preservatives, colours or flavour enhancers in food and personal care products. Humans have found or made millions of different chemicals, the vast majority over the past few decades. Do your research and make informed decisions. Many are classified as 'carcinogenic to humans'. (INFO: Cancer.org)

TOP TIPS TO AVOID CHEMICALS:

- Buy fresh and organic produce as often as possible.
- Avoid using chemical-based insecticides at home.
- Use natural cleaning products in your home. Go back to basics.
- Read the labels on products for the list of potential 'nasties' and get informed.
- Use BPA-free and phthalate-free plastics (to avoid BPA leach into water and foods) and use glass instead of plastic.
- Find the 'paraben free' and 'sodium lauryl sulphate free' labels in your cosmetics and skin care products.
- Choose natural organic brands for your toiletries and personal care products.
- Avoid using PVC material, and use more natural materials such as cotton, wool, linen, bamboo or hemp.
- Keep your home well-ventilated.

TIP

If you use any chemicals, read the instructions closely to avoid injury or poisoning.

Women's Voices 10 ways to avoid toxic chemicals, Dr Mercola dangers of aspartame, The Guardian things that can give you cancer, The Skin Care Clinic toxic chemicals in skin care,

Books on food allergies or intolerances: Sue Dengate. *Fed Up With Food Additives*, Peter Taubert. *Read the Label, Know the Risks*

PERSONAL CARE – TOP TIPS ON SKINCARE, HYGIENE AND MANNERS

SKIN CARE TIPS FOR UNDER 25s

Hormone surges can cause oily skin and enlarge pores, causing young people to fall into the trap of over-cleansing and using harsh cleansing products, which can disturb the skin's natural balancing act.

- Choose a natural cleanser designed for younger skin. If you've cleaned the daily grime from your face in the evening, it's usually sufficient to simply use water to rinse your face in the morning.
- Use products sparingly. Keep your skin hydrated with gentle, natural moisturisers formulated for your skin (e.g., if you have acne use acne-treatment products).
- Wash your hands before you touch your face, to reduce the transfer of germs.
- If you have dry skin, use a cream cleanser instead of a foaming product. Over-dry skin can stop the skin from breathing and can harden the epidermis, which can clog pores and cause breakouts. Keep the skin lightly moisturised with a chemical-free product.
- Gently exfoliate once a week (but don't scrub).
- See a doctor, skin specialist or dermatologist if you have large lumps and pimples. They can recommend prescription cleansers and acne treatments.
- Protect the skin from sunburn with natural sunscreens, like zinc.
- Don't share skincare or makeup, as you can share germs as well.

COSMETIC SURGERY

Before undergoing any elective (non-urgent) surgery, fully weigh up the benefits versus the risks.

Some surgeons are not forthcoming in advising all of the potential risks of surgery. Do your own due diligence and fully research the surgery you're considering. Look at previous clients' independent feedback and testimonials.

Be aware that any surgery under general anaesthetic comes with a risk of complications, and even death.

Ask yourself why you're considering surgery. Is it to boost your confidence or to please other people? Even simple cosmetic procedures come with a risk (e.g., Botox can cause droopy-eye or a crooked smile).

If things do go wrong, and you don't get the result you want, it can increase the financial burden and decrease your self-esteem.

Check if your surgeon is registered with the Medical Board.

Remember that 'beauty is only skin deep'.

Risks of cosmetic surgery, Flawless advantages and disadvantages of cosmetic surgery, FDA risks and complications of breast implants, Mayo Clinic breast augmentation

> "I think beauty comes from actually knowing who you are. That's real beauty to me."
>
> *Ellen DeGeneres*

TATTOOS

Research suggests a third (34%) of Australians regret their tattoos.

A tattoo is a significant lifetime artistic statement. Make sure you research it well, including the design and placement, and be sure you want to see it for life.

In particular, be mindful of putting partner's names on your body (just in case).

Also, carefully choose the tattoo artist (for style, reputation, quality of work and their portfolio).

Healthline tattoo regrets, Beard Brand tips for tattoo beginners, McCrindle tattoos in Australia - perceptions, trends and regrets

HYGIENE AND GROOMING

Good personal hygiene and grooming habits help you feel good and make you nicer to be around.

Because dirt and bodily secretions build up on our bodies, being clean and hygienic avoids getting sick or getting an unpleasant skin condition.

Hygiene has been under the spotlight since Covid-19, so we're all aware that washing hands properly helps reduce the spread of bacteria and viruses.

Looking after teeth (brushing and flossing) shows you value your personal care, plus it preserves your teeth.

Maintaining and cleaning your fingernails and toenails show the attention you place on personal hygiene. The same applies to having clean and well-groomed hair, including body hair.

TIP

Don't brush your teeth too hard as it can erode the gums and wear down the enamel.

MANNERS DO MATTER – DON'T LEAVE HOME WITHOUT THEM ☺

Even if you're not smashing out life too well right now, manners will *always* service you well. In fact, if you're not on top of your game, then a 'check-in' on manners and courtesy might be the very thing to do.

For starters, people who are courteous are nicer to be around (as opposed to selfish people who think the world owes them something). Being nicer means they usually have a better friendship-base and circle of contacts because they're proof that what they put out, they get back ('like attracts like').

When you start a day with good manners, you're more likely to gain brownie 'feel-good' points.

Try standing up for an elderly person on the bus so they can sit down. They will appreciate it, and you will feel good.

Try letting someone else in first in a lift, or at a door. Or letting a car merge in front of you.

Try sending a "thank you" text or note to someone who helped you.

Try doing something special for someone who has your back.

There are many more examples of manners and courtesy. It's a matter of practice... then being aware that good things return to you.

DON'T

- text or talk on the phone when you're in other people's company (unless you explain the reason first).
- discuss taboo topics, such as religion, politics, money or a person's weight or appearance.
- be too familiar with new people or swear excessively.
- talk about absent people (that's called 'gossip').
- chew with your mouth open.
- wear hats or caps inside (dress codes can be important and may require consideration).
- push into queues or lines.

DO

- turn up on time (respect people's time as being as valuable as yours).
- show courtesy to elderly or less advantaged people.
- let the person closest to the door exit first, and let elderly go first.
- when sitting down to eat, wait for everyone to be served their food before you start eating.
- be friendly, but not gushy, and respect people's personal space.
- pour other people's drink or wine first, then pour your own.
- call before visiting anyone at home or work.
- knock on a door before entering.
- make eye-contact and listen with interest when talking with others.
- learn proper table manners, such as using the correct cutlery and wine glasses.
- say "please" and "thank-you".

Very well family manners you should know, GT20 manners and rules of etiquette

FASHION ON A SHOESTRING BUDGET

10 WAYS TO ROCK YOUR LOOK

1. **Build confidence in your own style.** Know what works with your body shape. Check out what celebrities or friends with a similar shape/size to you wear. Look through Pinterest and magazines to find styles you like.
2. **Shop with a purpose.** What's missing from your wardrobe? Spend wisely on clothes that will complement and add value to those you already own. Start with the basics, like a neutral, black base or white base, and build up your wardrobe around some favourites.
3. **Only buy a bargain if you LOVE it** (not because it's cheap), otherwise it will sit in the wardrobe gathering dust. If it makes you feel confident, it's a good sign.
4. **'Quality over quantity'.** It's better to have ONE stand-out outfit or jacket (that you wear to death) than lots of cheaper items you can take or leave. One awesome piece can sometimes form the basis of your other purchases.
5. **'Op shops' and pre-loved stores.** You'd be amazed what people throw out, especially in wealthy suburbs. If you have the patience to fossick through some of the crappy odds and ends, you might come across a unique vintage piece that will be timeless.
6. **Clothes swaps.** Clothing exchanges are a fun way to get some new items and shed some old stuff.
7. **Internet bargains. e.g., Facebook marketplace, buy/sell/swaps and eBay.** Watch out for new or pre-loved clothes and shoes that come up on offer.
8. **Accessories can make or break a simple outfit.** It might be some bling, sunglasses, a necklace, jacket, scarf, bag, belt, watch or shoes. These are often the first things people notice.
9. **Subscribe to websites.** You'll get the latest offers and styles. Sign up for email alerts from your favourite stores or designers.
10. **Want to impress at a special occasion?** You can borrow from a friend or go to hire sites instead of spending a fortune on a one-time outfit. Or check out the direct factory outlets for designer clearance items.

TIPS

Hair tip: Remember to style your hair and makeup to complement the look you're after. Use some fun hair ties or clips or, if your hair is left out, ensure it's clean and brushed.

Make-up tip: When applying makeup, have either strong eyes or strong lip colour, but not both. 'Less is more', so that you accentuate your unique features, instead of distracting from them.

Busbee Style how to look expensive, Chloe Coriolan how to make cheap clothes look classy

HEALTH CHECKS FOR UNDER 25s

Preventative maintenance is an engineering term referring to maintenance performed on equipment to keep it running and lesson the likelihood of it failing.

The same applies to our health. It's far more proactive to monitor your health and nip issues in the bud before they become chronic illnesses, which rack up costly health-care bills and a stack of regrets.

WHY ARE HEALTH CHECKS IMPORTANT?

Health checks aim for early diagnosis and prevention of health issues. Knowing some key information about your health status lets you and your doctor know if there are any particular issues you need to start keeping an eye on. In health, as in car maintenance, 'prevention is better than cure'.

Although some checks can be uncomfortable, they provide your doctor or specialist with an opportunity to look at your lifestyle, medical history and family history to find out if you're at risk.

Seek second (or third or fourth) opinions if you're in any doubt

If you're not feeling right about a diagnosis from one doctor, listen to your intuition and seek a second opinion. General practitioners (GPs = doctor) come from all strengths, specialities and knowledge bases, and it's possible they do not have extensive knowledge of your condition.

Treat the cause, not the symptom

'Symptoms' and 'pain' are indicators that something is not right in your body, and 'treating symptoms' only masks the cause.

Before jumping on the medication bandwagon, ask yourself if you've addressed the underlying symptoms or if it's a quick fix. E.g., if you have anxiety, consider the cause of the anxiety and how you can minimise or manage it. Or if you have a sinus problem, consider the causes, such as allergies.

Psychology Today Are you simply treating your symptoms

WHAT DOES BULK-BILLING MEAN?

Most medical centres are bulk-billed (i.e., the service is free, as Medicare covers the cost).

Ask if it's a bulk-billed service before you attend a medical appointment, or if there's an additional cost to you.

> Take care of your body. It's the only place you have to live.
>
> *Jim Rohn*

HEALTH CHECKS TO PUT IN THE CALENDAR

This section is not medical advice and is provided as a guide only. Any health concerns should be discussed with your doctor.

HEALTH CHECK	BY	WHEN	WHY
Breast examination	Yourself and your GP	Self-check every three months after your first period	Breast cancer can occur at any age but the incidence in the 20s and 30s is low. For younger women, regular self-examination and a GP check are recommended at the time of cervical screening. Men over 40 should also do self-examinations. It is recommended to become familiar with the normal look and feel of your breasts and to contact your doctor if you notice any unusual breast changes.
Cervical screening test (CST)	GP or gynaecologist	Every five years, from 25, or as directed by your GP	Cervical screening test (previously known as a pap test) detects human papillomavirus (HPV) which causes cervical cancer. It is recommended to start tests from age 25, or 1-2 years after becoming sexually active. Women can be screened through the National Cervical Screening Program. Note: No matter what your age, if you are having abnormal bleeding (after sex or in between periods) you need to see your doctor.
Cholesterol levels	GP	As directed by your GP	High levels of LDL-cholesterol and triglyceride fats in your blood can help predict people at risk of heart disease. If you have a family history of heart disease or high cholesterol, then you will probably have these tests regularly.
Dental checks	Dentist or oral hygienist	As required or directed by your dentist	Taking care of teeth and gums can help reduce dental problems in the future. Dentists recommend brushing your teeth twice a day and flossing daily to remove plaque. Do you know how to brush your teeth properly? Hard brushing can cause gums to recede and cause tooth ache and sensitivity. Good oral hygiene helps prevent tooth decay, gum disease and bad breath, and other health risks. It is recommended to see your dentist every 6-12 months.
Glucose (blood sugar) levels	GP	As directed by your GP	If you have a family history of diabetes you may be tested more regularly. The normal blood glucose levels for non-diabetics are between 4.0–7.8 mmol/L.

Mind health checks	GP or mental health practitioner	As required	Mental health is as important as physical health. Each year, an estimated one in five Australians will experience a mental health illness. Sometimes, because the symptoms are hidden, there is a tendency to overlook this side of our health. A mental health check-up is a chance to tell your GP about any feelings, emotional concerns or inabilities in coping with relationships or work/study situations. This is also a chance to do blood tests to check that your general health is not affecting your mental health. A GP might recommend a mental health treatment plan, whereby Medicare rebates are available for up to 10 individual and 10 group allied mental health services per calendar year to patients who are referred by a GP or psychiatrist or paediatrician. (As of 11 October 2020, Medicare will rebate between $84.80 and $126.50 for a session. This is a guide only. If the cost of the service is higher than this amount, you will need to pay the difference.) Ask your doctor if you're eligible for free mental health care under the Primary and Community Care Service. Also contact headspace to inquire about free mental health care.
Sexually transmitted infections (STI) screening	GP	Depending whether you are sexually active. Some doctors recommend annual STI screening for people under the age of 30	STIs are infections or diseases that are passed on through sex or exchange of fluids with an infected partner. Most can be detected with a urine or blood test and can be treated with antibiotics. Some STIs, if left untreated, can lead to longer-term health problems, such as infertility. Chlamydia is the most common STI in Australia. If you are sexually active, it's recommended to get checked every 6-12 months, or when changing partners.
Skin cancer check	Yourself, GP or dermatologist	Every two years from age 18, or as required	The incidence of skin cancer in Australia is one of the highest in the world. The majority are caused by exposure to the sun. Early detection and treatment improves outcomes and survival rates. Get to know your skin and any spots that begin to change colour, shape or size; or become inflamed or painful. Be vigilant with sunscreen, especially when swimming and surfing.

Testes examination	You and your GP	Men should regularly self-check (4 weekly)	Testicular cancer is the second most common cancer for men between 18 and 39. With early treatment, more than 90% of men can be cured. It is recommended men get to know the symptoms, such as finding a lump or painless swelling and know the testicular cancer risk factors.
Weight assessments	GP or nutritionist	As directed by your medical practitioner	An estimated 60% of Australians are overweight or obese, which can increase the likelihood of weight-related disease. The body mass index (BMI) test measures weight against height to determine if you are in a healthy weight range (18.5-24.9 is considered healthy). Health direct bmi calculator

Health Direct health conditions explained, Cancer Screening healthcare providers, Diabetes Australia blood glucose monitoring

PLEASE NOTE: This information has been reviewed by a health professional; however, it is recommended you consult your doctor for your general health checks or any specific health concerns.

12. CHECKLIST WHEN MOVING OUT OF HOME

WHAT ARE THE COSTS OF LIVING INDEPENDENTLY?

When you're moving out of home, make sure you have a safe place to live and that you know and can afford all the potential costs of living independently.

Keep in mind how living alone will affect other parts of your life, such as your study and work.

> **TIP**
>
> Check if you're eligible for financial assistance through Centrelink.

Remember, it's likely your parents or guardians shielded you from the real costs of living alone. Don't say 'it'll be ok' and fudge the figures. Add up ALL the costs and check if you can truly afford them.

POTENTIAL COSTS

- Rent
- Utilities (gas, electricity, water, internet)
- Food and groceries
- Household goods
- Transport, car costs, fuel
- School fees, uni fees
- Clothes, phone and personal items
- Entertainment and going out
- Insurance

If you're living in a shared house and splitting these costs, you'll have to make sure you have a very clear agreement in place about:

- How much everyone will pay
- When they pay
- Who's in charge of collecting money and paying the bills
- How you will pay for shared household costs

(Also refer to the budget in the money section of this guide)

ASIC's MoneySmart moving out of home, Youth Central advice for life, Lawstuff becoming independent, ReachOut moving out of home

THINGS TO ASK WHEN RENTING A FIRST HOUSE (WHEN YOU'RE A TENANT)

How long is the lease? How much is the bond? When is the rent due? Can you break the lease? What are your rights? Can you have pets? What's the deal on parking? Is the managing agent reputable and on-the-ball?

If there are repairs to be done, you don't want to wait forever. What are the neighbours like (check them out if you can)?

8 TIPS FOR A WINNING RENTAL APPLICATION

1. Dress well, because first impressions count
2. Be on time. Don't rush in late to an inspection
3. Be honest, reasonable and pleasant
4. Create a 1form account and apply for multiple properties with just one application.
5. Keep your application to the point and transparent
6. Make sure you have the correct documentation
7. Have references (personal and tenancy)
8. Follow up the next day to show them you're keen

WARNINGS AROUND SUBMITTING A 'CONDITION REPORT'

After you sign a rental agreement, submit your condition report within 7 DAYS. If you don't, you might have to fix all the former tenant's damages.

Take photos of the condition of the property at the start of the lease to ensure you don't get hit with repair costs (or disputes) at the end.

HOW DO I TO SET UP A NEW HOME ON A TIGHT BUDGET?

- Access what you need, not want
- Decorate personally, not professionally
- Try Facebook first, ask for help from friends and family. Check 'buy sell swap' pages
- Head to opportunity shops and discount retail stores (e.g. Kmart and Target)
- Rummage around in council clean-ups
- Check specials, deals on utilities, phone, Wi-Fi, Foxtel. Ask about student deals. Search: compare the market

First grocery shop, Shopping list example, Realestate.com C. Jacobs – 8 tips for winning a rental application, Youth Central what you need to know when you move out of home

ESSENTIAL THINGS TO KNOW WHEN BUYING YOUR FIRST HOME

WHAT'S THE DIFFERENCE BETWEEN A PRIVATE TREATY AND AN AUCTION?

1. PRIVATE TREATY (ON THE MARKET)

Most residential properties in Australia are sold privately, where the owner sets the price for their property based on what they consider 'fair market value'. Usually, this is done with a real estate agent. The owner and the agent, if they have one, then negotiate with prospective buyers to agree to a purchase price.

2. AUCTION

When a property goes to auction, the owner sets a reserve price (the minimum price they'll accept for the property) and, together with the real estate agent, they select a date to go to auction.

On auction day the property is open to the market for bids and will go to the highest bidder. Sometimes, this method can push the price up in a buoyant market, due to competition and group interest. It will be passed in if the reserve price is not met, and negotiations can continue following the auction.

Remember, you can negotiate the terms of an auction contract, but this must take place prior to auction day. Also, the buyer can negotiate other terms beforehand such as:

- a smaller deposit (5%, instead of the standard 10%)
- a longer settlement period (12 weeks instead of the standard six weeks)

WHAT TO CONSIDER BEFORE CHOOSING A HOME LOAN

1. Which interest rate? Fixed or variable or split rates? Interest-only or principal and interest (P&I) repayment?
2. Ensure you get pre-approval (also known as conditional approval) before you start searching for a property, so that you know your budget. You'll need to provide all your financials, such as income and savings, current expenses, assets (term deposits and investments) and liabilities (like credit card and personal loans).
3. How much can you afford to borrow? Consider the size of deposit you can afford.
4. Are these *all* the fees? Consider what the fees are now, and the possible on-going or new fees in the future? Are there fees when exiting within that time, and what about discharge, break or settlement fees?
5. Compare apples-to-apples: When comparing lender options, make sure you compare the same information.
6. Consider using a mortgage broker, who will do the legwork for you and it's a free service to you (i.e., the lender/bank pays them the referral fee). Importantly, find an independent broker who's not aligned with a bank so that you get impartial advice, but first, check they're registered with ASIC Connect Professional Register website.

STAMP DUTY AND FIRST-HOME BUYER CONCESSIONS

Stamp duty is paid on all home property purchases. The amount is based on the market value of the property or the price paid, including any GST, which means the more expensive a property, the higher stamp duty rate.

Work out the rate using calculators, like the Realestate.com - stamp duty calculator

Buyers purchasing a residence they intend to live in as their home, or purchasing a property intended to be their first home, may be eligible for stamp duty concessions and first-home buyers' concessions.

THE 8 BIGGEST MISTAKES FIRST HOME BUYERS OFTEN MAKE:

1. Underestimating the real costs of the purchase (i.e. not factoring in stamp duty and conveyancing/legal costs), and therefore over-committing.
2. Falling in love with the property and not sticking to the purchase-price budget, or buying before selling (this is especially risky in a low-supply, high-demand market).
3. Failing to inspect the property thoroughly, therefore overlooking potential additional costs.
4. Believing a 'building inspection' covers all building issues (note: buyer beware). In fact, in NSW the Department of Fair Trading website states: "A building inspector would not normally check such things as: electrical wiring and smoke detectors; plumbing, drainage and gas fitting; air-conditioning; appliances; and hazards" (to name a few examples). Some building inspections have so many legal disclaimers they could wriggle out of most of what they claim to have inspected. TIPS Get a referral for an inspector from someone you trust, but not the real estate agent. Before choosing a building inspection company, ask for a sample of their reports, so you can see if it's readable or full of legal jargon.
5. Not taking advantage of first homeowner concessions. i.e., not checking if the government is offering first homeowner grants.
6. Buying at auction before ensuring finance is secured.
7. Failing to get expert independent advice, thinking they can save money 'doing it all themselves'.
8. Signing before they read the fine print. e.g., are there any caveats (notice of a legal claim to the property) to be aware of that may affect the purchase or delay the settlement?

TIP

There's no cooling-off period on auction purchases, which means you can't cancel the contract without a big penalty.

ASIC's MoneySmart borrowing and credit, Macquarie Bank Macquarie bank. The top 5 mistakes first home buyers make, Fair Trading buying property at auction, e.g. NSW property inspections, Mozo home loan terms glossary

QUICK AND HEALTHY COOKING IDEAS FOR THE TIME POOR

EASY-TO-USE COOKING APPLIANCES:

1. **Barbecue:** It's the easiest and most Aussie way to cook quickly.
2. **Pressure cookers or Tefal Cook4Me.** Pressure cookers are ways to fast-track healthy meals. (e.g., the Tefal cooks risotto in six minutes).
3. **Other electric cookware:** e.g., toastie-maker, sandwich press, air fryer, electric wok, rice cooker, etc.

DID YOU KNOW?

- Raw meats should be cut on a separate cutting board, or before vegetables, to avoid cross-contamination (from bacteria).
- When cutting meats and fish, wash cutting boards straight away to avoid bacteria, like salmonella.
- Let cooked meat rest before cutting, as it continues cooking after the heat is turned off (slice meat against the grain).
- Wash rice before cooking to rinse off the starch. Rice cookers are hassle-free. Google: how to cook perfect rice.
- Make sure your dishes are microwave-proof and oven-proof before using (e.g. some plastics are not suitable for the microwave).
- Don't cook an egg in the microwave, unless it's in water or a special container for that purpose, as it will explode.
- Don't use metal or sharp utensils on frypans, as it scratches the surface.
- Keeping knives sharp will reduce preparation time (also use the correct knife for its purpose).
- Wash all fruit and vegetables thoroughly to remove dirt and insecticides.

SUPER-EASY MEAL EXAMPLES

- Pasta-based meals – spaghetti bolognese, lasagne
- Rice-based meals – fried rice, risotto (cheat's version)
- Casseroles and stews
- Vegetable-based meals (with a protein), like stir fry or salad
- Egg-based meals – omelette, eggs on toast
- Wraps, tacos, noodles, pizza-bases
- Healthy frozen meals

Taste.com.au quick weeknight dinners, Greatist Healthy Dinner recipes for beginners, Budget Bytes top 10 recipes for students

LAUNDRY AND CLEANING TIPS FOR NEWBIES

Laundry (clothes and linen washing) is something that many of us do every day, but if you leave it a few days you can wash in batches, especially if you have 'whites' and towels. Wash bed linen at least fortnightly to avoid bed bugs.

General home cleaning is another chore we all love to do. Hmm, not. But it must be done, so it's a good idea to have daily and weekly routines.

Daily cleaning: If you have a good general routine on a daily basis, it will make the weekly clean easier.

E.g. wiping the bathroom basin and kitchen sink, keeping the kitchen tidy, and clearing and washing dishes at the time of use. (Note: this will also avoid attracting ants and cockroaches.)

Weekly cleaning: e.g. wipe the counters, dust surfaces, vacuum, mop, clean the bathroom and put the washing on. You can make it 'fun' by all doing a job (if you're living with flat-mates) and then going grocery shopping and having a cook-up.

TIPS

1. To avoid turning all your whites pink or pastel, don't wash whites with colours.
2. Wash towels separately from delicates or good clothes.
3. Be careful with bleach. It's a good idea to do cleaning naked or in your daggy underwear if you're using bleach, to avoid bleaching the clothes you're wearing. ☺ Seriously though, be careful when using any cleaning chemicals (i.e., read the warnings and instructions closely).
4. Clean up the kitchen and bathroom AS YOU GO. Give surfaces a quick wipe-down each morning.
5. Use a shorter cycle on the washing machine (to save water and power) if clothes or towels are not especially dirty.
6. A natural way to clean - use ½ cup baking soda and 1 cup vinegar. Vinegar is a natural cleaner and deodoriser, and baking soda dissolves grease and dirt in water.
7. Read the labels on clothing to see if there are special washing instructions, like 'dry clean only'.

ReachOut how to look after yourself and your home, laundry tips and tricks

COOLEST QUOTES AND MUST-READ BOOKS

ANTHONY HOPKINS

"None of us are getting out of here alive, so please stop treating yourself as an afterthought. Eat the delicious food. Walk in the sunshine. Jump in the ocean. Say the truth you're carrying in your heart like hidden treasure. Be silly. Be kind. Be weird. There's no time for anything else."

BRENE BROWN

Favourite books: *Dare to Lead* and *The Power of Vulnerability*
YouTube: Ted talk - Brene Brown on vulnerability

"You either walk inside your story and own it or you stand outside your story and hustle for your worthiness."

"True belonging is a spiritual practice; knowing you're part of something bigger yet having the courage to stand alone."

BRIAN TRACY

Favourite books: *Earn what you're Really Worth* and *Eat That Frog*

"The key to success is to focus our conscious mind on things we desire not things we fear."

BRYCE COURTENAY

Favourite book: *The Power of One*

"Sometimes the slightest things change the directions of our lives, the merest breath of a circumstance, a random moment that connects like a meteorite striking the earth. Lives have swivelled and changed direction on the strength of a chance remark."

DALE CARNEGIE

Favourite book: *How to Win Friends and Influence People*

"People rarely succeed unless they have fun in what they are doing."

"Inaction breeds doubt and fear. Action breeds confidence and courage. If you want to conquer fear, do not sit home and think about it. Go out and get busy."

DEAN GRAZIOSI

Favourite book: *Millionaire Success Habits*

"Successful people, whether they're working for somebody else or working for themselves, do whatever they do to the best of their ability—as if the boss is watching them every minute of every day. I learned that in everything you do, always do your best."

DEEPAK CHOPRA

Favourite books: *The Seven Spiritual Laws of Success* and *Super Brain*

"There are no accidents; there is only some purpose that we haven't yet understood."

ECKHART TOLLE

Favourite book: *The Power of Now*
YouTube: How do we break the habit of excessive thinking?

"Realise deeply that the present moment is all you ever have. Make the Now the primary focus of your life."

"Where there is anger, there is always pain underneath."

ESTHER HICKS

Favourite books: *The Law of Attraction, The Basics of the Teachings of Abraham* and *Ask and It Is Given*

"Look around less, imagine more."

"If you want it, and expect it, it will be yours very soon."

"Success is about a happy life, and a happy life is just a string of happy moments. But most people do not allow the happy moments because they are so busy trying to get a happy life."

JACK CANFIELD

Favourite books: *Chicken Soup for the Soul* and *The Success Principles*

"Don't worry about failures, worry about the chances you miss when you don't even try."

"Everything you want is on the other side of fear."

"You only have control over three things in your life: the thoughts you think, the images you visualise and the actions you take."

JACK MA

YouTube: Life advice
YouTube: Top 10 rules for success

"Help young people. Help small guys. Because small guys will be big. Young people will have the seeds you bury in their minds, and when they grow up, they will change the world."

"If you don't give up you still have a chance. Giving up is the greatest failure."

JASON LOUV

Blog: The 10 secrets of adulting

"Do not bear grudges. Let the past go."

"You need others. Life is a team sport."

JAY SHETTY

Favourite book: *Think like a monk*

"When nobody else celebrates you, learn to celebrate yourself. When nobody else compliments you, then compliment yourself. It's not up to other people to keep you encouraged. It's up to you. Encouragement should come from the inside."

JEN SINCERO

Favourite book: *You are a Badass*

"You are responsible for what you say and do. You are not responsible for whether or not people freak out about it."

JIM KWIK

Seminar: Unleash Your Brain mindvalley.com/superbrain
YouTube: The power of morning routine

"We need to understand how our minds work so we can work our minds better."

JIM ROHN

Favourite book: *7 Strategies for Wealth and Happiness*

"Formal education will make you a living; self-education will make you a fortune."

"Never wish life were easier, wish that you were better."

"If you really want to do something, you'll find a way. If you don't, you'll find an excuse."

JOE VITALE

Favourite book: *Zero Limits*

"NOW is the time. The Universe likes SPEED. Don't delay, don't second-guess, don't doubt. When the opportunity or impulse is there... ACT!"

"Smile. It is sunshine to others."

JOHN ASSARAF

"Your mind is a powerful thing. When you fill it with positive thoughts, your life will start to change."

"If you're interested, you'll do what is convenient. If you're committed, you'll do whatever it takes."

JOHN DEMARTINI

Book and seminar: *The Breakthrough Experience* (Demartini Institute)

"The more inspiring your purpose, the greater your power and the meaning of your life."

"Nobody is going to get up every morning dedicated to empowering and inspiring your life. That's up to you."

"Your innermost dominant thought becomes your outermost tangible reality."

"If you don't value you, don't expect the world to value you."

JOHN GRAY

Favourite book: *Men are from Mars, Women are from Venus*

"Men are motivated and empowered when they feel needed. Women are motivated and empowered when they feel cherished."

JOHN KEHOE

Favourite book: *Mind Power into the 21st Century*

"No-one has ever made money doing something they don't love."

"The beautiful thing about life, is we get to choose whatever goal we want."

"Don't end up as the one who is climbing the ladder of success only to find it is up against the wrong wall!"

"Negatives only have power over you when you react to them."

JOHN LENNON

"We live in a world where we have to hide to make love, while violence is practiced in broad daylight."

"Life is what happens when you are busy making other plans."

KENNETH ROBINSON (SIR)

Favourite books: *The Element: How Finding Your Passion Changes Everything* and *Our Minds: Learning to be Creative*
YouTube: *Do schools kill creativity?*

"If you're not prepared to be wrong, you'll never come up with anything original."

"Creativity is as important as literacy."

"My contention is that creativity now is as important in education as literacy, and we should treat it with the same status."

"We need to radically rethink our view of intelligence."

LAYNE BEACHLEY

YouTube: The power of self-belief

"You manifest what you believe."

LOUISE HAY

Favourite book: *You Can Heal Your Life*

"Love is the great miracle cure. Loving ourselves works miracles in our lives."

"Every thought we think is creating our future."

MARK MANSON

Favourite book: *The Subtle Art of Not Giving a ****

"Who you are is defined by what you're willing to struggle for."

"Living a good life is not about being extraordinary. It's about doing ordinary things really well."

*"You and everyone you know are going to be dead soon. And in the short amount of time between here and there, you have a limited amount of ****s to give. Very few, in fact. And if you go around giving a **** about everything and everyone without conscious thought or choice—well, then you're going to get ****ed."*

MARTIN LUTHER KING JR

"We must develop and maintain the capacity to forgive. He who is devoid of the power to forgive is devoid of the power to love. There is some good in the worst of us and some evil in the best of us. When we discover this, we are less prone to hate our enemies."

"Darkness cannot drive out darkness; only light can do that. Hate cannot drive out hate; only love can do that."

MAXWELL MALTZ

Favourite book: *Psycho-Cybernetics*:
Website psycho-cybernetics.com

"If you make friends with yourself, you will never be alone."

"Man maintains his balance, poise, and sense of security only as he is moving forward."

"You make mistakes. Mistakes don't make you."

MEL ROBBINS

YouTube: *How to stop screwing yourself over*

"You are one decision away from a completely different life."

"There will always be someone who can't see your worth. Don't let it be you."

NAPOLEON HILL

Favourite book: *Think and Grow Rich.*

"Whatever the mind of man can conceive and believe, it can achieve."

"Don't wait. The time will never be just right."

"A goal is a dream with a deadline."

OPRAH WINFREY

YouTube: Become the best version of yourself
YouTube: How to make someone remember you for a lifetime

"Be that fantastic at what you do that your talent can't be dismissed."

"Stop comparing yourself to other people. You're only on this planet to be you. Not someone else's imitation of you."

"When you are excellent, you become unforgettable. People remember you. You stand out!"

PAUL HANNA

Favourite books: *You Can Do It* and *Believe and Achieve*

"No one can upset you, unless you give them permission."

RHONDA BYRNE

Favourite book: *The Secret*

"There is no such thing as a hopeless situation. Every single circumstance of your life can change!"

RICHARD BRANSON

Favourite books: *Losing My Virginity* and *Screw It, Let's Do It*

"You've got to take risks if you're going to succeed. I'd much rather ask forgiveness than permission."

"Learn from failure. If you are an entrepreneur and your first venture wasn't a success, welcome to the club!"

"You don't learn to walk by following rules. You learn by doing and by falling over."

RICHARD CARLSON

Favourite book: *Don't Sweat the Small Stuff*

"Stress is nothing more than a socially acceptable form of mental illness."

ROBERT KIYOSAKI

Favourite book: *Rich Dad, Poor Dad*

"If you're still doing what mommy and daddy said for you to do (go to school, get a job, and save money), you're losing."

"It's not what you say out of your mouth that determines your life, it's what you whisper to yourself that has the most power!"

"It's more important to grow your income than cut your expenses. It's more important to grow your spirit than cut your dreams."

"Complaining about your current position in life is worthless. Have a spine and do something about it instead."

"The main reason that over 90% of the public struggles financially is because they play NOT TO LOSE."

SCOTT PAPE

Favourite book: *The Barefoot Investor*
Summary: The Barefoot Investor

"Debt is a four-letter word."

SETH GODIN

YouTube: Top 10 Rules for Success

"Being aware of your fear is smart. Overcoming it is the mark of a successful person."

SIMON SINEK

Favourite books: *Start with Why* and *Find Your Why*
YouTube: Top 10 rules for success
YouTube: Change your future
YouTube: Evan Carmichael 5 Lessons in life people learn too late

SPENCER JOHNSON

Favourite book: *Who Moved My Cheese?*

"The fear you let build up in your mind is worse than the situation that actually exists."

"The quicker you let go of old cheese, the sooner you find new cheese."

STEPHEN (AND SEAN) COVEY

Favourite book: *The 7 Habits of Highly Effective People*

"Begin with the end in mind."

"Find your voice and inspire others to find theirs."

"Seek first to understand, then to be understood."

THE DALAI LAMA

Favourite book: *The Art of Happiness*

"If you want others to be happy, practice compassion. If you want to be happy, practice compassion."

"Remember that sometimes not getting what you want is a wonderful stroke of luck."

"Sleep is the best meditation."

"Love and compassion are necessities, not luxuries. Without them, humanity cannot survive."

TIMOTHY FERRISS

Favourite books: *The 4-hour Workweek* and *Tribe of Mentors*

"People will choose unhappiness over uncertainty."

"A person's success in life can usually be measured by the number of uncomfortable conversations he or she is willing to have."

TONY ROBBINS

Favourite books: *Awaken the Giant Within* and *Unshakeable*
YouTube: Tips on changing the way you feel
Seminar: Unleash the Power Within

"Everything you can do now, there was a time you couldn't do it. Why wait to get confident? If it doesn't work out, you'll learn something."

"Change your belief system. If you think 'I've never done anything well!' that's a reinforcing belief. It does not serve you well and sets you up for failure."

WAYNE DYER

Favourite books: *The Power of Intention, Change your Thoughts, Change your Life* and *10 Secrets to Success and Inner Peace*
YouTube: 5 lessons to live by. Don't die with the lesson in you

"How people treat you is their karma; how you react is yours."

"If you change the way you look at things, the things you look at change."

"Be miserable. Or motivate yourself. Whatever has to be done, it's always your choice."

ZIG ZIGLAR

Favourite books: *Born to Win* and *See You at The Top*
Website: ziglar.com

"People often say that motivation doesn't last. Well, neither does bathing – that's why we recommend it daily."

"You can get everything in life you want if you will just help enough other people get what they want."

"You don't have to be great at something to start, but you have to start to be great at something."

DESIDERATA – WORDS FOR LIFE

BY MAX EHRMANN

Go placidly amid the noise and the haste *and remember what peace there may be in silence. As far as possible, without surrender, be on good terms with all persons.*

Speak your truth quietly and clearly*; and listen to others, even to the dull and the ignorant; they too have their story.*

Avoid loud and aggressive persons; *they are vexatious to the spirit. If you compare yourself with others, you may become vain or bitter, for always there will be greater and lesser persons than yourself.*

Enjoy your achievements as well as your plans. *Keep interested in your own career, however humble; it is a real possession in the changing fortunes of time.*

Exercise caution in your business affairs, *for the world is full of trickery. But let this not blind you to what virtue there is; many persons strive for high ideals, and everywhere life is full of heroism.*

Be yourself. *Especially do not feign affection. Neither be cynical about love; for in the face of all aridity and disenchantment, it is as perennial as the grass.*

Take kindly the counsel of the years, *gracefully surrendering the things of youth.*

Nurture strength of spirit to shield you in sudden misfortune*. But do not distress yourself with dark imaginings. Many fears are born of fatigue and loneliness.*

Beyond a wholesome discipline, be gentle with yourself. *You are a child of the universe no less than the trees and the stars; you have a right to be here.*

And whether or not it is clear to you, ***no doubt the universe is unfolding as it should.*** *Therefore, be at peace with God, whatever you conceive Him to be. And whatever your labours and aspirations, in the noisy confusion of life,* ***keep peace in your soul.***

With all its sham, drudgery and broken dreams, it is still a beautiful world.

Be cheerful. Strive to be happy.